Cover Art by Cover Reveal Designs

ISBN: 978-0-6487687-5-3

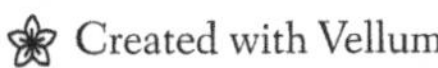

KERI ARTHUR

Broken Bonds

A LIZZIE GRACE NOVEL

With thanks to:

The Lulus
Indigo Chick Designs
Olivia / Hot Tree Editing
Debbie from DP+
Robyn E.
The Lulus
My mates from Indie Gals
Lori / Cover Reveal Designs for the amazing cover

CHAPTER ONE

The second full moon of the month rode high in the sky, filling the night with her light and her energy. For many, a blue moon was either a symbol of good luck or bad, depending on which part of the globe they came from and what superstitions they believed in.

For witches, it was a symbol of great power. A prime time in which to perform rituals of prophecy and protection.

It was also a symbol of great change.

And change was coming.

To this reservation, and to my life.

I shivered and wrapped the old woolen sweater tighter around my body. It filled my nostrils with a musky, smoky scent and made me wish it was the arms of the man to whom it belonged.

But tonight was the one night that couldn't happen.

Aiden O'Connor—the man I'd fallen in love with, the man I shared my life with—was a werewolf. While a full moon didn't force them to shift shape, or even become monsters, as so many old myths would have everyone believe, they nevertheless gravitated to their home compounds in order to run wild with their pack, enjoying the freedom and the power of the moon.

As a witch, I could never participate in that part of his life. I would never be invited onto pack grounds except in cases of emergency. And I would certainly never be welcomed into his family as his partner. Hell, his mother was having a hard enough time accepting me as his lover.

And *she* was the reason my life—and Aiden's—was on the cusp of change. The bitch had invited Mia—the werewolf he'd once asked to be his wife—to return.

She wasn't here yet, but she was close, maybe only a day or so away. It wasn't only the moonlit threads of destiny that whispered of her arrival, but also my precognitive senses and dreams.

Of course, I'd gone into this relationship knowing full well this day would come. Knowing he'd take my heart and then tear it into a million pieces. I'd nevertheless hoped for a few more years rather than just a few more days.

I sighed, closed my eyes against the sting of tears, and raised my face to the moon. Her caress was cold, and her power flooded my senses, expanding and strengthening them.

That's when I felt it.

Not the presence of the woman who'd shatter the current perfection of my life, but rather, evil.

It swirled through the chilled darkness, intent on bloody revenge.

My eyes snapped open and I scanned the inky waters of the lake directly opposite the balcony on which I stood. Moonlight glinted off the gentle waves that lapped at the shore, and the wind stirred through the trees, making the leaves whisper and moan. Neither held any sort of threat and yet ... and yet, I was certain trees played a part in whatever I sensed.

Which wasn't overly helpful when parks, forests, and bush covered a good proportion of the Faelan Werewolf Reservation.

There was only one way I'd have any hope of uncovering what was going on—without actually jumping in the car and driving around in the vague hope that proximity would strengthen the signal—and that was to use my psychic powers.

I sat down, crossed my legs, and then tugged the sweater over my knees in an effort to keep warm. After a deep breath to center my energy, I closed my eyes and reached down to that place deep inside where my psychometry and second sight lay leashed and waiting. When I provided psychic tracking services for clients, I generally used either touch or something personal to locate whatever it was they'd lost, but that was no longer really necessary. Thanks to the wild magic that infused my soul, my psychic talents had started mutating—a development that should have been impossible. Wild magic was an energy that came from deep within the earth's core and was not something that could safely be used, as it was possible for it to be forever stained by darkness. The reason all manner of dark entities continued to flood the Faelan Reservation was the fact that —for too damn long—the council had willfully ignored the necessity for the larger of the two wellsprings to be protected. That had been rectified quite a few months ago now, but the echoes of her power still washed across the distant shores of darkness and remained a siren call to all the things that lived and breathed evil.

Of course, an unprotected wellspring was also the reason I could now use wild magic in ways no one had ever thought possible. My mother had unknowingly been pregnant with me when she'd been sent to restrain and protect an emerging wellspring, and the energy that had almost killed her should certainly have killed me. Instead, it had fused to my DNA, giving me a deep connection to the wilder forces of this world, though absolutely no one—including me—had been aware of that until I'd come into this reservation almost a year ago.

Where the connection would ultimately lead was anyone's guess, but it continued to make changes to both my physical and psychic senses. If I was being at all honest, it scared the hell out of me.

I took another breath and tried to concentrate, but for too many minutes, nothing happened. The wind stirred around me, chilling my neck and toes, but there was no sense of the tenuous thread I'd sensed earlier.

Perhaps more power was required ... the thought had barely crossed my mind when the inner wild magic responded. It burned through every fiber, every muscle, sharpening not only my psychic senses but also my physical. It allowed me to hear the distant, joyous howls of wolves as they ran through the trees, let me feel the flickering pulse of the two very different wellsprings—a heartbeat of power that briefly matched my own—and tugged the heady scent of earth and forest and distant rain into my nose.

But underneath those scents ran something far more intense and abrasive, a blast that was rose and geranium mixed with something suspiciously overripe or rotten.

It was coming from the north, though I doubted it was anywhere near Castle Rock. Which meant I'd have to jump into the car after all if I wanted to track this thing down.

I swore, pushed upright, and walked back into the bedroom. The king-sized bed was a mess, a legacy of the hours I'd spent tossing and turning before I'd gotten up. I'd undoubtedly regret doing so in the morning, given Saturday was usually one of the busiest days at the café I co-owned and ran with Belle—who was not only my best friend and fellow witch, but also my familiar—but there was nothing I could really do about that. It certainly wouldn't be the first time I'd gone in there looking the worse for wear. In the early days of my relationship with Aiden, it had become something of a running joke with many of our customers.

I hurriedly dressed, then grabbed my coat and a thick woolly hat and ran down the stairs. After making a cup of coffee to take with me, I grabbed my keys and headed out to my car. It was a cheery yellow-and-black Suzuki Swift that I mainly used to travel to and from the café. While the council had replaced yet another of our vehicles—evil seemed to have a penchant for blowing them up—the SUV cost an arm and a leg to run, so we used it mainly for business purposes. Me having the Suzi also meant Belle had wheels if she needed them. Not that she did all that much these days, given the amount of time she was now spending with Monty, who was not only the reservation's resident witch but also my cousin. They tended to use his old Mustang to get around in.

Of course, these days Monty was also my boss, as I worked on a part-time basis as his assistant. By rights I should have contacted him about the brush of evil, but he and Belle had gone down to Melbourne to see the latest incarnation of *Oklahoma*. And *that* said a lot about how serious he was about his relationship with Belle, given he absolutely hated that particular musical.

But even if I *had* wanted to call him, it'd take them at least an hour and a half to get to Argyle—where Aiden and I lived—and by that time, whatever I was sensing might have disappeared. Though in truth, past experience with the various evil entities who'd found their way into this place suggested *that* was unlikely.

I did—for all of one second—think about ringing the ranger station. Despite the full moon, there would be someone assigned to hold the fort and take emergency calls. Aiden had done more than his fair share in recent months, preferring to be with me rather than his pack—or rather, his interfering fucking mother—but tonight the moon's pull had been too fierce for him to ignore.

Because destiny waits in the moon's cold light. The soft reply echoed lightly through my mind. *Even a wolf with a will of iron cannot ignore her forever. His choice lies before him.*

The voice belonged to Katie, Aiden's deceased sister. Her soul—and the ghost of her witch husband, Gabe—now inhabited and protected the reservation's second wellspring. As my connection with the wild magic had grown and strengthened, so too had my connection to her. Up until recently, it had taken a luminous thread of wild magic wrapped around my wrist for the two of us to converse. That was no longer the case—the wild magic just had to be in the area. Which it was—the moonlit, ethereal threads were floating across the dark waters of the lake.

Does that mean Mia is already here?

It does not.

There was something in her soft answer that stirred trepidation. *If she's not here already, why is he being given a choice tonight?*

You shall see soon enough.

Katie ...

I cannot give answers to what I cannot see.

That's avoidance, and we both know it.

Her laughter washed through my mind, warm and oddly encouraging. *You, of all people, should know how restricted second sight can be and just how damn frustrating that is.*

Does that mean when you do know something more, you'll tell me?

Perhaps, she replied, her voice growing distant as the threads moved away. *And perhaps not.*

Annoyance rose, but I tamped it down. I might be her voice and her weapon in this reservation, but Aiden was her brother. It was natural her loyalties would in the end be with him, even if she didn't always approve of his choices in life.

Thankfully, she *did* approve of me. It would have been awkward if she hadn't.

I jumped into the Suzi and slowly drove past the other five houses in the lakeside complex. Once on the main road, I flattened my foot and headed out of town. The moonlight silvered the landscape and, though storm clouds occasionally dimmed her light, it was currently so bright the headlights really only became necessary whenever the highway swept through a forest.

I slowed once I reached the outskirts of Guildford, then wound down the window and stuck out my hand. The moon's cold energy caressed my fingers even as the inner wild magic stirred. The tug of evil came from the right, from deep within the hills that made up part of the state forest, and an area that contained lots of old mines and diggings—something I knew from experience, having fallen down one of them. Thankfully, Aiden had been with me that time, and had saved both our lives by not only finding something to latch onto as we'd both dropped but also by one-handedly catching me.

I turned right at the pub and drove on. When I reached a T-intersection, I stopped and studied my options while I waited for the psychic tug to kick in again.

It sent me right, but it was so faint now it was little more than a flicker. I didn't know whether that meant evil was moving away or if it had done whatever it had come here to do. At least I wasn't getting anything to suggest the latter was a definite possibility; it would certainly be a rather nice change if one of these excursions *didn't* end in the discovery of death.

The road gently climbed for several kilometers and then swept through a number of gullies and past an old cemetery. I was rather relieved that the tug of evil didn't have me stopping at the latter. While cemeteries didn't as a rule scare me, there were many tales of the dead coming to life under the light and power of a blue moon. However unlikely it was that that's what was happening here, I had no desire to tempt fate and find myself confronted by a vengeful ghost or even a zombie. Been there, done that, and—particularly in the case of the zombie—had no desire to ever repeat the experience.

I drove through a small hamlet of houses, all of them dark and showing little sign of life. No surprise, given it was close to one by now and any sensible person would be tucked up in bed.

The road continued on, and the trees grew thicker, cutting out the moon's wash of power. I neared another intersection high up near the ridge and slowed, looking left before turning right. I continued on to the top and then down into a valley that was scrub on one side and moon-washed farmland on the other.

Then, without warning, that wisp of evil sharpened.

I hit the brakes so hard the tires squealed. As the sound

echoed across the silent night, my gaze was drawn to the left. In amongst the trees were a number of caravans. One had a lean-to attached, suggesting it might be in use, but the others looked empty. That impression might not be accurate, of course, given the hour.

At the very edge of the camping area, off to the right of the old dirt road that led into it, was a small brick building with a water tank attached. Toilet and washing facilities, no doubt.

I scanned the area one more time and then turned in. The headlights pierced the shadows and, just for an instant, I saw something white moving through the trees.

My heart began to beat a lot faster. I had no idea what that flash was—it had moved out of sight far too quickly—but I had no doubt *it* was the thing I'd been sensing.

I parked close to the building, then picked up my phone and climbed out. It was starting to drizzle, and the moonlight wasn't piercing the thick foliage of the surrounding trees, leaving much of the immediate surroundings layered in darkness. There was no hint of evil teasing the air, so perhaps the flash had been nothing more than the breeze stirring a plastic bag to life ... but the psychic part of my soul simply said no.

I hastily shoved on my coat and hat, and then grabbed the backpack—which not only contained my silver knife but an assortment of potions, as well as holy water—from the back seat and slung it over my shoulder. Then, after a quick look around the nearby camping area, I switched on the phone's flashlight and headed off. While the light would give away my position to anyone watching, I wasn't about to go traipsing through the dark in an area well known for its many mineshafts. My eyesight had certainly sharpened over the last few weeks, but I felt more comfortable relying on a good old-fashioned light.

I trudged on for a good fifteen minutes, following a very faint path in the forest, before I spotted something in the mud between a rock and a wave of leaf litter. I squatted down and moved the light closer. It was a footprint, human rather than animal, and almost skeletal in appearance.

Goose bumps shivered across my skin, though I wasn't entirely sure why when it was likely the maker of this print simply had skinny feet. Of course, he or she was walking around barefoot, which *did* imply a certain amount of ... well, not insanity but at least eccentricity. I mean, it was damnably cold *and* wet out here.

The other possibility was the print belonged to a werewolf. They did tend to run lean, and everything I'd heard about moon runs said they generally stripped off first. It might explain not only why this person was running around barefoot but also why I'd seen a flash of white. The O'Connors' compound was the closest to this spot, and they were silver wolves who ran the color gamut from an almost bleached blond to a muddy, brownish silver.

Of course, this print might not have anything to do with the flash of white I'd seen, even if it did look reasonably fresh.

I carefully touched the edge of the footprint. There was no response from the psychic part of my soul, which was a relief, even if it didn't really mean that much. Said senses had shown no inclination so far to provide any concrete information about whatever it was I'd been led up here to find.

I swept the light around the immediate area. The very faint path I'd been following petered out a dozen or so steps ahead, and there were several tailing mounds off to the left, suggesting I was about to enter an area that had been mined. It really wasn't wise to keep on going—not by myself, at any rate, and certainly not when there were no more footprints, human or wolf, to be seen anywhere in the immediate area.

I took a couple of photos of the print I'd found, on the off chance the drizzle got bad enough to wash it away, then pushed upright and made my way back down to the camping area. If there was one thing I had learned over the last few months, it was not to push my luck too far.

Unless, of course, it was absolutely necessary.

The camping area remained silent. I briefly eyed the nearest caravan, then walked over to the brick building. Both toilets were empty, but in the washroom, someone had strung a simple rope line between two hooks and hung several shirts and a pair of shorts over it. All items belonged to a male and were still damp to the touch. Obviously, at least one of the caravans was occupied.

I tossed the backpack into the Suzi and then walked through the trees to the first caravan. After a quick walk around the outside to see if there was anything that looked suspicious or odd, I walked up the steps and tried the door. Unsurprisingly, it was locked. I rose up on my toes and peered in. It was too dark to see anything, so I reluctantly shone the flashlight in. There was nothing in either the small kitchen or dining area to suggest it had been in use recently and no twinges from my psychic senses.

I jumped down and headed across to the next one. It was one of those old, almost bubble-like vans painted in a fading yellow, and wouldn't have had much room for anything more than a bed. It too was empty.

Which meant the guy who owned the clothes was either using the caravan with the attached lean-to, or was off camping somewhere in the bush and just coming back here whenever necessary.

I walked over, the stones crunching softly underfoot. The sound echoed, and somewhere out there in the distant darkness, expectation stirred. I paused and scanned the area, but I couldn't see or feel a threat.

I frowned and shone the light into the small lean-to. No threat and no spells, and yet there *was* magic here somewhere. It was a faint caress that skimmed the outer reaches of my senses. I had no idea of the spell's intent, no idea if it had been cast by the owner of the van, or the evil that had drawn me here, but the stirring unease nevertheless grew stronger. Past experience suggested if I was sensing magic in the same area as evil, it was a pretty safe bet one belonged to the other.

I took a deep breath and stepped into the lean-to. It housed a small portable gas stove, a larder that contained mainly tinned food, an Esky, and a couple of chairs. I unlatched the Esky and looked inside. There was an assortment of beer cans, a carton of milk and, rather weirdly, a selection of cheese. The ice meant to keep it cold had melted long ago, but maybe the guy living here saw no point in replacing it, given how damn cold it'd been over the last few days. It wasn't like any of the Esky's contents would go off overly fast in this weather.

I lowered the lid and walked over to the van's steps. The door was locked and the curtains had been pulled across the small window. While the place was utterly silent, the wisp of magic was stronger.

Until I could see the spell's threads, I really couldn't say what its intent was. But it didn't feel like any sort of protection spell. In fact, it really didn't feel like any spell I was familiar with at all.

I jumped down the steps, then ducked out of the lean-to and slowly walked around the rest of the caravan. The spell sharpened at the hitch end and faded again as I moved around to the other side. I'd have to go in to uncover what was going on, but I wasn't about to do *that* until I'd checked the entire thing.

At the rear, a large window stretched the full width of the van, but it was up too high for me to peer through. I looked around, saw the sawn-off ends of an old tree someone had obviously been cutting up for firewood, and went over to grab one. Once I'd rolled it into position and stood it up on its end, I carefully stepped up.

And saw the emaciated skull of a man whose mouth had been permanently locked in a silent scream—a scream that I could *see* rather than hear. I'd always been able to feel the emotions of others through either touch or the color of auras, but this was the first time emotion and sound had become visible.

It was just more evidence that the mutations continued within.

I pushed that concern aside and tried to concentrate on the dead man rather than the dark wave of fear and horror that filled his final moments. There was no sign of putrefaction and no obvious sign of trauma. His features were so gaunt, it was impossible to tell how old he was, and there were no identifying marks or tattoos on the skin that sagged across his arms and chest ... my gaze halted at his groin and widened in surprise. The damn man had an erection. Did that mean he'd been with a partner when death had found him? Or had he simply been masturbating?

And how the hell was it still erect in death?

If he *had* been with someone, was she—or he—still in the van somewhere? Or was his lover also his murderer, and possibly the flash of white I'd seen fleeing through the forest?

I shone the light deeper into the van. There was no indication of another body, nor did anything seem out of place or odd. There was also no sign of the magic I could sense. The spell, whatever its intent, had been hidden, and that couldn't be a good thing.

I glanced back at the emaciated form. While I guess anorexia couldn't be ruled out, this was more than simply muscle and fat wastage. There was actually no indication of muscle or internal organs at *all*. It was as if everything had simply melted away.

Or been *drained*.

Goose bumps skittered across my skin, and I fervently hoped we weren't dealing with some distant and deadly variation of the vampire. We'd already had more than our fair share of blood suckers here—hell, one of them even ran a popular nightclub, though she'd been missing ever since my ex had foolishly decided to bomb the place and she'd exacted bloody revenge.

I guess if there *was* a silver lining on the whole vampire possibility, it was the fact they were relatively easy to deal with—at least when compared to some of the other demons and ghouls we'd confronted recently.

I jumped from the log and returned to the lean-to. But as I stepped up to the door, I hesitated. I really should ring the ranger station. I needed to report the death anyway, and doing so now at least meant someone would know where I was if things went belly up. And aside from the fact it was better to be safe than sorry, it'd also save me from having to deal with Aiden's annoyance. Like all alpha wolves, he tended to be a little overprotective when it came to those he cared about.

I dragged out my phone and made the call. It rang on rather than switching over to voicemail as it usually did, and I was just about to hang up when a breathless but familiar voice said, "Ranger station, Jaz Marin speaking."

"Hey Jaz, it's Lizzie—"

Her loud groan cut me off. "Don't tell me you've found a body. Not tonight."

"Technically, it's more bones than body, and I have no idea if he was murdered or died naturally, but—"

"Your instincts are twitching, which likely means the former rather than the later," she finished heavily.

"Yeah. Sorry."

She blew out a frustrated breath. "Where are you?"

I gave her the directions and then added, "There's a spell of some kind inside the van, so I'll have to go in—"

"No," she said firmly. "Not until we get there."

"But—"

"Is Belle with you?"

"Well, no—"

"Then you've no one to take a record of events should things go ass up—and let's be honest here, they quite often do in this sort of situation."

"I've been recording everything I've discovered so far," I said, "I've got this feeling that if I don't go in, we'll lose evidence of what happened in there."

She swore. "Fine. Just be careful, and try not to disturb anything."

"I'm not a newbie at this sort of stuff, Jaz. Not these days."

"I know, and I'd be offering the same damn warning to Monty had he been on the other end of this call." She drew in a breath and released it slowly, the sound vibrating with frustration. "It'll take me twenty minutes to get out there. You want me to bring you out a coffee or hot chocolate?"

"Chocolate would be good." I paused. "Sorry to ruin your night."

"It's fine. Levi will just have to finish off matters by himself. See you soon."

She hung up on my laugh. After quickly returning to the rear of the van to make good my lie and record what I'd seen, I tugged a sleeve over my fingers then pressed them lightly against the door and murmured a quick incantation. Magic spun around the lock and, a heartbeat later, the door clicked open.

I stepped back to fully open it, but didn't immediately enter. Instead, I carefully scanned the darkness, all senses on high alert.

The soft pulse of magic was coming from the left. I shone the light that way, spotlighting a small galley kitchen on one side and a seating area on the other. There was a closed door at the far end and, though I wasn't entirely sure whether it led to the bathroom or something else, that's where the spell was located.

I shifted positions and swept the light through the rest of the van. Nothing appeared out of place, and the air was free of the scent of death—which I supposed wasn't that much of an oddity considering the state of the body and the fact it was winter.

I hit record again, then stepped into the van and slowly panned the phone, making sure I recorded absolutely everything.

Everything except the floating fragments of fear and horror that had filled this man's last moments.

I shivered and did my best to both ignore *and* avoid them as I walked toward the double bed under the window.

That was when I caught the faintest whiff of sweat and sex; he definitely *hadn't* been masturbating. Someone had been here with him.

I slowly panned the camera down his body, then hit pause and returned to the front of the van, pressing sleeve-covered fingers against the door. Not to open it this time, but rather to gain some sense of what lay beyond. My psychic senses remained mute, but the pulse of magic was now a whole lot stronger than it had been.

There were no threads of magic on the door or the handle so, after a brief hesitation, I opened it. The room beyond was so small that there were only a few inches between the door and the wall. There was a toilet to my left and a washbasin directly in front. The pulse of magic was coming from the right.

I stepped in and closed the door. The spell sat in the base of the small shower and was a revolving, twisting mess of dark purplish threads—a color I'd not seen before and one that suggested evil even if it wasn't radiating darkness in any way. I hit record again and softly described what I was seeing, as the orb wouldn't show up on the video. With that done, I moved closer.

The spell's pulsing jumped several notches, and so did my heart rate. While I'd yet to pinpoint its intent, I had a bad feeling it was something *other* than a protection spell.

And *that* meant it was far too dangerous to leave it active. I had to dismantle it if I could.

I squatted down and, through narrowed eyes, studied the thing. In many ways, spell creation was similar to weaving—each magical thread was a combination of words and energy that were spun together to make a whole. And, just like in weaving, its success often depended on the skill of the weaver.

The person behind this spell was very skilled indeed.

I shuffled closer and propped my phone against the shower's frame so the light shone on the spell. Its magic crawled across my skin, feeling vaguely like midges that bit and stung. It was decidedly unpleasant, and I had to fight the desire to back away—which might well have been the intention.

There were, as far as I could see, eight layers within the spell. Its purpose wasn't immediately obvious, which no doubt meant one of the layers was a concealment spell of some kind. I carefully reached out and untwined the first layer of the spell from its brethren. As I did, the charm at my neck sprang to life, its warm pulse telling me there was indeed a dark intent behind this spell, even if I couldn't immediately see it. Tension wound through me as I deactivated the opening line; nothing untoward happened, but that didn't ease the tension levels in any way. I repeated the process with the next four, but as each thread came free, the spell's hum increased and the biting sensation got stronger. It felt like I'd stepped into the middle of a swarming bull ant nest, and *that* was the opposite of what was supposed to be happening.

It also meant that the main event spell-wise actually lay within the three remaining threads.

I dismantled another thread, leaving two. The bottom one—which was also the final line of the incantation—definitely looked "heavier" than it should have. Most closure lines were nothing more than a list of limitations and exemptions, but this definitely held a whole lot more than that.

It also *wasn't* the first time I'd come across something like this.

My very first "case" in this reservation had been helping

to track down a magic-capable vampire hell-bent on revenge, and the explosion spell he'd set to blow me up had a very similar feel to this.

Fear gathered, but I tried to ignore it and studied the penultimate line. It was, as far as I could see, the concealment portion of the spell and was almost too easy to deactivate.

One thread to go.

It hovered in the air, dark, heavy, and extremely unhealthy in its feel. Just like the vampire's final spell line, this one consisted of three heavily entwined spells. One of them was certainly the limitations and closure line, but the other two felt unclean and dangerous.

The urge to leave the thing alone and get the hell out of there hit, and it was all I could do to remain in place. While Monty might not be within range to help out, he and I weren't the only witches in the reservation now. But neither Ashworth nor his partner Eli would get here in time. This spell, whatever the hell it was, was working up to something.

I just hoped it wasn't another damn explosion.

I pushed the fear back down once again and forced myself to concentrate. Despite the chill in the air, sweat trickled down the side of my face. I swiped at it with the back of my hand, then carefully pulled the closing thread away and murmured a spell to isolate it without breaking its connection to the other two.

I had no idea which of them I should tackle next, and very much suspected it might not matter.

Before I could decide, the spell came to life.

A dark wave of its energy hit so hard, it threw me back. I crashed into the toilet bowl with bruising force, and my breath left in a huge whoosh of air. The remaining threads of the spell were twisting—growing—washing waves of fierce power and heat through the air, making it sparkle and burn. I swore and scrambled upright, ignoring protesting back muscles as I grabbed my phone and then wrenched open the door. The whole van was now shaking. Cupboard doors flapped wildly back and forth, spilling their contents out onto the floor, the cans of baked beans bruising my feet even as they impeded my progress to the main door. The heat was now so fierce, the painted paneling was beginning to bubble and, on the bed, the mounds of skin barely hanging from white bones burned.

The whole van was on the verge of destruction.

I stumbled toward the door and reached for the handle. A heartbeat before my fingers clasped it, I felt the heat and jerked my hand away. The whole handle glowed.

I stepped back and kicked the door with every ounce of panic and strength I had. It didn't immediately open. I swore at the thing and kicked it again and again, until the damn thing tore off its hinges and went tumbling into the lean-to.

The spell's buzzing was so loud it was all I could hear, all I could feel. I leapt out and ran.

I was barely four meters away when the whole damn caravan exploded.

CHAPTER TWO

A fierce wave of heat and debris hit my back and sent me flying toward a tree. I twisted my body to avoid the trunk but crashed instead into the shrubs and stones that lay to the right of it.

I didn't move. I didn't dare. Bits of metal and wood and God knew what else continued to spear through the air, but the tree and the rocks protected me from most of it. The stuff that did hit was mostly splintered and didn't hold enough force to pierce my clothes, let alone my skin.

After a few more minutes, the magic ebbed away. Ash continued to dance through the air, and a small plume of smoke drifted skyward, though there couldn't have been much of the caravan left to burn.

I pushed upright, then screamed as pain unlike anything I'd ever felt before hit. Nausea surged and sweat broke out across my brow. Sucking in great gulps of air helped calm my stomach, but there was no calming or controlling the pain. It felt like someone had shoved a white-hot poker into my right shoulder and was gleefully twisting it deeper into muscles and tendons. My body shook, my arm burned, and my fingers were going numb—a sure sign I'd done something rather serious.

I shifted carefully, making every effort to keep the arm still, and then dragged the phone out of my pocket. It had, thankfully, survived both the explosion and subsequent crash relatively unscathed. After switching the camera to selfie mode, I raised it high in an effort to see what the hell was wrong with my shoulder.

And immediately wished I hadn't.

A three-inch piece of metal as thick as a finger stuck out of my skin. Weirdly, it didn't feel or even look like the wound was bleeding, though wounds further down my back definitely were. I tried to check them, but couldn't bend my arm around enough. I swore and put the phone away.

Light swept across the trees lining the road below. A heartbeat later, an SUV appeared. Jaz, I hoped.

I took another deep breath that did little to help the pulsing agony or the growing fear, and then, as carefully as I could, extricated myself from the rocks. Nausea surged once more, and this time there was no controlling it. I braced my good arm against the tree in an effort to keep upright and was violently sick.

The soft sound of footsteps broke through the haze of pain, but before I could react in any way, a familiar voice said, "Lizzie? Are you okay?"

I weakly shook my head. I couldn't look up; it was all I could do to remain standing right now. The metal seemed to be sapping all my strength.

"A bit of metal has speared my shoulder," I somehow croaked. Goddammit, even talking was an effort. "I need you to get it out, Jaz."

"That's not a wise move, given we have no idea if that bit of metal is the only thing stopping you from bleeding out." Her feet appeared in my line of vision and stopped several feet away. "I'll call an ambulance. You do look like shit."

"Do it *after* you pull the bit of metal out." The burning was worse and I was starting to feel light-headed and dizzy.

"Lizzie, honestly—"

"Jaz, trust me, you need to do this. *Now*."

She made a low growly noise and then moved closer "Okay, but it's against my better— Oh fuck, Liz, that's *silver*."

I frowned. "What is?"

"That bit of metal sticking out of your back. It's silver."

"Why on earth would a caravan have silver in it?"

"I've no idea, but it means I can't touch the damn thing."

"You have to. It feels like it's killing me."

"Yeah, well, it will *definitely* kill me."

"I know, and I'm sorry, but I need it out."

"Fine," she bit back, "but I'll have to grab some pliers from the back of the SUV. And if you bleed out, I'm going to be very pissed."

"Hurry," I said hoarsely, but I was talking to air.

My legs gave out and I dropped heavily to my knees. The waves of heat radiating from the silver shard were now so fierce, sweat dripped down my face and spine, even though I was shaking with cold.

If I didn't know any better, I'd say I'd somehow developed an allergy to the damn stuff. And yet both my knife and my athame were silver, and I handled them on a regular basis without problem.

Jaz returned and squatted next to me. "This is going to hurt, I'm afraid."

"Not as much as leaving it in will, trust me."

"I daresay we'll discover the truth of *that* soon enough."

She gripped the bit of silver with the pliers and, without fanfare, ripped it from my flesh. A scream tore from my throat; for several seconds, I couldn't breathe, couldn't think, couldn't do anything but feel. And, God, it *hurt*.

But with the shard of silver gone, the waves of burning heat and thick nausea quickly eased. I still felt like crap, but at least it no longer felt like I was dying.

I finally looked up at Jaz. She was tall and slender, with lightly tanned skin and short, dark brown hair. She held the pliers and the bit of silver at arm's length, her expression one of revulsion.

"I expected it to be bigger," I said. "It certainly felt bigger."

"It doesn't take much silver to kill a werewolf."

"I'm not a werewolf."

Her gaze jumped to mine. "Indeed. So why were you reacting to silver like one?"

"I have no idea."

I did have plenty of suspicions, however, and they all revolved around the wild magic and the changes it was making to my body.

But I wasn't going to give them voice. Not to Jaz. Not to anyone. Not until I talked to Katie. She'd already told me that the wild magic would never alter my DNA to the point where I'd be able to shift shape, so why had I suddenly developed a werewolf's vulnerability to silver? It made no sense.

But then, that could be said about many things happening of late.

I drew in another breath that did little to ease the lingering remnants of pain and added, "Maybe I've been hanging around Aiden too long."

She snorted. "Maybe. Do you want a hand up or are you happy to remain right where you are until the ambos get here?"

"I'd rather move away from the vomit. It's rather odorous."

"That it is."

She tucked her hand under my good arm and gently helped me rise. Niggles of pain flared down my spine, but I suspected they were due more to bruising than anything serious.

"Ready to walk on?" Jaz asked softly.

I nodded and did so. My legs remained wobbly, but I made it over to her SUV without them giving way again.

"Right," she said, once I was safely sitting on a rock. "You want to tell me what the hell happened here?"

"The van blew up."

"Obviously." Her voice was dry. "The question is, why?"

"The most logical reason would be to destroy evidence of the crime."

"I thought you said you'd discovered human bones? That normally means the crime is an old one."

"This reservation rarely does anything normally—at least not when it comes to murder." I tugged out my phone and transferred all the video files across to her. "Despite the state of the victim's body, he'd only been dead an hour or so. If it had been any longer, his fear and horror wouldn't have lingered in the air."

She opened the files and silently viewed them. "The way his flesh is hanging off his bones suggests he was drained." Her gaze came to mine. "Could we be dealing with a vampire?"

"A variation of, possibly, though I've never heard of one

that drains not only muscle and fat, but every single organ like this thing did."

"Yeah, but as you've already said, this fucking reservation doesn't do anything normal. Would Monty know?" She paused and frowned. "Why isn't he here? It *is* his job, after all. You're only supposed to be a part-time assistant."

"Yes, but I had no idea what I'd find when my psychic senses tugged me out here. It might have been—"

"Nothing?" she cut in with a snort. "When has that ever been true of late?"

Almost never. "As to where he is, he and Belle went down to Melbourne for the evening. Even if I *had* called him, he wouldn't have gotten back here in time."

"Melbourne, you say?" Speculation glittered in her golden eyes. "Does that mean they've finally stopped the verbal foreplay and plunged into the more intimate phase of their relationship?"

A smile tugged at my lips. "That's a rather polite way of asking if they're finally fucking."

She laughed. "And do we know the date of when it happened? I have a fiver riding on it."

My smile grew. "You and half the damn town. You didn't win."

Her eyebrows rose. "And you know this how?"

"Mike's running the betting book, remember? Seeing he banned me from participating thanks to the possibility of insider knowledge, I helped keep track of all the bets. Notification of the winning date will be going out later today."

"Suggesting their relationship only progressed recently."

I nodded. "You were out by three days."

"Damn." She put her phone away. "Will you be all right

here until the ambulance arrives? I need to section off and record what's left of the crime scene."

"I promise I won't fall off the rock or otherwise collapse on you."

Her expression suggested she wasn't convinced, but she nevertheless rose and walked away. I shifted in an effort to find a more comfortable position, without much success. My butt cheeks were as tender as my back, and both would no doubt be displaying a wide range of colorful bruises tomorrow.

The ambulance and the fire brigade arrived a few minutes later, their red and blue lights lending the caravan's remnants a bloody glow.

While the firemen strode over toward the still smoking remains, the two paramedics helped me into the back of the ambulance and did a full check.

"It appears you've gotten away with nothing more serious than a few cuts and bruising," the older of the two said. "But we'll take you to the hospital so they can fully check—"

"No," I cut in. "Definitely not."

He frowned. "Aside from the fact we can't be certain the blast didn't cause any internal injuries, silver sickness is a real possibility."

"What the hell is silver sickness?"

"It's a type of blood poisoning that sometimes happens after wolves have been stabbed with silver."

"I'm not a werewolf."

He blinked. "Then the silver shouldn't have affected you the way it has."

"Tell me about it," I muttered. "In the unlikely event that I do develop said sickness, what sort of symptoms should I be on the lookout for?"

"It mirrors the symptoms of sepsis, so dizziness, fast heartbeat or breathing, vomiting, slurred speech, that sort of stuff."

"If anything like that happens, I'll head straight to the hospital."

He didn't look at all pleased by this statement, but we both knew he couldn't actually force me to seek further medical attention.

"Don't drive yourself there," he said, a slight bite in his voice. "Call us."

I nodded. "I can drive home now, though, can't I?"

"Yes."

"Good." I rose somewhat stiffly. "Thanks for patching me up."

He nodded and helped me from the ambulance. I slowly walked over to Jaz, who was standing to one side of the van's front end. All that actually remained of it was the floor substructure, two of the four tires, and the bed's metal frame. The mattress and the body were nowhere to be seen. The spell had certainly done a damn fine job of getting rid of whatever evidence might have been here.

It would also have erased me if I'd been any slower.

"Whatever the hell caused this blast, it did a damn good job," the darker-haired fireman was saying. "I doubt forensics are going to find much."

"Which is exactly what the spell was designed to do."

He glanced at me sharply. "I had no idea spells could do this sort of thing."

"Spells can do just about anything you want them to." I glanced at Jaz. "Do you need a statement or anything?"

A smile tugged at her lips. "Aside from the fact you recorded everything, Aiden would have my hide if I delayed you longer than necessary—especially when you're obviously hurting like hell."

"I'm not—"

"Liar. You want someone to drive you home?"

"I'd have to hang around and wait for that someone to arrive, and I honestly can't be bothered. Besides, the painkillers should kick in soon and make everything better."

She nodded. She knew me well enough now to know when it was pointless to argue.

"Just be careful. And if your psychic radar happens to go off again tonight, please ignore it."

"Rest assured I will."

She raised an eyebrow, expression disbelieving. "Rest assured you likely won't—especially when you've shown no inclination to ignore the radar up until now."

A fact I couldn't deny. I waved goodbye and slowly walked back to my car. By the time I let myself into Aiden's house and trudged up the stairs to the bedroom, the painkillers really *had* kicked in, and I was feeling almost normal—in a floaty, spaced-out sort of way. After a quick shower to erase the smell of smoke and destruction from my skin, I dropped into bed and was asleep within seconds.

Strident music woke me a few hours later. I muttered obscenities at the offender and, when *that* didn't work, swept my hand across the bedside table and eventually found my phone. I wearily turned off the alarm and then pried open an eye to see if there were any messages from Aiden. There weren't, and disappointment slithered through me. Which was ridiculous given he often *didn't* make contact on the morning after a moon run with his family. Besides, Jaz wouldn't have had time to make her report yet, so it was likely he didn't know about last night's events.

I ignored the inner whisper suggesting that had nothing to do with the lack of a message, and slowly climbed out of bed. I was as stiff as hell, but I could at least move without too much wincing, and that was always a bonus. A quick look in the mirror revealed I was indeed sporting an interesting array of bruises, but the numerous cuts and scrapes were already well on the way to healing. The area where the silver had stabbed me remained red and puckered, but there was nothing to indicate infection had set in, and both the burning ache down my arm and the numbness in my fingers had disappeared.

I might not be able to shift shape, but the werewolf-like ability to fast heal was definitely getting stronger. Which was probably just as well, given the dangerous situations I kept finding myself in.

I slowly got dressed, then headed downstairs. After making myself a quick breakfast—crumpets slathered with butter and an instant coffee to keep me awake on the drive to our café—I jumped into the Suzi and drove to Castle Rock.

Belle hadn't arrived home from Monty's by the time I got there. Either they'd slept in or were too involved in the pursuit of pleasure to realize the time. They *were* in the first blush of their relationship, after all.

I grinned and headed into the kitchen to do the prep for the day. Mike, Frank, and Penny—our chef, kitchen hand, and main waitress—all arrived before Belle did. When she *did* make an appearance, her thoughts were all sorts of chaotic, but her eyes sparkled and there was a decidedly bright glow of satisfaction swirling through her aura.

"Had a good night, did we?" I said, as she threw her coat over the nearby hook and then tossed her bag under the counter.

"The best," she said, silver eyes bright with happiness. "*Oklahoma* was just amazing."

"So the review said." A smile twitched my lips. "But I'm thinking the show isn't the reason for the glow."

She gave me a stern look and raised a warning finger. "Go no further."

"Oh, I won't."

"Good."

"Decidedly so, I'd say."

She whacked me. I laughed and added, "Oh, come on, after all the dancing to and fro between you two, you've got to expect a little ribbing."

She sighed. "I suppose I should. And yes, before you ask, he's very ... adept in the bedroom."

"A polite way of saying he got your rocks off multiple times."

She grinned and didn't deny it. "So, what happened to you last night? I had a vague sensation of trouble about one o'clock, but when I reached out, you were locked down tight."

"Because I didn't want to disturb your night."

"That doesn't answer the damn question."

I waved a hand. "We had an event—"

"Define event." Her voice was dry. "Because in *this* reservation, that could mean many things."

I gave her a quick rundown and then added, "I'm a little stiff this morning, but otherwise okay."

"And that niggling worry I can feel at the far reaches of your thoughts? The one you're keeping from me?"

"I'm lucky I can keep anything from you."

"Stop avoiding the question."

I grinned. Belle wasn't only a witch, but also a spirit talker and a strong telepath. She also happened to be my familiar—an event that had never happened before in all witch history and something that had not only changed my life but also saved it.

"I've just got a few things I need to ask Katie—nothing serious."

Belle harrumphed. "Yeah, believing *that*."

I smiled and nudged her with my good shoulder. "I wouldn't lie to—"

"No," she cut in, voice dry. "But evade the truth? Hell yes."

I laughed, and we both got down to work. The morning rush came and kept us busy, though I mostly remained behind the counter making coffee, as it required the least amount of movement. I checked my phone a number of times over the course of the day, but there was nothing from Aiden. Had something happened within the O'Connor compound or during the run last night? It wasn't like any of us outsiders would know—the wolves might share the bulk of the reservation with us, but the three home compounds were out of bounds.

At three on the dot, Monty made his usual appearance for afternoon tea. He was tall and well built, with crimson hair that gleamed like dark fire in the afternoon sunlight streaming in through the windows. He was also grinning like a cat that had just lapped all the cream.

A poker player he would never be.

"You can do the honors," Belle said. "I don't want to be starting any untoward rumors."

I snorted. "Little late for that. Half the gossip brigade is here, three of whom won a sizable amount of money correctly guessing when you two would become an item, and all of them will know exactly what that satisfied grin of his means."

"Yes, but I have no desire to add further fuel to the gossip mill fire. And I probably would, if I went out there." She slipped his coffee and a thick slice of black forest cake on the tray with my cup of tea and pushed it toward me. "Off you go."

I rolled my eyes, but picked up the tray and slowly wound my way through the tables to the one he'd claimed in the corner. There was a backpack sitting on one chair and his wet coat slung over the other.

I slid the tray onto the table and handed him his coffee and cake. "Heard a good time was had last night."

"Heard you hit some problems last night," he replied evenly. "Why didn't you ring me?"

I just gave him the look—the one that said "don't be daft"—and sat down on the remaining chair.

He grinned. "Well, okay, I'm glad you didn't, because oh boy—"

I held up my hand to cut him off. "Details are not required."

He chuckled softly. "I, however, *do* require them. I didn't get much from Aiden this morning—"

"He was at the ranger station?" I said, surprised and perhaps a little hurt.

"Yes—Jaz was giving everyone a rundown of what happened last night." He studied me with a slight frown. "I take it you haven't seen him yet?"

"No, but he did start work reasonably early." I was making excuses for him, and we both knew it. And as much as I wanted to believe his lack of contact had nothing to do with Katie's warning, I knew in my heart it was a false hope.

Or was I looking for problems that didn't currently exist, and doing him a disservice?

It was possible something had happened during the

moon run last night—something that had taken precedence over everything else in his life. Especially given that, even at his busiest, he would normally have sent a text message asking if I was okay.

I slid the teapot and cup off the tray, then leaned it against the chair leg, out of the way. "Did they find any body fragments?"

He shook his head. "Though that's hardly surprising, given the force of the explosion just about obliterated the caravan. You were damn lucky you weren't more seriously hurt."

"I can run very fast when the situation requires it."

"One of these days, that's not going to be enough."

"One of these days, the echoes of an unguarded wellspring will stop washing onto darker shores, and this reservation will finally be free from the constant threat of evil." I shrugged. "Until then, however, I have no choice but to do what I can to keep this place safe."

"That task isn't yours alone—"

"No, but I *am* the only one who can communicate with the wilder forces that inhabit this place."

He grunted. It was not a happy sound.

I poured my tea, then picked up the cup. Like many of the items we'd salvaged from secondhand stores to use in the café, this cup had a history and a presence the sensitive could feel. While most would scoff at the thought that a mere cup could make a difference to a person's mood, I knew from experience the *wrong* choice could have an unsettling effect. This particular cup had become a favorite of mine lately, simply because it held echoes of the loving relationship the woman who'd previously owned the set had been in. It had become my daily reminder that happiness was possible even if everything was threatening to fall apart.

"Did Jaz say anything about the footprint I photographed?" I added.

"They're presuming it's human rather than wolf."

I frowned. "Why?"

He shrugged. "Something about the bone structure and weight distribution of a werewolf's foot in human form being slightly different to that of an actual human."

"I'll have to investigate Aiden's foot more closely." I sipped my tea. "Did she say whether she managed to get out there and check it?"

"She did, but the drizzle had basically washed everything away, including whatever scent might have remained."

"Bugger."

"Yeah." Monty scooped up a big bit of cake. "I take it you think the print belonged to whoever set the explosion spell?"

"I can't be positive, but my gut says it does."

"And your gut is rarely wrong."

I couldn't help but hope that when it came to Aiden and me, it was.

"Did you get any sense of what it was?" he continued.

I shook my head. "It was just a flash of white. I have no idea whether that meant he—or she—was clothed in white or simply had very pale skin."

"And the magic? I know you said in the video you didn't recognize the spell, but what about its feel?"

"It was dark, but not evil as such, if that makes any sense." I sipped my tea. "It was also dark purple, a color I generally associate with revenge rather than magic."

"There *are* dark witches who walk the line between good and evil—their magic tends to be more purplish, rather than the dark red of either blood witches or those who deal with demons."

I frowned. "How can dark witches walk the line? If they trade with evil, they can't be good."

A smile touched his lips. "Not everything falls on one side or the other, Lizzie, especially when we're dealing with magic."

It did when a dark sorcerer was responsible for your sister's death. "I take it you've met such a person?"

"Once—sort of—up in Canberra." He shrugged. "He'd come to the archives looking for a book. According to Brenda—a fellow archivist who practically trampled me in order to serve the man—he was charismatic, powerful, and a complete enigma."

I raised my eyebrows. "The fact he was in the main archives suggests he was there with the council's permission."

"He was."

"But ... how?"

He shrugged again. "Something to do with his parentage."

"Meaning he came from one of the royal lines?"

"That was the talk." He scooped up the remaining bit of cake. "I don't suppose any of Belle's books catalog the various types of vampires?"

The books he was referring to were the ones Belle had inherited from her grandmother. Nellie might have been one of the so-called "common" Sarr witches, but she'd gathered together a vast collection of extremely rare books on magic and the supernatural over the many years of her life. The collection *should* have been gifted to the Royal Witch Library on her death, but the majority of it had instead gone to Belle—something I suspected the High Witch Council might now be aware of. Which was why we were on the final stretches of converting them all to electronic format. If the council *did* demand we hand over the library, we'd still have a full record of every book.

"None of the ones I've read mentioned this sort of vampire," I said. "But I'll check the index and see what I can find."

He nodded. "It'd be handy to know exactly what we're dealing with when this thing hits again."

"It could be a one-off event for a change."

He gave me a wry look. "Since when has that ever happened?"

I couldn't help smiling. "Well, never, but there's always a first time."

"Not in this reservation, there's not." He leaned across to the other chair and opened his backpack. "I brought you a present."

"Me?" I raised my eyebrows. "I'd have thought—given the very new relationship status—you'd be showering Belle with presents rather than me."

Oh, came her amused comment, *he is.*

Oh? Do tell.

I'll tell my secrets if you tell me yours.

I have no secrets.

Liar.

I didn't bother denying it. She knew well enough when I was and wasn't keeping something from her.

Monty dragged a rather heavy-looking book out of the pack and dumped it on the table. It was a thick, leather-bound volume that looked older than Methuselah. The gold writing on the cover had faded so badly it was unreadable, but my heart nevertheless beat a whole lot faster.

My gaze jumped to Monty's. "Is that ...?"

"It is indeed." He spun the heavy book around. The title was no clearer, but it didn't matter, because I knew exactly what it was. *Earth Magic: Its Uses and Dangers.* This was the book we'd been waiting for—the one that would hopefully give us some idea of what to expect when it came to the wild magic and its impacts on the human body.

I *couldn't* be the only one to have survived a merging with the wild magic. There *had* to be others, especially given earth magic—as they'd called it at the very dawn of time—had been less volatile and more widely used by witches at the time.

I drew the book closer and reverently ran my fingers down the front of it. Images had been carved into the thick leather, but the book was so old and the leather so worn they were barely visible. I tracked the faint outline of a tree —the tree of life, I suspected.

"Have you read any of it?" I asked softly.

"Nope, because the damn thing is written in Latin."

My gaze jumped to his again even as my heart sank. "Do you know anyone who can translate it for us?"

"Apparently, Eli can. He said he'd read through and convert the relevant sections for us as quickly as he could. I'll drop it off to him as soon as I finish my coffee."

"Good." I finished my cup of tea, then collected the tray and pushed stiffly to my feet. "Are you and Belle heading out tonight?"

His grin was full of devilment. "I think it more likely we'll stay in. Things to do, places to explore, and all that."

"An image I did *not* need in my mind," I said. But I certainly got them—at least until Belle abruptly shut the line down. The silence echoed with her amused embarrassment.

He laughed. "We're all adults here."

"Yeah, but you're also my cousin, and I don't want to be envisaging you all naked and sweaty with my best friend."

He raised his eyebrows. "I never mentioned naked and sweaty."

"You didn't have to."

His gaze shot past me. "Belle?"

"Didn't shut her thoughts down fast enough."

He laughed again. "Then *I* am definitely looking forward to tonight."

I snorted softly and placed the empty plate and cups on the tray. After dropping them off in the kitchen, I headed back behind the counter to continue making the coffee orders and doling out cakes.

Aiden still hadn't contacted me by the time we'd closed and cleaned up, and it was all I could do not to send him a text asking if everything was okay.

"And why shouldn't you?" Belle handed me a coffee and leaned a hip against the counter. "You are in a relationship, after all."

I scooped up some of my cheesecake. It was a triple chocolate sort of day. "Yes, but it's one that is ending."

"If that *is* what's happening here, you need to find out."

"Agreed, but we both also know I have a long history of sticking my head in the sand when it comes to relationships falling apart."

A smile twitched her lips. "Hard to forget when you've had so few of them."

I contemplated flicking a bit of cheesecake at her but decided it was a waste of good cheesecake and ate it instead.

"What are you going to do, then?" she asked. "Go home and wait for the man?"

"Absolutely not. I'm going to talk to Katie."

"Can't you contact her through the wild magic?"

"It has to be present. It's not." Besides, there were some discussions that were best done in person.

Belle frowned. "You won't get any sympathy from her. Aiden is her brother."

"I won't even broach the subject of her brother." At Belle's rather disbelieving arched eyebrow, I grinned and added, "Well, maybe a little. But I also need to head across to the new storage unit and see if we've anything that mentions entities that can literally suck a man dry."

"You don't think it was a vampire?"

I shook my head. "It just didn't have that feel."

"I didn't think it had hung around long enough for you to get any real sense of it."

"It didn't, but I have confronted vampires before, and this thing felt nothing like them."

A car horn blasted outside before she could say anything. She glanced at her watch and then drained the remains of her coffee. "That'll be Monty."

"Enjoy your evening."

"Oh, I will." She picked up her overnight bag and then touched my shoulder lightly. "I'm here if you need me. Remember that."

"I know." I placed my hand over hers and squeezed lightly. "But I want you to lock down your thoughts and stop worrying about me. If I get into trouble and need your help, you know I'll reach out."

"Promise?"

"Yes."

She studied me doubtfully for a moment. "I sense a 'but' in that agreement."

I couldn't help smiling. "Because I'll only reach out if

the situation is something you *can* help with. I don't want to be a spoilsport."

"I'd rather you be a spoilsport than dead."

"I'm not going to get dead." I crossed mental fingers that I hadn't just tempted fate.

She hesitated and then left. I finished my cheesecake and coffee, then locked up and jumped into the SUV. The Suzi might be cheaper to run, but all the recent rain had washed out the road up to the second wellspring. The SUV, with its bigger wheelbase and all-wheel drive, was definitely the safer option.

Once I was out of Castle Rock and on the open road, I turned up the music and happily sang along. I knew it was nothing more than a means of avoiding too much thinking, and I had no problem with that. I'd spent far too much of my life so far second-guessing not only other peoples' motives and actions, but also my own. No matter what I feared, no matter what I thought, Aiden deserved the benefit of the doubt. The constant gnawing over what it all meant was absolutely useless.

Of course, telling myself that and actually believing it were two entirely different things.

The second wellspring lay within the St. Erth forests, which ringed the small town of Maldoon and was Marin Pack territory. Thankfully, I'd been given permission to visit the site as often as needed, but only as long as I went absolutely nowhere else.

I turned onto a gravel road a few minutes out of Maldoon and did my best to avoid the many potholes while keeping well away from the soft roadside edge and the long drop into the heavily treed valley below. But as I turned onto the track that led up through the scrub and the second wellspring, the psychic part of my soul stirred.

Something was out there.

I hit the brakes, turned down the music, and studied the shadows gathering beyond the headlight's bright beams. Nothing moved through the trees, and there was no other sound aside from the rumble of the SUV's engine. I glanced in the rearview mirror. The red glow of the brake lights lit tree trunks lining the road, and for no good reason, a vision of blood rose.

On the trees. On my face.

I blinked, and the vision disappeared. The trepidation didn't. It suddenly seemed a very *bad* idea to be climbing this bitch of a road with night coming on and more rain on the way.

Besides, it wasn't like I couldn't come up here any other time. Wasn't like I couldn't call in a thread of wild magic and contact Katie if I absolutely had to.

The *only* reason I'd come up here was simply to avoid going home to emptiness. Which was dumb when I had plenty of times in the past.

I scanned the shadowy trees one more time, then put the SUV into reverse and carefully backed away from the goat track.

As I swung the wheel around, the lights caught a flash of white, and my heart leapt into my throat. The inner wild magic surged through my body, and sparks danced across my fingers, ready to be deployed against whatever moved out there.

The white thing tumbled closer, and I couldn't help a sharp, somewhat nervous laugh.

It was a goddamn plastic bag.

I flexed my fingers in an effort to release the pent-up energy, then shifted the gear into drive and carefully drove back down the road.

Another flash of white, this time in the trees to my left. My breath caught, and I braked, tension pounding through me. It didn't ease when I saw it was just another bit of plastic.

I scanned the growing shadows, looking for the threat I could feel.

Nothing.

But it was definitely out there.

What "it" was, and what it intended, were two questions the psychic part of my soul couldn't answer.

I watched the plastic float off over the edge of the steep drop to my right, then drew a shaky breath and continued on.

I'd barely gone more than a few more meters when energy surged.

Energy that was dark and fierce and full of determination.

My own responded, exploding from my body so fiercely it tore a gasp from my throat.

But before I could do anything else, something hit the side of the SUV and sent it tumbling.

Straight over the edge of the road and down into blackness.

CHAPTER THREE

The thick smell of smoke and burnt material woke me. For several seconds, I did nothing more than dazedly wonder where the hell I was and why there was moisture on my face.

Then recognition hit.

It was blood.

My blood.

Consciousness abruptly sharpened, and I became aware of the roaring of an engine and the heavy groaning of metal. The blood on my face was running *up* my cheek, which suggested I was hanging upside down—a fact supported by the seat belt digging fiercely into my shoulder as it held my full weight.

I carefully ran my fingers across my face, finding a cut on my chin and a deeper one near my temple. There was plenty of glass tangled up in my hair too, which meant at least one of the windows must have shattered.

A brief sense of déjà vu hit. This wasn't the first time I'd been upside down in a goddamn truck, but at least *that* time, I'd known exactly who'd attacked me.

And why.

I swiped at the blood dribbling up my face, then carefully reached past the deflated airbag and switched off the engine. The vehicle continued to groan and, though I couldn't smell petrol or see flames, the urge to get the hell out of the cabin hit.

I pressed a hand against the roof, my feet against the upside-down floor, then carefully undid the seat belt and dropped somewhat inelegantly down. The front of the SUV shifted, then the whole vehicle began to slide. I screamed and gripped the handbrake above me in an effort not to add my weight to the vehicle's momentum. The headlights briefly illuminated each of the saplings and shrubs we crashed through before pinpointing the thick trunk of a tree. We were heading straight for it ...

I braced as best I could and shut my eyes at the last moment, just in case the windscreen shattered and sent glass flying into my face and eyes. We hit the tree hard enough to rattle my teeth and, for one heart-stopping moment, the SUV slid sideways, as if to continue its downward journey. My pulse rate didn't decrease any when the momentum eventually stopped. Though my situation was damn precarious, for too many minutes I simply couldn't move, fearing that even the slightest twitch would send the vehicle skidding on.

When that didn't immediately happen, I sucked in a very shaky breath and looked around. There was only one headlight working now, and it highlighted the steep, rock-strewn slope beyond the tree. Thunder rumbled ominously overhead and, a few seconds later, the rain hit, drumming on the undercarriage so loudly it was deafening.

It was the very last thing I needed. This area had

already suffered one major mudslide. Another wasn't beyond the realms of possibility.

I did *not* want to be in the SUV if that happened.

Slowly, carefully, I inched toward the driver door and tried to open it. It refused to budge, and after a moment, I saw why. There was a rock resting hard up against it. I swore again and turned around, but the shift of weight sent the SUV into another slide. When it stopped this time, there was nothing visible in the beam of the remaining headlight except airy darkness.

I gulped and tried not to wonder just how far the drop might be. If I didn't get out of this vehicle, I'd be finding out the hard way.

The passenger door wouldn't open either, though there didn't seem to be anything blocking it. But the window had shattered, and though there were sharp shards of glass still clinging to the rubber, it wouldn't take much to clear it.

I reached across to the backpack—which had fallen from the passenger seat and was now lying hard up against the still-intact front windshield—and drew out my knife. Thankfully, I didn't react to the silver in the blade, maybe that was because the hilt was offering my skin protection. Or maybe it was simply a matter of silver needing to be in my flesh rather than merely touching it. I wasn't a werewolf, after all, so what applied to them wouldn't necessarily apply to me.

I knocked out the remaining glass with the blade, then tossed it out the window. After shoving the backpack after it, I lay on my stomach and cautiously followed.

I was halfway out when, with a deep, metallic groan, the SUV slipped again.

Taking me with it.

I yelped and desperately searched for something,

anything, to grab. One hand caught a thick root of some kind and I held on tight. Breath hissed from my lips as the lower half of my body was brutally ripped free from the vehicle.

But I was out. Free. Maybe not safe, but at least safer.

The resulting surge of relief was so fierce that my body shook and tears flowed. I angrily swatted them away, then twisted around. The SUV was nowhere to be seen. It had obviously plunged over the drop only meters away from where I lay and disappeared into the darkness.

I rested my forehead against the waterlogged ground and gulped in air, trying not to think about how close I'd come to serious injury or even death.

That, I thought sourly, was the last time I tempted fate in any damn way.

I pushed onto my haunches and looked around. From my current position, I couldn't see the road, though it wouldn't be hard to find—all I had to do was follow the trail of destruction the SUV had left in its wake.

I drew in another shaky breath and reached for my phone. It wasn't in my pocket. I swore and—somewhat frantically—looked around. It was nowhere to be seen. The damn thing must have fallen out of my pocket sometime during the rollover.

Which meant I'd have to contact Belle and ruin her evening if I wanted to get out of here ...

"Hello!" a youngish-sounding voice said from somewhere above. "Anyone down there?"

My head snapped up even as my heart leapt. "Yes!"

"I saw the taillights as I was walking past and wasn't sure. Are you injured? Do you need help?"

"My SUV rolled, but I'm okay. Could you contact Aiden O'Connor for me, please?"

"Sure thing. You want me to call a tow truck as well?"

"There's little point—the SUV went over the drop."

"You all the way down there? Fuck, you're lucky to be alive."

"Tell me about it."

"You'd better stay put. Once I call the ranger, I'll contact my pack and get them to bring down some climbing gear. We'll likely need it to get you out. Sit tight."

"I will." I paused. "You got a name?"

"Ryan Marin. You?"

"Lizzie Grace."

"The witch who runs the amazing cake place in Castle Rock?"

It was interesting he mentioned *that* rather than my relationship with Aiden, but maybe he simply cared more about cakes than relationships. He sounded more like a teenager than an adult. "The same."

"Then I'm glad I happened by. We definitely can't afford to lose your cake-making skills."

I laughed. "You won't."

"Good. Hang five. I won't be long."

Silence fell, and the darkness closed in. The rain continued to pound down, dripping from the canopy above and running in little rivers past my thighs. I might be wearing a coat, but it wasn't covering my legs, and my jeans were utterly soaked.

But at least the rain was all I had to worry about right now. The energy that had sent the SUV off the road had disappeared, and I had no sense that anything or anyone else was near—not even the wild magic. Which was rather odd, given how close I was to Katie's wellspring.

Obviously, something else had her attention.

Was that something her pack? Her family?

Aiden?

I shoved the thought away and told myself to stop worrying over every little thing beyond my control. But it was a hard thing to achieve when I'd spent half my life doing just that.

I looked around again, this time for my backpack, and spotted it a few meters further up the slope. I crawled toward it, alternating between digging my fingers into the soft soil and gripping onto the sharp but crushed needlewood branches to keep balance. The effort left me shaking. There was no way known I was going to get up the rest of this hill without help.

I found my knife not too far away from my pack, and once it was safely tucked inside to ensure there was no chance of it harming my werewolf rescuers, I sat back and waited.

Getting wetter, colder, and more miserable by the minute.

Eventually, the musky scent of wolf touched the cold air. I wiped the rain from my face and looked up. Though I couldn't see anything, I knew there were three of them up there.

"You still okay?" Ryan asked.

"I am."

"I've got my dad and brother here. They're going to rappel down and rescue you. Won't be long."

"Awesome. Thank you."

A few minutes later, two men appeared out of the rainy gloom. They were both wearing full wet weather gear and were coming down the slope at a speed that would have alarmed the hell out of me.

The bigger of the two jumped to the right when he neared my position and then stopped. Teeth flashed in his brown, handsome face. "You got yourself into a bit of a pickle, didn't you?"

"I did. Sorry to drag you both out on a night like this."

"Wouldn't be the first time we've had to rescue someone from a rollover," the second—and younger of the two—said. "I dare say it won't be the last. The road is utter shit in this sort of weather."

It hadn't been the weather or the road that had caused the rollover, but I didn't bother telling them that.

"You're the local rescue unit?"

The older man nodded. "The name's George, and this is my eldest, Harry. Ryan—my youngest—will be working the pulley to help you up."

I took a deep breath and released it slowly. "Good, because I'm not sure I'd keep my footing too well on this damn ground."

"Even we werewolves struggle in shit weather like this. You able to walk?"

I nodded. "The airbags and the seat belt did their jobs, thank God."

"And the blood I can smell?"

"Small cuts on my face from the broken side window."

He grunted and pulled a second harness over his head. "You able to slip this on?"

I handed him my backpack and did so. He checked all the clips were properly secured, then snapped on a rope. I instantly felt a hundred percent better, even though I had a long climb still ahead of me.

"Right," he said evenly. "Ready to go up?"

When I nodded, his smile flashed. "Good. Ryan, we're all set down here."

The rope instantly tightened, and I slowly began the

ascent up the steep hillside. The two men kept close, catching my arms to steady me when my feet slipped.

It took ages to reach the top. A tall, lanky figure came into view, and his wide smile briefly lit the gloom. But he continued to work the pulley system until I was back on solid ground.

I undid the harness with shaking fingers and handed it to him. The sheer and utter sense of relief had tears stinging my eyes and my legs threatening to collapse.

I sucked in another of those breaths that really didn't do a whole lot and then said, "I'm not sure I can thank you all enough, but you can expect free cake and coffee whenever you're in my neck of the woods."

Ryan grinned. "You can keep the coffee, but cake never goes astray."

"And he can eat mountains of the stuff," Harry said with a laugh. "You may end up regretting that offer."

"I'd have regretted going over the edge of the cliff more."

"*That* is a certainty," George said. "We called an ambulance, but they won't be able to traverse this road. We'll be meeting them at the turnoff instead. Are your legs stable enough now to walk to the truck?"

I smiled. "No, but I'll nevertheless make it over there. The sooner I'm out of here, the better."

"A sentiment I totally agree with," Harry said.

Once I was safely tucked into the back of their four-wheel drive, they retrieved all the climbing gear and then jumped into the truck and headed down the road. There were several sections that had been partially washed out or were covered by the rubble of a landslip. If it hadn't been for that rush of energy I'd felt just before the SUV tumbled, I might have been tempted to believe it was an accident.

But it wasn't, and I needed to find out why.

Of course, it was possible that the thing that'd drained the man in the caravan simply wanted me out of the way, but that then begged the question ... how had it even *known* about me?

Had it spotted me in the forest behind the van and investigated who I was? Or did the wild magic have something to do with it? Given dark entities could sense its presence, maybe it could feel me through it.

Katie might know, but to ask, I needed to get hold of her.

Which reminded me ... "Ryan, did you manage to get hold of the ranger?"

He twisted around to look at me. "Yes. He said he'd be waiting at the top of the road with the ambulance."

The goddamn tears threatened again. I blinked and told myself to get a grip. I was *not* going to fall apart the minute I saw the man. The relationship might or might not be teetering on the edge, but I had more pride than that.

I hoped.

We continued on, our pace by necessity slow, but eventually the ambulance's red and blue lights washed across the darkness ahead. And parked to one side of it was Aiden's truck.

All I wanted to do was jump out and run into his arms.

The four-wheel drive stopped, and I climbed somewhat stiffly out. A frisson of heat and awareness rolled over my skin, and I turned to see Aiden striding toward me. Like most werewolves, he was tall and rangy, but his shoulders were lovely and wide, his arms lean but muscular, and his sharp features very easy on the eye.

His expression held little in the way of emotion, but his

aura practically crackled with it. Fear, relief, guilt, concern, and deep, deep worry ... the latter *not* aimed at me.

I frowned, knowing then something bad must have happened, but before I could say anything, he wrapped me in a hug that was fierce and warm and oh-so wonderful.

"What the fuck have you been doing to yourself?" His voice was gruff with emotion. *Love*, an inner voice whispered, but that was something I didn't dare hope for. It was a path that could only lead to tears. "You look and feel utterly drained."

"It's been a busy few nights."

"You should have rung me—"

"I rang Jaz. She was the ranger on call, not you."

"Yes, but—" He stopped, took a deep breath, then kissed the top of my head and pulled back. "Thanks for saving my girl, Harry. Appreciate it."

"No problems, Aiden." Harry handed Aiden my pack, then looked at me, his amber eyes bright with amusement. "Perhaps next time you should think twice about driving on shitty roads in shittier weather."

I laughed. "Oh, you can be sure of that."

"Good." With a nod at the two of us, he jumped back into his truck and headed off down the road.

Aiden took my arm and guided me over to the ambulance. "I'll meet you at the hospital. We can talk there."

There was a note in his voice that sharpened the inner worry. "Is everything alright?"

"*That* is the question on everyone's lips right now." He ran a hand through his wet hair, his blue eyes bright with worry. "Dillon was badly injured during the moon run."

Dillon was his youngest brother, and only fourteen, if I remembered correctly.

I gripped his arm, and his muscles briefly tensed—a

reflexive action that suggested he didn't want to be comforted right now. "What happened?"

"Tree fell on him. His legs were ..." He took a deep breath and released it slowly. "Well, mangled is the only word that is in any way appropriate."

My breath caught. "But he's a werewolf—"

"Yes, but to heal, a werewolf has to shift shape, and Dillon is comatose."

"Isn't the change normally automatic in this sort of situation?"

"There is *nothing* normal about this situation." It was sharply said, but he immediately grimaced and placed his hand over mine, squeezing lightly. "Sorry. It's been a long day. I should have called but—"

"Your mother wouldn't have appreciated my presence at such a moment, Aiden."

One of the paramedics cleared his throat. "Um, hate to interrupt, but we need to get you out of this rain and down to the hospital."

"Go," Aiden immediately said. "I'll see you down there."

I hesitated, then nodded and accepted the paramedic's help. The ambulance door was slammed shut and, once they'd done a preliminary check, I was strapped in and driven away.

When we arrived at the hospital twenty minutes later, I was shoved into a gown and whisked through various scans and tests. Thankfully, they all came back clear; there was no sign of internal injuries, and neither of the cuts on my face was deep enough to require stitches. The doctors were more surprised than me, I think, at the lack of injuries given the severity of the rollover. They tried insisting I remain overnight for observation on the off chance the seat belt had caused internal injuries they'd missed, but I was having none of that. After a good deal of arguing and a promise to return if I developed any sort of abdominal pain, they grudgingly released me.

I reluctantly pulled on my wet jeans, then dragged on my sodden shoes, collected my pack, and headed out.

Aiden was waiting in the seating area just outside the main emergency department entry, but rose when he saw me. His eyes—a deep blue rather than the usual amber of a werewolf—were haunted.

"Dillon's condition has taken a turn for the worse." He scraped a hand through his wet hair. "I'll have to stay, just in case."

"I'm so sorry, Aiden." I gripped his arm, but once again muscles tensed under my touch. "You may need your truck, so I'll grab a cab—"

I stopped abruptly, my gaze caught by the flicker of a moonbeam.

Only it wasn't. It was a glowing, silvery thread of wild magic.

Katie was here.

You can save him, she said. *You are, in fact, his only hope.*

Not to put any pressure on me or anything, I muttered mentally. *And in case you missed it, I'm not a healer. Neither is the wild magic.*

He doesn't need a healer. He just needs to shift shape. His body will do the rest.

And how am I supposed to force him to shift?

You'll need to use your precognition and psychometry skills in much the same way as you use them to read the memories of the newly dead.

That particular skill was one I used only in extreme

circumstances, as it was a rabbit hole a psychic could easily get lost in. While most thought the brain died the minute the heart stopped, there was in fact up to a six-minute window of survival, after which memory deterioration began if the heart wasn't restarted. But deep diving into a living mind that was dying presented a whole raft of new dangers I really didn't want to think about.

I can't see how that will help. I can read memories, but I can't alter them or his mind.

No, but Belle can with my guidance. We need to hurry, though. I can hear death's footsteps, and she draws far too close.

"Lizzie?" Aiden said softly. "What are you seeing?"

"Katie. She wants me and Belle to help her save Dillon."

"*What?*" The word exploded from him, filled with a deep mix of disbelief and hope. "Does she seriously believe that's possible?"

"Yes, but neither she nor I can give you a hundred-percent guarantee."

I raised my hand, and the glowing thread curled around my wrist, as fragile as a moonbeam, but pulsing with power. Ancient power. This thread had come from the old well-spring rather than Katie's, which suggested her influence over both was increasing. I couldn't help but wonder where it would all end—for her, and for me. Because within that power was an acknowledgment of kinship with me, and it was stronger now than it had ever been.

"If that's the case, we need to get to intensive care, and fast." Aiden twined his fingers through mine and quickly tugged me forward.

My bruised and aching muscles protested the sudden movement, but I ignored them as we ran through a myriad of corridors that all looked the same. *How exactly is this supposed to work, Katie?*

You, Belle, and I will have to become one.

Meaning you'll be acting through us? Because that's dangerous.

For all three of us.

How could it be dangerous for you when you're a soul locked in the wild magic?

What is locked can be unlocked if I step beyond the limits of strength.

What was dangerous for her would undoubtedly be doubly so for me. *Is that why you were absent for so long after our confrontation with your mother at Aiden's party?*

Yes. It drained me to the point where I was little more than a shade.

A statement that held a warning for me, and one that confirmed fears that overusing the wild magic could literally result in me fading away.

But we have no choice. It is the only way to save Dillon's life. She paused. *It might also have the side benefit of proving your worth to my mother.*

I snorted in silent disbelief. *You really believe that?*

Well, no, but stranger things have happened.

I think that is one step too far, even for a reservation that specializes in strange.

Her laughter bubbled through me, though it held a sharp edge. *Indeed. We are near the ICU. You should contact Belle, so there is no further delay once we are in his room.*

I reluctantly reached out, and immediately hit a mental wall so damn strong it would have kept even the strongest telepath out. But she was my familiar, and that was a connection no distance, no barrier, and very few spells could break.

It took a few seconds, but I did get through.

What's happened? she immediately said.

All sorts of shit that I can tell you about tomorrow. Right now, I need you to get comfortable and form a full connection with me. Aiden's brother is in hospital, on the cusp of dying, and the only way we can save his life is by you, me, and Katie forming a three-way connection and diving into his brain to force a shape shift.

Well, fuck.

Yeah.

Let me get comfortable and warn Monty.

Sorry to spoil your evening.

You haven't.

The deep undertone of satisfaction running through that statement very much suggested they'd enjoyed themselves more than once this evening.

Indeed, she said. *It's actually excellent timing on your part. We were just taking a refuel break.*

A secure-looking door loomed ahead of us. Aiden punched through it and immediately set off a series of alarms. Nurses came running from everywhere, but Aiden held up a warning hand. "Liz can save my brother. Get in my way at your own peril."

One brawny nurse stopped in front of us and crossed her arms, practically daring Aiden to run her over. "She isn't getting near intensive care until she's fully masked, gloved, and gowned. And I will take you down, Ranger, if you take one step further."

Aiden made a low sound deep in his throat, but nevertheless stopped. "Fine. But hurry."

The nurse nodded and motioned us to follow her. In almost no time at all, we were both kitted up and ready to go. Aiden grabbed my hand again, his fingers so warm against mine despite the gloves. I appreciated that warmth. Appreciated the strength of his grip.

I was going to need every little bit I could scavenge.

The ICU door slid open. A sharp array of different sounds hit, the noise so loud it was briefly overwhelming. Monitors and machines surrounded every patient, and some had so many tubes in their bodies it was hard to see the person. At least five patients were intubated; Aiden's brother was one of them.

His bed lay at the far end of the room; Karleen and Joseph—Aiden's parents—stood on one side of the bed and a nurse on the other. The nurse's expression was remote and businesslike, but worry and concern ran all through her aura. As Katie had said, things were going downhill fast.

Karleen abruptly stiffened. Before Aiden could say anything, she spun around and bared her teeth. If she'd been in wolf form, I suspected she might have launched herself at me.

"What," she said, her voice quivering with rage, "is *she* doing here?"

"She came here to help Dillon—"

"And what the fuck can she"—Karleen pointed a stiffened finger at me, her sapphire eyes glowing with a ferocity that was almost manic—"do that a multitude of specialist doctors cannot?"

"Maybe nothing," I cut in, voice calm despite the inner rage—rage that was more Katie's than mine. "But your daughter believes it's possible, and I'm not going to gainsay her."

"Aside from the fact she's *dead*, Kate is no more a healer than you." Her gaze snapped to the woman standing on the other side of the bed. "Nurse, call security and get her the *fuck* out of here."

"Do not obey that order," Joseph said. He was an older, gray-haired version of Aiden and, at least at a surface level, taking my intrusion a whole lot more calmly than his wife. "What is all this about Katie being able to help?"

"There is no time to explain, Father," Aiden said. "Please, trust Liz. Or at least trust the fact that I wouldn't do anything to endanger Dillon's life, and let us get this done."

The older man hesitated and then nodded. Karleen made another low sound, but Joseph gently touched her arm. Her gaze snapped to his, but after a moment, she said, "Fine. Let it be done. But do not think this will in any way change anything."

My smile was thin and humorless. "Oh, I'm more than aware of that. Your loss, not mine."

Her gaze narrowed, but she didn't say anything. I followed Aiden around to the nurse's side of the bed. The wash of Karleen's fury was sharp enough to burn my skin, but I had no choice except to ignore it. Anything else would have the bitch launching at me.

Dillon's face was drawn and pale, his aura awash with agony despite the drugs they were pumping into him. It also pulsed, and that meant the damage to his body was so bad his soul was in the process of giving up the fight. If we didn't force his shift, he *would* die.

He had minutes left, if that.

Do whatever it is you do to slip into the dead's mind, came Katie's urgent response.

I moved around to the head of the bed, stepped carefully past several monitors, and then pressed my fingers to Dillon's temples.

My gaze rose to Aiden's. "What we're about to attempt is a mix of mind-reading the dead, and Belle, Katie, and I merging. You've seen how both affect me."

He nodded. "I'll catch you."

"And take me home."

He hesitated, and that hurt. But then, what did I expect? I was his live-in lover rather than family, and he would always put them first.

Always.

Concentrate, Katie admonished softly. *The clock ticks. Connect with Belle.*

I immediately reached out for her. *Okay, Belle, let's do this.*

The connection instantly deepened between us. This was far more than just a sharing of thoughts and energies. It was all encompassing—a merging of metaphysical beings. There was no me here in this connection, and no her. There was simply *us*, even if her spirit remained anchored to her body via a tenuous ethereal thread—to do otherwise would mean her death. A heartbeat later, the moonlit thread around my wrist began to burn, and two became three.

Enter his mind as you would the dead, the portion of us that was Katie said.

We closed our eyes, took a deep breath, and reached for my psychometry abilities.

His agony hit us, a wave so fierce it tore a gasp from our lips and sent our heart into overdrive. We gulped and pressed our fingers tighter against his skull, using it as an anchor to hold against the force of his emotions. Tears slid down our cheeks but there was nothing we could do about that.

He was already dying.

We had to hurry.

We pushed past the barrier of his unconscious agony and entered his mind. It was chaos itself. His thoughts were everywhere, scattered by the broken agony of his body.

Deeper, came Katie's comment. *We must go deeper*.

We sucked in a breath and pushed harder. The deeper we went, the more chaotic it became. He might be dying, but there was some fragment of his unconscious mind, some part of his soul, that wanted to fight, wanted to live.

That was what we had to find.

The blood now pounded so loudly through our body, it erased all other sounds. Pain bloomed—not Dillon's, but ours. In our head, in our body. It was a warning that this link drained us way too fast.

Belle, there, Katie said. *See it?*

"It" was a faint pulse of light that appeared in the chaotic darkness of Dillon's mind.

What I see, came Belle's response, *is that we'll have to step fully into his mind—join him, as we are joined, however briefly—to force his change.* That *could kill us all.*

Because by going that deep, we could lock ourselves into his spiral of death.

Yes, but I will not see my brother die without doing all that I can to save him. Would you not do the same for each other?

We said nothing. There was nothing we could say against a truth like that.

Reach for his spirit, Belle, Katie said. *Connect. I will take it from there.*

She reached out, telepathically encompassing that bright pulse, drawing it into us, fusing it to our body, our thoughts and our minds, and three became four.

And, oh God, the memories ... they were hammer blows that hit multiple times, their force so hard our whole body shook. The tree, the crush of its weight, the mind-numbing agony that forced the shutdown of instinct that was now threatening his very life ...

Energy swept through us, energy that spoke of both the earth and the wolf. Not Dillon this time, but Katie. It flooded into that bright pulse, giving it strength even as it took the reins of control and forced the change.

It was a moment unlike anything we'd ever experienced. Energy swept through us, energy that came from within, a force that stung even as it concealed. Limbs and bones and muscles twisted and altered as they reformed and reshaped. Our skin twitched and crawled as hair retreated and fur sprouted. It hurt and yet it didn't.

We became wolf, and the scents and the smells and the noise overwhelmed us, and we didn't want this, didn't want the pain ... Again, the electric force that was Katie took charge, reversing the change, once again claiming Dillon's human form. Awareness stirred, despite the drugs, but it hurt, everything hurt. Our heart, our mind, our body ...

Belle, came Katie's distant cry, *pull us out. Now!*

Somehow we did. Somehow, we ripped our hands from the side of Dillon's temples, and four dissolved, leaving one.

That one collapsed.

CHAPTER FOUR

I woke to the nagging sensation that something was different. That something had changed, within rather than without.

And I had no idea what that something was.

In truth, I physically felt no different. Other than the faint pulse of a headache, I seemed to have come through the whole merge thing relatively intact.

Of course, relatively was a far cry from absolutely.

I shifted and stretched; cotton rustled as the top sheet slid across bare skin, a sensation that was close to sensual. Light shone into the room from the windows to my left, pressing coldly against closed eyelids. In the distance, thunder rumbled, a promise of an incoming storm, and one I could smell. The thick, heady scent of musk and man filled every breath, but Aiden wasn't in the bedroom, and I couldn't hear him moving about downstairs.

I opened my eyes and immediately spotted the note on the bedside table next to my phone. I reached out and grabbed it.

Just in case you wake and discover I'm not here, it said,

I've gone to the bakery to get some fresh bread. Won't be long. A.

Sadly, there were no XX substitutes for kisses after his initial. Romantic, he was not. Or maybe he just wasn't inclined to be so with me. I frowned at the thought, dropped the note back down, and reached out for Belle. *You there?*

Always, came her response. *Glad you're finally awake. You had me scared for a little while there.*

How long was I out?

Three days.

Three! Holy fuck.

Her amusement bubbled through me. *Indeed. Aiden didn't know which way to turn.*

I'm guessing family won. There was no bitterness in that statement, although I couldn't deny hurt lingered deeper down.

Until Dillon came out of his coma, yes. But he did take you home as he promised, and he arranged for Ashworth and Eli to come over and watch you while he was at the hospital.

They're not here now.

No, they went home yesterday, after Dillon had fully woken and Aiden felt it was safe to leave his side.

My eyebrows rose. *Have you been reading his mind from a distance?*

Belle hesitated. *Didn't need to. There was a lingering connection between my mind and Dillon's. It gave me some insight into what he was seeing and hearing.*

Alarm slipped through me. *Have you severed the connection?*

Yes, though it was rather interesting eavesdropping for a while there.

I just bet.

She chuckled. *Karleen is a piece of work. I believe you're right in thinking there's more behind her hatred of witches than just Gabe helping Katie become one with the wild magic.*

I suspect it has something to do with someone close to her dying—someone from her past. One of her parents, perhaps, or maybe even a sibling.

Possibly. I'll certainly find out if the bitch ever gets within reading range.

A smile twitched my lips. *The only reason the bitch would ever get within reading range is if she's on the attack.*

Belle's surprise flitted through me. *What makes you think she'd ever physically attack you? Alphas have far more control than that. Besides, you're not a pack member, and she's well aware attacking a civilian could have serious consequences for both the pack and the reservation.*

I hesitated. *It's a niggle, nothing more.*

Unfortunately, your niggles have a tendency to become fact.

Maybe this will be one that won't. As you said, she's well aware of the penalties involved. I took a deep breath and pushed away the inner voice that said she wouldn't care. *What about you, Belle? Aside from that lingering telepathic link, how did you pull up after the immersion?*

I was out less than a day. You were the host, so it affected you far more than me.

But you're okay now?

She hesitated. *Yes.*

Meaning no.

Honestly, it's nothing to worry about.

A statement guaranteed to make me worry more.

Her smile ran through me, a bright, warm wave. *Seriously, it's probably just a soon-to-fade consequence of our souls being joined with Katie's when she forced Dillon to go through the shape shift.*

But?

My senses have sharpened.

All of them?

To the point where I was close to telling one customer yesterday she seriously needed to stop bathing in her goddamn perfume. Belle paused. *It didn't happen to you?*

My senses have been sharpening for a while.

And yet, until this morning, I'd never been so aware of the sensual caress of the sheets against my skin or known without even looking that Aiden wasn't downstairs.

It made me wonder what else might have altered or sharpened in our four-way merger, especially given the awareness of change that had hit when I first woke.

Katie might be positive the DNA adaptations caused by the wild magic *wouldn't* end with me gaining the ability to shape shift, but what if *that* was the only thing I couldn't do? What if I became a wolf in all other ways *except* that?

And would it matter in the long run? Would it make any damn difference to my relationship with Aiden?

Probably not.

Frustration stirred, and I wished—not for the first damn time—that there was someone we could ask about it all. But unless Monty's book on the earth magic came through with some sort of information, we were very much in the dark as to where all this might end.

It's entirely possible that only time will answer any of your questions, Belle commented.

And time is taking entirely too damn long to do so, I grouched. *I may well lose him before she motivates herself.*

According to Katie, that'll happen anyway. The question

that lingers, however, is whether the break will be permanent. Right now, I've a feeling fate is undecided.

I don't feel inclined to trust my future to the whims of fate, thank you very much.

She laughed. *It's not like you've any other choice.*

That's a truth I have no desire to acknowledge right now. I scrubbed a hand through my hair, snagging several knots in the process. *I need to grab a shower and some food, so I might be a little late getting into the café—*

There's no need for you to be here today, she cut in. *Rest up and come in tomorrow. We've been slow all week anyway. Besides, given the shit that happened yesterday, the rangers will probably need you at full strength.*

I groaned. *I take it we have another murder?*

Yes, but Aiden will no doubt fill you in. After you ride that man senseless, of course.

I grinned. *Sounds like the perfect plan to me. Catch you tomorrow.*

Indeed.

I tossed off the sheet and climbed to my feet. Aside from the slight pinching of skin across my shoulder blade where the silver shard had dug in, there were no lingering aches or pain from the caravan blast. The bruising—which had promised to be spectacular—was also very absent. I might not be able to shift shape, but my healing capacity was almost wolf strong these days.

I padded into the shower and washed the days of grime and sweat away. My hair was a mess, and it took a fair bit of conditioner and a whole lot of swearing to detangle it. By the time I'd finished and stepped out, the soft whistle of a kettle and the sizzle of frying bacon told me Aiden had returned and was now making breakfast.

I pulled on a T-shirt but didn't bother with

anything else, and padded barefoot down the stairs. The warmth in the air sharpened as I neared the ground floor, and the rich scents of frying bacon and musky male filled every breath. Hunger flicked through me, and I wasn't entirely sure which scent it was responding to more.

Aiden was busy flipping eggs, but glanced up as I jumped down the last couple of steps and strode toward him. His gaze skimmed me and came up hot and heavy. Hunger strengthened, and this time there was no doubt as to its cause.

"Morning," I said cheerfully. "Hope there's plenty of that bacon cooking, because I'm famished."

His grin was decidedly wicked. "And not just for bacon, from the smell of things."

"Well, no, but I do have my priorities, and you, Ranger, sadly come second to bacon and eggs."

He shook his head, though his woebegone expression was somewhat spoiled by the sexy glint in his eyes. "And a sad state of affairs that is, too. I'm not sure how I'll ever get over it."

I laughed, wrapped a hand around his neck, and pulled him into a kiss that was as hot and needy as I felt. A low rumble rose up his throat, and desire surged—a warm and delicious wave that had tiny beads of sweat dancing delightedly across my skin. I briefly—and seriously—reconsidered my priorities, but a loud grumble from my stomach soon put paid to the idea.

"That," Aiden murmured, his breath warm against my lips, "sounds like I'd better put on more bacon."

I laughed and moved around him to make the coffee. "How's your brother?"

"Not fully out of the woods just yet, but at least recovering, thanks to you." His amusement fell away. "Honestly, Liz, my family—"

"Owes me nothing." I shrugged as I reached for a coffee filter. "It was Katie's doing, not mine or Belle's. We were just her conduits."

"Maybe, but we both know the toll it takes on you and Belle." He hesitated. "I also owe you a personal and very deep apology."

I frowned at him. "What for?"

"For all but dragging you into the ICU. For giving you little choice when you'd just survived a dangerous rollover and were wet, tired, and undoubtedly sore."

"It's fine, Aiden."

"No, it's not. At the very least, I should have *asked*."

A smile tugged at my lips. "Do you honestly think Katie would have allowed me to walk out of that hospital without helping Dillon?"

Confusion touched his expression. "How on earth would she stop you? She's a spirit."

"One who controls wild magic ... and wild magic resides in my soul."

"Does that mean she could control you if she wanted?"

"In all honesty, I don't know. Nor do I honestly believe she'd have forced me, but ..." I shrugged. "Spirit or not, she *is* a wolf, and family is absolutely everything to a wolf, is it not?"

It was a barb, even if a very gentle one, and he grimaced. "That doesn't excuse our behavior. At all."

"I'm fine, Aiden." I paused and frowned. "Why isn't Dillon out of the woods? By forcing his shape shift, shouldn't his body have healed all his wounds?"

"Normally, yes, but his legs were so badly smashed that the shift—while it saved his life—only partially reset his legs." His eyes were clouded with worry. "He's already had one surgery to reset his right leg in the hope that another shift will knit the bone in the correct position, but they can't guarantee it'll work. He may be left with a permanent limp."

"Better a limp than death."

"I guess."

My eyebrows rose. "What the hell does that mean?"

He hesitated. "To a wolf, running with the pack is everything. It's a time of deep bonding—a reaffirmation, if you wish, to family and pack. To be unable to participate—" He sucked in a breath and released it slowly. "It will affect his future when it comes to mate possibilities."

I snorted. "Any woman who discounts a man because he has a limp isn't fucking worth the time of day."

"Yes, but that does not alter the fact that there are some who will *always* judge him—and treat him as less—because of it. But enough of Dillon." His gaze skimmed me again, this time more critically. "Are you truly okay?"

"More than okay, to be honest."

He raised an eyebrow, seeming to sense there was something more to that answer. "Does that include the silver wound you forgot to tell me about?"

I gave him the look. The one that said "don't be dumb." He raised his hands. "Okay, stupid comment. But that doesn't negate the question."

"Yes, it does. And before you ask, I can't tell you why I'm suddenly reacting to silver—especially when it *isn't* all encompassing. I can still handle both my knife and my athame without problems." I hesitated. "What I *can* say is that not only are my senses sharpening, but I'm now healing far faster than I should. For example, I should be sporting a colorful array of fading bruises right now, and I'm not."

"Bruises? From the explosion?"

I nodded and glanced at him. "Jaz did tell you about that, didn't she?"

"Yes, but she didn't say you'd been hurt."

"I guess she figured it wasn't her place, especially given everything else you had going on." I shrugged again and decided to change the subject. If we continued down that particular path, we'd end up at the whole "I'm not a wolf and will never be pack" discussion and I wasn't quite ready for that yet. "When I was talking to Belle just before, she mentioned there'd been another murder."

He nodded, though the brief flicker of relief that crossed his expression suggested he also wasn't ready for the confrontation we both knew was coming. "Hale Letts. At least this time it wasn't accompanied by an explosive attempt to get rid of evidence."

"Maybe because, in the process of trying to defuse that first bomb, I think I exposed my presence to the killer." I shrugged. "Maybe they've decided not to waste magical energy on a spell that could be used to trace them."

His gaze cut sharply to mine. "Why would you think the killer is aware of your presence?"

"My rollover wasn't an accident. I was forced off the road by a bolt of magical energy that appeared to come from the same entity I sensed up near the caravan."

"*What?*"

"Yeah." The coffee machine started spluttering. I concentrated on it rather than the man whose concerned anger washed over me in waves.

"Why on earth would it be targeting you? And why didn't you mention it to Jaz?"

"Because I don't believe the explosion was aimed at me. And it's not like you and I have had any time to talk."

"No." He drew in a deep breath and released it slowly. It was a somewhat frustrated sound. "If the rollover was an attempt to get rid of you, it might be wise if you stayed out of the investigation."

I snorted and switched cups to fill the second. "And how will that help? This thing is clearly aware of my presence and is intent on nullifying me. What makes you think I'll be any safer on the sidelines?"

"Misplaced hope?"

I grinned. "At least you recognize it as such."

He started plating up our meal. I picked up both cups, walked around the counter, and sat on one of the stools. "Have you made an ID on the van victim?"

"There was nothing left of him to hang an ID onto—not even teeth. But Jason Martin owned the caravan, and we believe the body was his. According to his parents, he'd been living there for the last two months after losing his job and his rental."

"Did he have any connection to the second victim?"

"Initial forensics suggests Hale might actually be the first victim." Aiden slid a filled plate across the counter, then handed me a knife and fork. "But no connection that's immediately obvious."

He moved around to sit on the stool beside me. His leg brushed mine and sent my pulse rate skittering again. The small smile that tugged at his lips suggested he was well aware of my current state of hypersensitivity where he was concerned.

I pulled my leg away a fraction to allow concentration on the food rather than the man.

"Any theories?" I asked in between mouthfuls. To say I was famished would be the understatement of the year. It was probably just as well he'd also readied a stack of toast.

"Not at this point. Jason wasn't local—his parents live in Bendigo. The second victim was born and raised here."

"Either of them wolf?"

"No." He shrugged. "It wouldn't be the first time something nasty has stepped into this reservation to hunt for the hell of it."

"No, but if it was here to do nothing more than hunt, why go after me? Why bring attention to itself like that?"

"You ask that like you expect me to have an answer."

His voice was wry, and a smile tugged my lips. "Well, you usually do."

"Maybe they're as attracted to your luscious body as I am."

"Attracting evil's attention isn't something I want, thanks very much."

And we both know there's more between us *than mere attraction.* But I kept that thought well and truly to myself. He'd admitted he cared for me—deeply cared—but that was all he was willing to admit, now or probably ever. I had to accept that, like it or not.

And I certainly didn't.

With a little more force than necessary, I swished my bacon through the yolk then shoved it into my mouth. "Has Monty come up with any theories as to what we might be dealing with?"

He eyed me for a moment, perhaps sensing the brief flicker of anger. "Other than some sort of vampire? No. I believe he and Belle have been searching through her books to see if they can find anything."

I grunted. "Hopefully that'll work."

"It has in the past."

Which didn't mean it would continue to do so. The library was extensive, but I suspected there were far more evil entities out there than anyone knew. "What about our SUV? Has it been found yet?"

He grimaced. "Yes, and it's a write-off."

"I suspected it would be." I reached for a bit of toast and slathered it with butter. "That's not going to make the council happy."

"They've nevertheless ordered you a new one." He shrugged. "You could write off a hundred vehicles, and it wouldn't make the slightest impact on the reservation's finances."

"How full the reservation's coffers might be has no relation to how pissed off they become over constantly having to replace my vehicles."

He waved his fork at my plate. "How about you concentrate on the rest of that rather than talking. You haven't eaten anything for three days—I'm amazed you even had the strength to bounce down the stairs so damn energetically."

"Oh, I have the strength to do much more than just bounce down stairs," I teased. "And if you hand over that piece of bacon sitting all uneaten and forlorn on your plate, I might just prove it later on."

He laughed and immediately handed over the bacon. He finished relatively quickly after that, but I had several more slices of toast. Maybe I was changing into a Hobbit rather than a werewolf. I seemed to have gained a stomach that required more than one breakfast.

Eventually, I did push my plate away with a contented sigh. "That was lovely, thank you."

"No problem at all." He caught my hands, then tugged me off the stool and into his arms. His teeth grazed my earlobe and sent a delighted shiver through my entire body.

"And now," he murmured, "I do believe the time has come for you to confirm your earlier statement."

"Shall we retreat to the bedroom?"

It came out husky, and he chuckled, his breath so warm against my skin. "Why waste precious time climbing stairs when we have a luxurious rug in front of the fire?"

I raised an eyebrow, even though the rapid cadence of my heart was so damn loud it seemed to echo all around us. "The floor is hard."

"The rug is not."

"You're fully dressed."

He rose and quickly stripped off.

I let my gaze dawdle down his long, lean length and sighed in appreciation. "It's still not the bed."

He laughed and pulled me close. His body was warm and hard against mine, his erection fierce. "No, and that's the whole point."

I trailed my tongue across his chest until I found a nipple and then gently pulled it into my mouth. He shuddered, and the scent of desire—both his *and* mine—became so thick it was almost liquid.

"And what if someone walks by?" I murmured. "There's a public path around the lake, after all, and you don't believe in window coverings."

"If there's one truth about werewolves none of us can deny," he said, kissing his way toward my ear, "it's that we are all exhibitionists."

The sweet heat of his tongue delved inside my lobe, and a helpless sound of pleasure escaped my lips. He chuckled again, a throaty sound as seductive and as arousing as his touch. He slipped his hands under my T-shirt and trailed his fingers up my stomach, setting me alight. Then his big hands cupped my breasts and lightly pushed them together, his thumbs teasing the engorged points. I groaned and squirmed, every inch of me vibrating with the hunger flowing through my veins.

"Okay," I said breathlessly. "Rug it is."

He laughed, lifted me up, and carried me over to the rug. Once he'd divested me of my T-shirt, he pressed me back into the thick rug and straddled my body.

I wrapped my arms around his neck and pulled him down, squashing my breasts hard against his chest. I didn't care. I simply claimed his lips and kissed him with all the urgency that surged through me. It was an urgency he shared, if the wild beating of his heart was anything to go by.

The kiss went on and on, becoming a deep exploration of heat and desire, fueling the inner flames and making me ache for his touch and his body.

Then, with a low and very sexy growl, he pulled away. "I think we need to pace ourselves. You've been unconscious for almost three days, remember."

"Which also means I haven't had sex for three days, Ranger." I slipped a hand between us and caressed the hard length of him. "That's almost drought territory these days."

He laughed and pulled away. "No touching the goods just yet, young lady. Let's explore how well you've recovered first."

I sighed in a very put out sort of way. "If you insist—"

"And I do."

I airily waved a hand to indicate my body. "Then by all means, have your wicked way with me."

His blue eyes gleamed with hunger and need, but when his mouth once again met mine, it was little more than a brush of heat—a tingling, tantalizing promise of what was to come. Slowly, ever so slowly, he kissed his way down my neck, then lingered on my breasts, licking and nipping until I was once again shuddering and moaning in pleasure. Then he continued on down my stomach, discovering a pleasure zone I had no idea existed. Which was odd considering this was not the first time he'd explored my body in such a manner.

Then his tongue flicked across my clit, and all thought disappeared. I groaned and thrust my hips toward him, wanting more, needing more, but knowing full well he wasn't about to fulfill the promise his tongue was making. Not yet.

He chuckled softly, his breath hot and heavy against my skin, and continued on, bringing me to the edge so very quickly. But he offered no release; instead, he claimed my mouth and kissed me until the threatening tremors subsided. Then the slow process started all over again, until desire was all-consuming and all I wanted was him inside. He didn't comply, but this time, he didn't withdraw, using tongue and breath to push me over that glorious edge.

The waves of my orgasm had barely eased when he thrust inside. It felt so damn good, so damn right, that I wanted to cry.

He began to move, not slowly, but fiercely, his body hot and needy against mine. The delicious, low-down pressure began to build again, fanning out in thick waves until it was a molten force that would not be denied.

He came with me, his lips capturing mine, kissing me urgently as his warmth spilled into me and his body went rigid against mine.

When I could finally breathe again, I took his face between my palms and kissed him long and slow. "I think we both needed that."

His grin was that of a man who knew a task had been

well done. "Yeah. Though I have to admit, it was a little too fast for my liking."

I raised an eyebrow. "If that was your definition of fast, I can't wait to see what you call slow."

He raised a lazy eyebrow. "Shall we take this upstairs and find out?"

"I'm yours for the entire day, Ranger."

"Then I shall certainly ensure we use the day wisely."

And he most certainly did.

Belle was already in the kitchen doing the day's prep when I walked in the following morning. I glanced at the clock and feigned surprise. "Did Monty kick you out of bed for snoring? It's barely seven."

She tossed a carrot stick at me. "As if he'd ever dare."

I grinned and waved a hand at the full containers of cut vegetables on the counter. "You've obviously been here for at least an hour, so what happened?"

She grimaced. "He got a damn phone call from an old friend. She's arriving in Melbourne this afternoon and wanted to arrange a quick catch-up."

There was a very slight edge in her tone that had my lips twitching. "She?"

"Yes." The terse response was accompanied by a rather brutal decapitation of a carrot.

"That wouldn't be a smidge of jealousy in your voice, would it?"

She kept her gaze down and thoughts locked. "Don't be ridiculous."

"You do remember that I can read auras, don't you? Because yours, right now, is a dead giveaway."

"Fine," she muttered. "I won't deny there might be just a smidge of that odious emotion."

I smiled. "A serious understatement, if you ask me."

"And I didn't."

My smile grew. "So, what was it about the call that raised the green demon?"

She blew out a breath. "The familiarity. The warmth. The overly friendly natter."

"So, basically, everything."

"Basically."

"Oh, Monty is going to be *so* pleased to hear—"

"You dare mention it, and I'll curse your libido for the next year." She glared at me. "And you *know* I can."

I laughed. "So didn't he suspect anything was wrong by your abrupt departure from his bed?"

"He's a man. They tend not to notice annoyed snits. Besides, I did warn him I had to get in early today."

"Are you going down to Melbourne to meet said friend with him?"

"Of course not. It's not like we're an item or anything."

Oh, definitely *not*.

She glared at me, hearing the thought despite all her barriers being up.

Another laugh escaped. "And would you, if he asked?"

She hesitated, and then smiled somewhat ruefully. "To be honest, probably not. I was just caught by surprise, that's all. It wasn't even so much the fact a past lover was ringing him, but rather the warmth in his tone and their obvious closeness. I just wasn't expecting it."

"Why on earth not? He is an attractive man and a rather good catch."

"Yes, but he was never serious about anything or anyone —at least when we knew him."

"He was utterly serious about you."

She rolled her eyes. "We were only teenagers. But even if he *was*, his parents would never have allowed him to get deeply involved with a mere Sarr witch."

While that was undoubtedly true, neither of us could say whether Monty would actually have listened to them. He might have toed the family line back then, but only up to a certain point.

"Enough about me," Belle said. "What about you and Aiden? Did he apologize for his actions at the hospital?"

"He did, in fact."

Her eyebrows rose. "Well, that's encouraging."

"I don't see how." I grabbed a board and a knife and tugged the large tub of peeled potatoes toward me. We had Parmentier potatoes—which were basically mini roasted spuds cooked in butter, garlic, and herbs—on the menu today, and they'd proven extremely popular in the past. "I mean, it wasn't like Katie gave us a lot of choice either."

"She didn't drag you like a wet sack through hospital halls."

"But she might have, if I'd refused to help."

Belle shook her head. "She needs you more than you need her, remember."

Maybe. I swept a pile of cubed potatoes into a tray and started in on the next lot. "Did you find anything in your gran's books to suggest what we might be dealing with?"

"A couple, but the most likely one is the *hone-onna*."

I raised my eyebrows. "Which is?

"A female skeleton that apparently lures men into her lair and seduces them. According to Gran's notes, her victims often don't discover her state until after they've had sex. She then drains them of their life force, until they become skeletons themselves."

"That suggests it's a type of energy vampire."

She nodded. "One that can either take on or at least project the illusion of humanity."

"Any notes on how to kill it?"

Belle shook her head. "But Monty seems to think what will kill a vampire should kill this."

"Then he can be the one holding the stake to finish her off."

She laughed. "I said the same thing."

I grinned and got down to the business of finishing the potatoes. The usual breakfast crowd came through, but things quietened down after nine, which at least gave us time for some cake baking. My phone rang just after ten-thirty, the tone telling me it was Monty. My pulse rate immediately skipped into a higher gear. There could be only one reason for him to be calling right now.

I hit the answer button and said, "I thought you were supposed to be heading down to Melbourne to meet an old flame? What's happened?"

But even as I asked the question, I knew.

"We've another murder on our hands," he said, voice tight. "And this time, the victim's kid has gone missing."

CHAPTER FIVE

I swore and rubbed a hand across my eyes. "How long ago did it happen?"

"Only half an hour. The trail should be fresh enough for you to pick up."

"The rangers had no scent to follow?"

"No. There was some sort of magical interference. I tried to track it, but they were in a car and the trail faded out about a block away."

"If we're dealing with a skeleton spirit, why on earth would it be driving a car?"

"Why would I know?"

A smile tugged at my lips. "Of the two of us, you *are* the more knowledgeable witch."

"More knowledgeable when it comes to spells, maybe, but definitely not when it comes to this sort of stuff. How soon can you get here?"

"That depends on where 'here' is."

After he'd reeled off the address, I added, "It'll take me about ten minutes. Is Aiden there?"

"No. He's at the hospital again. Tala's taking the lead on this one."

Which wasn't a surprise given she was second in charge. But Dillon having another setback wasn't good news. I wished there was something more I could do to help, but neither Belle nor I were healers. I wasn't even sure that witches who *did* have that capacity would be able to do anything that a werewolf's own inbuilt healing system couldn't. "Be there soon."

"Bring your kit, just in case."

"Will do."

I hung up and pushed to my feet. Belle emerged out of the reading room, backpack in hand. "It's definitely not a good sign that her killing spree is ramping up."

"No." I accepted the pack with a nod of thanks. "Unless this is nothing more than another attempt to get rid of me."

"She surely won't catch you unawares a second time." She paused and gave me a severe stare. "Will she?"

A faint smile teased my lips. "No, because she also won't be expecting me to be able to track her through the kid."

Belle's eyebrows rose. "And how do you figure that?"

"Well, she's obviously aware of my presence through my magical aura—"

"If that's how she's tracking you, she would have also come after Monty, Ashworth, and Eli."

"Not if it's the wild magic that drew her here. If she's sensitive to it, it's possible she'll sense me through it. But that won't tell her about my psi skills."

"Yes, but that's something of a moot point when there's such things as tracking spells."

"They're often not as reliable as my psi abilities, though."

"Tell that to Monty. He swears by them." She plucked my coat from the hook and handed it to me. "Just promise to be careful. I've got a bad feeling about this whole thing."

I rolled my eyes. "I promise to be careful."

"You say that, but we both know the demons and other nasties that come a-hunting in this reservation don't often play by the rule book. As this one has already proven —twice."

"Yes, but this time I'm not alone. Monty and Tala will both be there."

"That isn't as comforting as it sounds."

"I'll tell him you said that."

"Like he'd care."

"True." With a laugh, I headed out.

It didn't take me long to arrive at the crime scene. The house in question was a modern timber-and-concrete building with a flat roof that melded surprisingly well into the surrounding bush.

I stopped behind Monty's old wagon, then climbed out and walked down the driveway. As I ducked under the crime scene tape and moved toward the front door, Duke—another of the rangers—stepped out.

"How bad is it?" I asked.

He shrugged and offered me gloves and crime scene booties. "As far as these things go, we've seen far worse."

I leaned against the wall to put on the booties. "So definitely another vampire-type attack?"

He nodded. "All skin, bones, and boner."

I smiled, despite the seriousness of the situation. "Any clue as to the time of death?"

"Not yet—Ciara has only just arrived. Tala is with her now. The kid is our priority. This way."

Ciara was the head coroner here on the reservation and

Aiden's sister. That she was here rather than at the hospital was a little surprising, but I guess there were limits on the number of people allowed into an ICU.

We walked inside. The corridor was light, and the mild aroma of pine and smoke dominated the air. But underneath them ran the darker scents of sex, death, and agony. The victim hadn't died quickly, but he *had* died quietly.

For the son's sake. To keep the son safe from the monster he'd welcomed into their home.

I frowned at the insight and tried to chase it down for further information, but it disappeared as quickly as it had arrived. My psi senses might be strengthening, but they remained as annoying as ever.

We turned left into a long corridor that ran at right angles to the main section of the house. Again, intuition stirred.

There were secrets in this place.

Lies.

And they centered on the little boy who'd been stolen.

But, once again, intuition didn't provide anything else in the way of information. It was damnably frustrating.

We walked past three bedrooms and a bathroom and entered the room at the far end of the hall. The walls were painted pale blue and decorated with a multitude of train and truck stickers, while toy tractors, cars, and fire engines battled with Lego bricks for dominance on the floor. In a small cleared space in the center of this chaos was a plate on which a half-eaten Hundreds and Thousands sandwich and several empty Freddo Frog wrappers sat. Beside it was a Tetra Pak juice container with a straw sticking out of it. At least the father had ensured his son was fed and occupied before fucking the woman who'd taken his life ...

Monty was staring out the window, but turned around

as we entered. His expression was apologetic. "Sorry to drop this on you so soon after the hospital session, but—"

"It's a kid, Monty. I'm never going to be 'not available,' no matter what state I'm in physically." I raised a hand and then walked slowly around the room, trying to find something that held enough of the kid's resonance to track him. "Do we know his name?"

"Jack," Duke replied. "Jack Mason."

"And the dad? Is much known about him?"

Duke pulled out a small notebook. "Kyle Mason was an ex-copper who arrived here with his son a couple of months ago. According to the neighbor who reported Jack's kidnapping, he kept mostly to himself."

Aside from inviting back the occasional sleeping partner, obviously. "Did the neighbor give you a description?"

"No. She said there was some sort of haze around the two of them that made it hard to see them."

I looked over to Monty. "A concealment spell?"

He nodded. "A haze suggests it was hastily constructed, perhaps as a result of the kid screaming."

None of the toys on the floor held anything major in the way of resonance, so I moved on. "Was Jack old enough to go to school?"

"Yes. Went to the primary school just down the road, and was picked up by his dad every day." Duke frowned, something I felt more than saw. "Why do I get the feeling there's something other than curiosity behind these questions?"

I hesitated. "It may be nothing, but I'm picking up some weird vibes from this house."

There was nothing in the wardrobe or the nearby small bookshelf that held even a vague flicker of a connection.

"What sort of vibes?" Monty asked.

I hesitated again. "I get the distinct feeling there's a whole lot of secrecy and lies when it comes to the life of the father and his son."

"You can sense such things?" Duke queried, surprise evident.

"Not usually."

"So why are you sensing them now?" Monty asked. "Or is this another side effect?"

"I suspect it is."

"Well, fuck."

And well and truly fucked is what I might be before all the changes were over.

"What sort of lies or secrets are we talking about, then?" Duke asked.

"That I don't know, but it would definitely be worth looking deeper into the father's history."

"Which we do as a matter of course during a murder investigation, but I'll flag it anyway."

I moved across to the bed and ran my hand above it. As I neared the pillow, I finally felt the slight beat of a connection. I tugged the blankets back to reveal several stuffed toys; the old teddy in the fireman's jacket held the strongest resonance.

"Got it." I picked up the somewhat threadbare teddy and waved it lightly.

"Is the kid alive?" Duke immediately asked.

I strengthened the connection and then followed the tenuous pulsing thread that linked the teddy to the little boy. Though I didn't go deep enough to become one with Jack—to see and feel whatever he was—it was nevertheless obvious he felt safe.

"He's not only alive, but also happy."

Duke frowned. "If the person who snatched him is

responsible for the death of his dad, how on earth is that possible? Unless, of course, the two are *not* linked."

"Given the shadows of deceit that haunt this place, that might well be the case," I said. "Shall we go? He's not that far away."

Duke immediately turned and led the way out, his footsteps echoing sharply on the polished concrete floor. Once we'd stripped off the crime scene booties and gloves, we strode over to the line of ranger SUVs. Duke's was the last in the line; he opened the passenger door and ushered me in, then ran around to the driver side while Monty climbed into the back.

As we sped down the old road, I tightened my grip on the old bear and listened to the secrets that lay within his shaggy, threadbare fur. There'd been a fair bit of sorrow in Jack's young life; the teddy had been the recipient of many tears.

"Left, and then through Castle Rock," I said. "I can pinpoint his position once we're closer."

Duke turned and flattened the accelerator. Though he wasn't using the siren, the emergency lights were on, and the traffic quickly got out of our way. The teddy's signal abruptly sharpened when we reached the far side of town.

"Slow down. We're close."

As Duke obeyed, I studied the road ahead. Just for an instant, a glittering silvery thread spooled out in front of the SUV. It wasn't magic. It was a physical emanation of the link between Jack and his teddy, and something that had never happened before when it came to my psi talents. Guide ropes such as this were usually only visible when it came to active *tracking* spells.

It would seem the wild magic was now blurring the line between the two.

I sucked in a breath and tried to ignore the spurt of trepidation. "Next left."

The road became narrower and wound up an incline. Once we'd crossed over the bridge that spanned the railway tracks, the teddy's link with the kid sharpened and expanded. Vague images of two women talking flitted through my mind. One was a stranger to Jack. The other was not.

"He's with his mom," I said, unable to keep the surprise from my voice.

Duke's gaze cut to mine. "*What?*"

I hesitated and rechecked. "I could be wrong, but that's what I'm sensing."

"But if it was his mom who snatched him," Monty said, "why was he screaming when he was being put in the car? That makes no sense."

"He was in the house when his dad was killed," I said. "Maybe he saw the thing that murdered his dad."

"Why would the father be fucking another woman if the kid's mother was also in the house?" Duke growled.

"They could have an open relationship," Monty said. "Some folks do like that sort of thing."

Duke snorted, a sound that very much suggested he didn't believe *that* was the case here. And to be honest, I agreed with him. There was nothing in that house that suggested a woman's touch. Nothing in the air that indicated a woman had ever spent any serious amount of time there.

"The three of them are in that weatherboard house with the rubbish bins sitting out the front."

"Three?" Duke said sharply. "Who's with them?"

"Don't know. I'm only getting vague impressions."

"So one of them could be our killer?"

"Could be."

He swore. "You can't go deeper?"

I hesitated. "I can try to widen the link, but I don't want to risk a full connection. Not when the wild magic is changing and strengthening my psychic senses."

While joining the mind of another might generally be more dangerous for me than the subject I was tracking, I had no desire to risk anything going wrong when we were dealing with a little boy.

"Do what you can," Monty said. "The more we know going in, the less likely it is that any of us will get hurt. Especially when we have no idea what we're really dealing with."

I took a deeper breath, then glanced down at the teddy and deepened the connection, allowing myself to drift lightly into Jack's mind. A short woman with curly brown hair was talking to another, taller woman with crimson hair.

Fuck.

"The third woman is a witch. A *royal* witch."

"That would at least explain the magic that obscured the scent trail. That sort of spell is generally only taught at the academy." He unclipped the seat belt and leaned forward. "Can you hear what they're discussing through the link?"

"Not without establishing a full connection." I glanced at Duke. "We'll have to go in at the same time, otherwise you might get hit by a spell."

He nodded, then leaned forward and switched off the lights as we cruised past the house. It was a run-down, white-painted weatherboard building with a rusting red tin roof. There was no door at the front, just two half-windows with curtains tightly drawn. The entrance was at the side, up a couple of steps that didn't look as if they'd hold any real weight. No cars sat in the driveway, but the barn at the back of the property was big enough to hide several.

"The place gives all the appearance of being deserted," Monty said.

"That's no real surprise if they *did* kidnap the kid," Duke replied. "They wouldn't want the neighbors knowing they were holed up there, especially when news of the kidnapping gets out."

Which it no doubt would, and pretty damn quickly. The reservation had a very active gossip brigade, and they rarely missed a juicy morsel.

Duke pulled over several houses farther up and switched off the engine. "Give me a couple of minutes to get around the back of the property before heading in. We'll see what happens."

"They're not going to open the door to strangers," Monty said.

"Locked doors have never stopped you before. I don't expect they will now." Duke smiled. "It will also have the advantage of drawing their attention away from me."

"A normally sound plan, but this reservation?" Monty shook his head. "Be prepared for things to go ass up, my friend."

Duke rolled his eyes. "You two are turning into fatalists."

"We prefer to call ourselves realists," I said.

Duke snorted and climbed out of the SUV. Once he'd shifted shape and disappeared into the yard of the nearby house, we climbed out. The wind hit hard, its touch like ice. I shivered and hastily zipped up my coat, then reached back into the SUV to grab the teddy. Jack would be happy to see it, even if the two women were unlikely to be so happy to see *us*.

As we walked down to the house, a curtain twitched in the window just down from the door, briefly revealing the soft blur of a face. It quickly fell back into place, and a second later came the sound of sharp footsteps moving in different directions.

"They've seen us," I said.

"If they're going for the back door, Duke will stop them."

"If we weren't dealing with a royal witch, I'd agree."

He glanced at me sharply. "You think she'd attack him?"

"They've split up, so yes."

"I'll go back him up, then. You hit the front door."

He'd barely taken three steps when magic surged, thick and fierce on the air. Monty swore and bolted for the rear of the house. I gripped the teddy tighter and, through it, felt the kid and the mother retreating into a room on the other side of the house.

I ducked under the half-size windows and then paused at the corner of the house and peered around. There was no immediate sign of them, but as I frowned at the teddy, a soft scrape echoed. A heartbeat later, the mother's head appeared out of a window. I drew back sharply, my heart racing and my fingers twitching with the force of information coming from the teddy. The kid wasn't scared; he thought it was all part of the adventure.

Magic surged again, this time Monty's. It was some sort of barrier spell, but I had no idea if he was protecting Duke or merely using it to deflect whatever spell the royal witch had cast.

The window slid up further, then the woman climbed out and dropped to the ground. I moved around the corner just as she was reaching up for her little boy.

"Please don't be alarmed, and please don't run," I said quickly. "I'm with the rangers, and we need—"

She launched at me, catching me unaware. She drove her shoulder into my stomach, hitting hard enough to send me flying backward. I hit the ground with a grunt of pain, felt the movement of air and the heated surge of anger. Swore, and quickly raised my arms. Her fist hit my forearm rather than my face.

"Damn it," I yelled, "I'm here to help you."

She didn't listen, and her aura pulsed with fury and fear. Magic burned across my fingers unbidden and leapt at her, hitting her as forcefully as she'd hit me only seconds ago, lifting her off her feet and sending her flying backward. She hit the ground with a sharp "oomph" but scrambled up and came at me again. I swore and quickly cast a rope spell, wrapping the golden thread of magic around her waist before lashing it to a nearby tree and pulling it tight. It stopped her in her tracks.

"You fucking bitch," she screamed, throwing herself forward against the spell so hard it rippled and pulsed. "You'll not take him, I tell you. Not again."

Her expression was filled with hate and the desperate need to retaliate, to hurt. While the spell was currently holding her in check, there was no way known I was going anywhere near her. Not until she calmed down.

A small boy with a mop of thick brown hair and eyes as dark as his mother's leaned out of the window and said, slightly tremulously, "Mommy? Is everything okay?

She sucked in a breath that did little to ease the murderous glint in her eyes and nodded. "Yes, Jack, everything is fine. Just go back inside and wait for me, okay?"

"Here," I said, sweeping the teddy from the ground as I walked across to the window. "Take this with you."

A happy smile bloomed across his cute, chubby features as he reached for the threadbare teddy with a chocolate-smeared hand. "It's Freddie, Mommy."

"That's good, darling," she replied, voice still vibrating with barely contained fury. "Now go inside and wait, like I asked."

As Jack obeyed, I turned to the woman. "What in hell did you hope to achieve by attacking me like that? We're in a werewolf reservation, for God's sake. Even if you had gotten past me, tracking is second nature to them."

"Which is why I hired a fucking witch." Her gaze raked me. "You'll not take my son from me—"

"I have no intention of taking your son, so calm the fuck down. I'm just here to ask—"

"Then you're not working for him?"

My eyebrows rose. "Him? Do you mean your *husband*?"

"He's an *ex*," she spat. "And *he* stole Jack from *me*."

Understanding hit. "So this is a *custody* battle?"

"No. I *won* custody, but that bastard disappeared with him during a weekend visitation. After a year of relying on the goddamn law to find him, I took matters into my own hands and hired a witch."

"The one who was inside with you?"

"Yes." Her gaze raked me again. I had a feeling if she hadn't been leashed, she'd be tackling me again. "You didn't answer my question."

It took me a second to remember what question she meant. "No, I'm not working for your husband."

She blew out a breath. It was a frustrated, angry sound. "If he didn't report Sabine snatching Jack to the rangers, then who did?"

"His neighbor."

"Nosy bitch," she muttered. "I guess Kyle was too damn

busy fucking his blonde tart to find out why his son was screaming."

I stared at her for a long second. "You don't know? The witch didn't tell you?"

"Tell me fucking what?"

I sucked in a breath and released it slowly. "Your husband is dead."

A weird mix of hope, joy, and horror ran across her expression. "Really? The bastard's gone, and I never have to fear him snatching Jack again?"

"Yes," I said. "Look, I'll explain inside, but first—if I release you, are you going to be sensible and not attack me?"

She hesitated. "Yes."

As affirmations went, it wasn't entirely convincing, but it wasn't exactly practical to remain out here, either. I untied her from the tree, but kept hold of her leash just in case. It was always better safe than sorry when it came to mothers protecting their young.

I motioned her to proceed, then followed her around to the front door. Despite looking ready to collapse, the old steps held our weight without problem. I spelled open the front door and waved her on.

"So when did he die?" she asked, her footsteps echoing against the old wooden floors. "Because he was definitely alive when Sabine went in to get Jack."

"The coroner hasn't had a chance to give us a definite time of death, but it obviously happened not long after your witch kidnapped your son."

"*Reclaimed*," the woman spat. "I was reclaiming him."

The little boy came running out of the front room and launched himself at his mother's legs. She stooped and picked him up.

"Say hello to Freddie, Mommy," he said, shoving the old teddy into her face.

Her brief smile was tense, but she nevertheless dropped a kiss on the bear's threadbare nose. "I'm glad you're back with us, Freddie."

Jack glanced at me and, with all the upfront curiosity of a young child, said, "Who are you?"

"I just need to ask your mom and her friend a few questions—that okay?"

"Are you the police?"

"No. I'm one of the reservation witches."

"You can do magic? Show me."

"Perhaps later. I really need to talk to your mom."

He regarded me steadily for a second, then nodded solemnly. "You brought Freddie back."

Obviously, bringing Freddie back put me in his "to be trusted" books. It was a shame his mother definitely did *not* hold the same opinion.

She bent and placed her son back on the ground. "You go and watch TV while this lady and I have a chat in the kitchen. Okay?"

The kid nodded and raced off. I once again motioned her to lead the way. There was no way known I'd trust the bitch to walk behind me. Not when her aura remained a roiling mess of emotions.

Up ahead, a door slammed and three sets of footsteps echoed. Monty had obviously caught the royal witch, but I had no sense he was using any sort of spell to contain her.

The three of them entered the kitchen the same time as we did. The other witch was thin and pale and older than I'd presumed. Her eyes were also blue rather than silver, which suggested there was human blood in her background somewhere. It didn't make her any less proficient at her craft, of course, as the spell she'd cast at Duke confirmed.

He led her across to the small table and sat her on one of the four chairs. His left cheek was scraped and bloody, and his golden eyes filled with annoyance. "Move," he growled, "and I might just be tempted to toss you as far as you tossed me."

"That's against the law, and we both know it," the woman said, somewhat snippily.

"Not in a reservation, and not when we're dealing with a murder. Sit quietly unless you're asked a damn question."

I motioned my captive toward the two of them, then dismantled the rope spell and stopped beside Monty. "I don't believe either of them were involved in the murder, Duke. It's more a case of unfortunate timing. The mother—"

"Jessica," she muttered. "Jessica Brown."

"—won custody of Jack during divorce proceedings, but the father disappeared with him during an access visitation a year ago. Police had no success in tracing him, so Jessica hired our witch here in a last-ditch effort to find them."

"We didn't do anything wrong," Jessica said. "And there *is* a warrant out on Kyle."

"We'll check," Duke said.

The witch shot him a glance. "Feel free, but I don't undertake a job that's likely to land me on the wrong side of the law. I fully checked Jessica's story *before* I started looking."

"And do you have a name?" Duke asked. "Or are you happy to be called witch?"

She snorted. "When you say it in *that* tone, most certainly not. It's Sabine. Sabine Fitzgerald."

My eyebrows rose. The Fitzgeralds weren't a royal line,

so her mom had obviously married down. It also explained her blue eyes, because the so-called "lesser" witch lines tended to marry humans more often.

"When did you track Jack down to the reservation?" Duke asked.

"A week ago."

"Then why wait so long to grab him?"

Sabine gave him a dark look. "And you call yourself a ranger?"

"Just answer the damn question."

"Because I wanted to document the daily pattern of Kyle's life to discover the best time to grab Jack."

"You're a witch," Monty commented. "You could have just walked in and spelled him into compliance."

"Yes, but I knew there were reservation witches here. Spelling Kyle would have left a tangible trace of magic that could have been used to either identify or track me. I had no desire for anyone to be aware of my involvement, even if Jessica does have rightful custody."

"Kyle has friends in high places," Jessica said. "It's why he was able to avoid detection for so long."

"So, what went wrong today?" Duke asked. "Why was Jack screaming?"

"Is this a formal interview?" Jessica asked. "Are we going to be charged?"

"You'll be asked to make official witness statements," he replied. "I'm also recording our conversation. But if what you say is true about Jack's custody, I doubt it'll go any further."

The two women shared a glance, and then Jessica nodded.

Sabine grimaced. "Kyle picked Jack up from school around three-thirty. About fifteen minutes after they'd arrived home, this blonde appears and knocks on the door—"

"Describe her," Duke cut in.

"Tall, extremely thin, spiky-style haircut, weird way of walking."

"Define weird," Monty said before Duke could.

"It wasn't fluid, if that makes sense." Sabine shrugged. "She looked to be in her late twenties, but she walked like an old woman with hip problems."

"Was there any indication of magic?" I asked.

She hesitated. "There was no spell that I could see, but there was a weird sort of shimmer around her. If I had to guess what it was, I'd say an energy field of some kind."

"There *are* vampires who are capable of producing illusion shields," Monty said. "It's possible we're dealing with one of those."

"Sunshine vaporizes vampires. Undisputed fact," Duke said.

"In this reservation, *nothing* can ever be considered undisputed." Monty's voice was dry.

"A vampire?" Alarm touched Jessica's expression. "My son was in the same house as a *vampire*?"

"Possibly," Monty said. "But it obviously wasn't after him, as evidenced by the fact Sabine was able to get him out."

"What happened when the blonde knocked at the door?" Duke asked.

"Kyle answered and invited her in. I figured they knew each other, because by the time I got there, they were in the bedroom having sex."

"And nothing seemed ... odd to you?" I asked.

She raised an eyebrow, amusement lurking. "I didn't go

check how they were going about their business, if that's what you mean."

I half smiled. "No. I meant magically."

She hesitated again. "There was a slight whiff of wrongness, but to be honest, I just grabbed the kid and got out of there."

"So why was he screaming when you put him into the car?" Duke asked.

"Because I unwisely took my hand away from his mouth and he started yelling for Freddie. I had no idea who Freddie was, and there was no fucking way I was going back into that house, just in case Kyle got nasty."

"Why would that bother you?" Monty asked. "You're a strong enough witch to cope with anything a human could throw at you."

"Anything except a bullet."

"Kyle kept a number of handguns when we were married," Jessica said. "We had to presume he was still doing so; he was on the run, after all."

"So neither Kyle nor the woman came out of the house when Jack started screaming?" I asked.

Sabine shook her head. "Though to be honest, I didn't look. I just drove away from that place ASAP."

"And there's nothing else you can add?" Duke asked. "You were tracking Kyle for a week—did you see him interact with the blonde at any other time? Or anyone else?"

"No. He pretty much kept to himself. Aside from school runs and shopping, his only other activity was a drink at the Railway Hotel every Saturday night."

"Did he meet anyone there?"

"Not when I was watching, but he might have previously." She shrugged.

"Did he take Jack with him?"

"No. The next-door neighbor watched him—Doris Hamberly, her name is. Middle-aged, retired teacher."

"What did you plan to do once you had Jack?" I asked curiously. "If your ex was so well connected, it probably wouldn't have taken him that long to track you down again."

Jessica's expression was cagey. "It's not hard to completely disappear if you have the money and the right connections."

Something *I* could certainly attest to.

"Right," Duke said. "If there's nothing else, I'll take you both down to the station to make formal statements. You'll need to stick around for a few days, just in case we have further questions, but I can't see any reason for either of you to be charged."

"Seriously?" Jessica asked, a mix of surprise and hope crossing her expression.

Duke nodded. "We werewolves don't take kindly to people kidnapping kids and disappearing with them. I will point out, however, that if you'd come to us and explained the situation in the first place, we would have retrieved Jack from his father without any problem."

"You really can't blame her for not trusting rangers when the police were of little help," Sabine said.

"And that's the sort of thinking that will get you into trouble one day." Duke glanced at Jessica. "Go collect your son and whatever you need to keep him happy at the station while we take statements."

"We'll accompany you, then catch a cab back to the crime scene," Monty said. "Just in case."

"Just in case what?" Sabine snapped before Duke could reply. "I'm not stupid enough to cause any trouble now that we're both on tape."

Monty raised an eyebrow, amusement evident. "We

both know there're spells that force compliance, and you've already admitted to having put in place the means to disappear."

"Jessica and the kid, not me. I certainly wouldn't risk the reputation of my business by spelling and stealing evidence."

"Pleased to hear it," Duke said. "But we'll nevertheless all squash into the SUV, just to be safe."

Sabine flashed him an annoyed look, then, with a muttered "Fine" crossed her arms and leaned back in her chair.

In little more than ten minutes, we were heading back to the ranger station. Monty and I then cabbed it back to the house.

Tala appeared as we walked back inside. "Did you find the kid?"

Monty nodded. "He was with his mother, and we don't believe she had anything to do with this murder."

"Then why was she here?"

"The victim disappeared with the kid during visitation a year ago. The mother hired a witch and had them tracked down to the reservation."

"Ah."

"Yeah," Monty said. "Duke's at the station now with the mother and the witch she hired, taking their statements."

"Good." Tala stepped to one side and motioned toward the bedroom. "You two want to go in and see if there's any sort of magical or creature clue that might help track this thing down?"

"Creature clue?" I said, amused.

She half smiled. "We *are* dealing with some form of creature or spirit, are we not?"

"Well, yes—"

"Then creature clue fits."

I snorted and walked into the room. A thick wash of pleasure, pain, and fear slapped across my senses, and I stopped so abruptly Monty had to do a quick side step to avoid running into me.

"What's wrong?"

"Nothing. The room is just so thick with emotions, I can practically taste them."

I could certainly *see* them.

"Is it just fear? Or something else?"

"It's a mix." I hesitated, psychically sorting through the wash of scents and pulling the various layers apart. "He was killed during sex, though."

"Would the timing have anything to do with the arrival of the witch?" Tala said.

I hesitated. "Unclear. It could be that she just gets bored and likes to alter up the way she kills them."

Monty walked over to the bed and stopped beside Ciara. "Well, there's one thing that's different to the second victim—she's used magic on Kyle."

"Really?" I studied the body for a second but couldn't see anything that suggested he'd been spell affected. "How can you tell?"

"There's a faint spell thread tangled in his hair."

I narrowed my gaze and, after a moment, saw the sliver of purplish magic. "Do you recognize the spell? Or isn't there enough of a thread to tell?"

He hesitated. "It has the feel of a silencing spell, which is rather odd."

"Not if she didn't want the kid involved."

Ciara's gaze met mine. "You think she was protecting the kid?"

"I do."

"Why?"

"When I first walked into the house, I got the impression that the victim had died in silence to protect the son. Not his son—*the* son. The phrasing only makes sense if it was the killer who was thinking it."

Ciara's eyebrows rose. "Why would she be worried about protecting the son if she's busy sucking the life out of the father?"

"I'm afraid that's a question I can't answer. Not until we know for sure what sort of entity we're dealing with."

Tala grunted. It was a displeased sound. "I suppose I'll get the same response if I ask about a possible reason for this ... spirit or specter or whatever the hell it is ... being drawn here?"

"It would actually depend on whether there're any links between the victims or not," Monty said.

"The only one we can currently find is that all three were divorced after having had affairs."

"So the divorces weren't amicable?" I asked.

"No," Tala said. "They weren't."

"Then that right there could be the reason," Monty said. "Though there'd have to be a whole lot of hate involved to draw a vengeful spirit here."

"Jessica's hatred alone could have done that," I said, voice wry.

"Yes, but she wasn't living in the reservation." He glanced at Tala. "I take it the other exes were?"

She nodded. "Does that mean we could be dealing with another white lady?"

"White ladies generally don't suck the juice out of their victims," Monty said.

"But it's not just juice, is it?" Ciara waved a hand at the skeletal body. "Which begs the question—how the hell is this thing liquefying not only muscle and veins, but also organs?"

"I have no idea," Monty said.

"What about stopping it?" Tala said.

"Anything that stops a vampire should also stop this."

"The uncertainty in your voice isn't filling me with a whole lot of positivity."

Monty smiled. "Until we know for sure what we're dealing with, I can't give you a guarantee. But holy water and salt will work as repellents against evil—be they demons or spirits—in a tight situation."

"Just as well the station has stocked up on both."

I walked over to Monty and studied the still-glowing thread of magic for a second. "Why would a spell get tangled in his hair like that? And why would it remain active when the rest had faded?"

"She might have done it deliberately." He plucked the tiny thread free. "There does appear to be just enough spell left to create a tracker."

"Meaning it might well be bait."

"Possibly."

"I gather we *are* taking the bait?" Tala said.

"You should know us well enough to know the answer to that question." Monty's gaze narrowed. "The magic is an older style, and reeks of darkness."

"The latter is unsurprising, given what we're dealing with," I said.

"Yes, but it does mean we're not dealing with a white lady. They're generally not evil from the outset." He glanced at me. "Do you think you could read it psychically?"

"Is that wise given her attack on Lizzie?" Tala said.

I held out my hand. "She's well aware of my presence, so touching this thread likely won't make any difference."

And I crossed all mental fingers even as I said that.

Monty dropped the fragment into my palm, and even though I was wearing gloves, my skin tingled. It *wasn't* a pleasant sensation. I narrowed my gaze and studied the fragment, but it didn't reveal its secrets to either my psychic senses or my witch.

"Anything?" Monty asked.

I shook my head. "If it's a lure aimed at me, it's a pretty poor one."

"Looks like it's up to me, then." He glanced at Tala. "You want me to track it now?"

"Do werewolves run wild and free at the full moon?"

He grinned. "Who knows? You lot are extremely secretive when it comes to that sort of stuff."

"Not that secretive." Her voice was dry. "Ciara, you right to finish off things here? I'll need to go with our witches."

She nodded. "We should be able to give you an official report by the end of the day."

Monty quickly caged the thread in magic to keep it active for as long as possible, then wound a tracking spell through his net of magic. I watched with crossed arms, admiring both the speed and the proficiency of his spelling. He might not have been as powerful as his parents had hoped, but he certainly wasn't underpowered by any stretch of the imagination. He and Belle were going to have some pretty powerful kids.

Let's not get ahead of ourselves. Her mental tone was dry. *We've only just started having sex.*

That may be true, but we all know that marriage and babies lie in your future.

Indeed they do, she agreed evenly. *Whether that will happen with Monty is a matter yet to be decided.*

Not according to Monty.

He hasn't spent any great time with me. Let's wait and see how compatible we really are once we've lived together for a while.

That she was even *mentioning* such a possibility was a huge leap forward.

"Right," Monty said. "I've got a directional pulse, but it's faint. No guarantee it won't fade before we locate her."

"A small chance is better than none," Tala said. "Let's go."

She quickly led the way out. Once we were all in her SUV, Monty activated his spell. His magic shimmered through the air and the cage around the tiny thread of magic began to pulse.

"It's pulling us toward Campbell's Creek."

"Not toward the diggings area again, is it?" Tala asked, as she sped off.

"Could be. Why?"

She shrugged. "I was just wondering what it is about that area that attracts supernatural nasties."

"It's the remoteness," I said. "And the fact there's plenty of nice dark holes to hide in."

"Then maybe we need to fill said dark holes," Tala said. "Maybe it'll ease some of their traffic."

"Sadly, it doesn't work that way," Monty said. "Besides, isn't a good portion of the diggings areas heritage listed?"

"Yes, but this is a reservation, and we have the final say."

"Unfortunately, it's not the diggings but the fact the wellspring was unprotected for so long that's drawing them here," I said. "Until the ripples of its energy stop washing across the shores of darkness, we'll continue to be inundated."

"Not what I needed to hear right now." She paused. "Or any damn time, really."

"It will eventually get better," Monty said. "Left up ahead."

We continued on, moving through Castle Rock and then on toward Campbell's Creek. The road got progressively narrower and rougher the deeper we moved into the mountainous, scrubby area that surrounded Campbell's Creek. The ripple of energy coming from the cage was fading fast, however. We drove through a crossroad and then up a steep incline. The trees crowded closer to the road and the gloom and the rain closed in. It was the perfect sort of day to be hunting a supernatural nasty, I thought wryly.

As we crested the incline, the pulsing caress of thread's energy ceased, and the fragments of the spell that had given it life for this long drifted away.

Monty swore. "I've just lost the signal."

"Is there anything in the area that might be worth searching?" I asked. "Buildings or even a mine site, perhaps?"

"There's an old mining settlement at the bottom of this gully," Tala said. "It has something of a rep too."

"What sort of rep?" Monty asked. "Is it haunted?"

"No, cursed," she replied. "According to legend, a Chinese Wu—which I believe is a type of shaman—was murdered on the site. She apparently laid a curse on the entire settlement with her dying breath."

"What kind of curse?"

"That neither the town nor the men in it would ever prosper."

"And did any of them?" I asked curiously.

Tala glanced at me, amusement evident. "The settlement was abandoned only a month or so after her death, but it's hard to say whether it was through her curse or the lack of gold. I suspect the latter, as there was a large and successful Chinese settlement in Vaughn, which is not that much further on."

"Given she cursed all the men, it's unlikely they prospered in any way for the rest of their lives," Monty said. "Only the very foolish mess with a Chinese Wu, trust me. They can be fierce."

"I'll remember that, if I ever come across one." Tala's voice was dry. She pulled off the road and stopped. "The old settlement is a ten-minute walk through those trees."

I climbed out and zipped up my coat. The wind wasn't as fierce up here—though it still held a definite bite—and it held an almost mournful note. It didn't take much imagination to think it was the cry of a woman who'd been murdered long ago.

I shivered and followed Tala through the trees. The settlement turned out to be little more than a few straight rock lines and a couple of rotting timber posts. Mining settlements in the very early days of the gold rush were mostly poorly sanitized, hastily erected tent cities. The wooden structures that did exist were generally for the necessities—merchants, churches, and pubs.

I walked past a couple of building remnants on the outskirts of the settlement, into what had probably been the main street—though calling it that was something of a misnomer, given it was only slightly wider than the average footpath. I stopped and scanned the area. After a moment, a vague shimmer caught my attention.

"There's a ghost here."

Tala glanced at me sharply. "Where?"

"Over by that building on the left with the three remaining roof struts."

"That's where the Chinese woman was murdered." She studied the area with narrowed eyes. Werewolves were often sensitive to the presence of spirits or ghosts, but I had the feeling she had no sense of this one. "Can you talk to it?"

"With Belle's help, yes, but I don't think it's necessary."

Tala gaze came to mine again. "Why not?"

"Because there's no feel of evil in this area," Monty said before I could. "And because evil spirits rarely use an area that is already occupied."

Tala's eyebrows rose. "Does that mean the answer to our evil problem is to employ some ghosts?"

I laughed. "Maybe."

We continued on. The old woman followed, but she made no move against us, and there was no feeling of threat or anger. Just curiosity and perhaps a sense of loneliness.

"There's nothing here," Monty said, as we reached the far end of the settlement. "There's not even a damn curse to lift."

"So all those stories of bad things happening to trespassers are just that—stories?" Tala asked.

"Well, maybe not, because shamans of any kind are not something you want to piss off, be they alive or dead," he said. "But there's nothing to suggest our skeleton spirit has ever been here."

"I should have known tracking this thing down would not be easy." Frustration ran through Tala's voice. "I guess it also means we have no choice but to wait for the next attack?"

"I might be able to construct a sensor spell centered

around the way our killer constructs her spells," Monty said. "But it wouldn't lead us directly to her; it'd only activate if we're in her vicinity or if she casts a spell."

"If we need to conduct a grid search, we will," Tala said. "It might take forever, but it's better than doing nothing. How long will it take to construct the spell?"

"A few hours. I'll have to check the logistics of it beforehand, because the only time I've done this sort of spell was at uni."

"So, will we be hunting tonight? Or tomorrow night?"

"All things being equal—tonight," he said. "But if she follows the pattern of previous kills, she's not going to be active for a couple of days, and that will make finding her harder. She knows there're witches in the reservation and will be guarded against it."

"Even so, we need to try and stop her *before* she attacks again."

Monty nodded and glanced at me. "You in?"

"It'd be safer if I am," I said. "Besides, you can't track and drive."

"Ring me once you're ready," Tala said. "With Aiden caught up in family stuff, I'm acting head ranger."

I raised my eyebrows. "He's temporarily stepped down? When did that happen?"

Surprise flitted across her expression. "Yesterday. He didn't tell you?"

"No."

And he'd certainly had plenty of opportunity yesterday. We hadn't spent all damn day in bed.

"Ah."

One word that spoke volumes. It was just another reminder that I wasn't a wolf and didn't factor into his thinking when it came to pack and family.

I took a deep breath and released it slowly. It didn't ease the hurt and certainly didn't ease the anger.

Wolf or not, he should have told me.

Monty touched my arm, a comforting gesture that didn't really help. I smiled, briefly pressed my hand over his, and then glanced at Tala. "We might as well head back. There's nothing more we can do here."

Tala nodded and led us out of the settlement. It didn't take us long to get back to the crime scene but, by the time we got there, the rain was bucketing down.

I raced to my car, my coat protecting my upper body but my lower jeans getting soaked. The café was in the midst of an afternoon rush, and a good half of the people inside looked as wet as me, suggesting they'd run in here to get warm and wait out the storm. I wasn't about to complain, given how'd quiet we'd been of late.

I went upstairs to change out of my wet clothes, then headed back down to help out. We barely had time to clean vacant tables before someone was claiming them again.

I placed a tray on the counter ready for the two lattes Belle was making, then crossed my arms and leaned on the edge of the cake display. "Do you get the feeling there's an edge of expectation to the wolf portion of our customers this afternoon?"

"There definitely is." She designed a tulip in the milk froth, then placed the two lattes onto the tray. "I've been resisting the urge to deep read their minds all afternoon."

I raised my eyebrows. "Why on earth would you be doing that?"

She gave me the "don't be daft" look. "Because my mother taught me manners."

I laughed. Her mother had absolutely no problem using her telepathic skills whenever she deemed it necessary. And *this* definitely was. "Every instinct I have is telling me we need to know what is going on. Besides, skimming isn't against the rules of politeness."

Amusement gleamed in her silver eyes. "Which is exactly why I did it."

"And?"

"And, it's got something to do with Aiden."

A hard, cold lump formed in my gut. I sucked in a breath and said, as calmly as I could, "Something called Mia?"

"Her name isn't appearing directly in anyone's immediate thoughts, but they're definitely all coming in to watch a fire show." She grimaced, and silently added, *They're goddamn ghouls, the lot of them.*

That's no real surprise, given he is an alpha in waiting. What he does in regard to a mate will affect the future of the pack.

Yes, but why on earth would they think there'd be a confrontation here? Surely they know Aiden would never air his emotional laundry so publicly.

He mightn't, but his goddamn mother certainly would.

Would even she be such a cow?

Oh hell, yes.

A smile tugged her lips. "I guess we'll find out soon enough." She placed two double-chocolate cheesecakes onto the tray. "You know, I'd love to send the lot of them away, but it's been a slow couple of weeks, and we could do with the bank boost."

"Aiden won't break up with me in public." Of that I was sure.

Penny arrived with another order. I picked up my tray, then stepped around her and walked across to the table in the far corner to deliver the lattes and cakes to the old couple. They were human rather than wolf, but this was the first time I'd seen either of them here. I was tempted to ask them if they'd come to see the show, but the gentleman's dour expression had me holding my tongue. He really didn't look the sort to take a joke.

The bell above the door chimed merrily as another customer stepped in. The wind whipped briefly around my ankles, oddly filled with the cold sensation of destiny.

My gaze leapt up.

The woman who stepped inside was several inches taller than me, with a slim but shapely physique and strawberry blonde hair. Her golden gaze swept the room and stopped on mine. Her expression was one of polite friendliness and suggested she had no idea who I was.

But I certainly knew her.

Mia Raines.

Aiden's ex.

CHAPTER SIX

A hush fell over the café, and it felt like the gaze of every person in the room pinned the two of us. It was a weight that made me tremble. Or maybe *that* was caused by the thick mix of anger and despair boiling through me.

The bitch has some cheek, Belle growled. *Coming in here, as bold as brass, when she has to know you're in a relationship with Aiden.*

I'm not so sure she does. Remember who invited her to the reservation.

Of course, she might also be a very good actor, and I might be reading her completely wrong. Especially given she'd strung Aiden along so very easily the first time she'd come into the reservation.

More than happy to read her mind and find out, Belle said. *Or, better yet, force her ass out back into the storm.*

It was tempting. So *very* tempting. I drew in a breath and resisted. *No. I need to handle it.*

After all, I'd have to do exactly that. Not just today, but every other minute, hour, and day in my life, for the rest of my life, if she and Aiden married.

I hugged the tray close to my chest and walked over to the door. "A table for one?"

She hesitated. "I was told that Aiden O'Connor might be here."

Her voice was smooth and mellow; definitely not the harpy tones I'd been half expecting.

"He's not here at the moment, but usually comes in after his shift. Would you like to wait?"

She hesitated again and then nodded. She obviously hadn't talked to Aiden as yet, otherwise she would have known he'd taken time off from work.

Maybe it wasn't just me he left in the dark.

"This way."

I led her across to the table we kept reserved for whenever Monty, Ashworth, or Eli decided to call in. A soft murmuring trailed behind us, a wave of surprise and expectation. I wasn't going to give them their show; not here, not now, not ever.

"What can I get you?" I said once she was seated.

She picked up the menu and, after a moment, said, "A long black and the lemon meringue pie, thanks."

"Won't be long."

"Thank you."

I headed back to the counter. Belle was already making her coffee. *You sure you don't want me to force her ass and too-perfect hair out into the storm?*

I smiled, even though all I wanted to do was scream and shout and weep. *I can't talk to her if you force her ass out into the rain.*

Belle's eyebrows rose. *Why the hell do you want to talk to her? She's the opposition.*

That doesn't alter the fact we need to talk. I walked around the counter and pulled the pie from the cake fridge.

Gut instinct is telling me all is not as it seems—at least when it comes to her appearance here.

Your gut instinct is crazy.

Could be. I cut a slice of pie, plated it up, and then decorated it with cream and strawberries. *I still need to talk to her.*

The gossips are going to have a field day.

Which will happen no matter what I do.

True.

I put Mia's order onto the tray, grabbed a green tea for myself, and then walked over. Once I'd placed everything on the table, I raised a shield to prevent our watchers from hearing anything we said, and then sat down opposite her.

She raised an eyebrow. It was an elegant gesture. "Is there a problem?"

"I suspect there will be."

Curiosity and perhaps a touch of wariness crossed her pretty features, but her golden eyes showed little in the way of emotion. It just reinforced my suspicion she had no idea who I was.

"And why is that?"

"Because of who I am, and who you are."

She studied me for a second. "You're a witch. I've been told that much."

"By Karleen O'Connor, no doubt. Did she also send you here?"

She hesitated and then nodded. "She said Aiden generally drops by for a coffee after an early shift."

I am so going to rain curses down on that bitch the next time I see her, Belle growled.

She's hardly worth the karma blowback. To Mia, I added, "Which is extremely interesting, considering she's well aware he's taken leave from work and is currently at the hospital by his injured brother's bedside."

"I did know about Dillon." Mia picked up her coffee cup and studied me over its rim. "But why on earth would Karleen lie like that?"

A smile tugged at my lips, though it held little in the way of humor. "For the exact same reason that she invited you back into the reservation."

"And why is that?"

"Because she wants me out of Aiden's life and has become so desperate to achieve that aim that she'd invite the woman who broke his heart back into his life without informing him."

Surprise flitted across her face, but there was very little else in the way of reaction. After a few moments, she put her coffee down, crossed her arms on the table, and leaned forward. "You and Aiden are in a relationship?"

"Have been for a few months now."

"But you're a witch. Surely you're aware it could amount to nothing."

Anger boiled down the mental lines, a force so fierce I winced. *Belle, you need to control it.*

Oh, I am. If I wasn't, she'd be naked and walking barefoot out of the reservation right now.

The whole naked thing is a bit extreme, methinks.

Not given she's thinking you're a little too well rounded for Aiden's tastes.

I snorted and said, "He appreciates the bigger tits, Mia."

Her gaze widened even as pink flushed through her cheeks. "You heard what I was thinking?"

"I didn't. My friend and co-owner did. I take it Karleen didn't warn you about that, either?"

She drew in a breath and placed her hands on the table,

obviously intending to leave. Belle's mental energy surged; a heartbeat later, she was in Mia's mind and preventing her from moving.

"What the hell ...?" Mia said, a mix of anger and fear flickering through her eyes.

"As I said earlier, we need to talk. You'll be free to go after that." I motioned to her coffee and pie. "Consider those on the house as a means of compensation."

She glared at me. I picked up the teapot and poured myself a cup, maintaining appearances for all those watching so avidly.

"Look," I said. "I mean you no harm. But you need to know what the situation is."

"I think I can guess what the situation is." Her mellow tones held a bite. "You're in a relationship destined to go nowhere, but it's one you're very desperate to hold on to. You no doubt intend to warn me off."

I picked up my cup and took a sip. "Actually, no. I'm well aware that my relationship with Aiden will end. What you and I need to talk about is the means through which that happens."

She raised an eyebrow. "Meaning what, exactly?"

"That until Aiden tells me himself it's over, you won't do anything to undermine us. You will not come on to him or bad-mouth me to him."

Frost touched her golden eyes. "I have no idea what you've heard about me, but I'm not the type to ever willingly sleep with a man in a committed relationship—be it with a wolf, human, or witch."

"The key word there is 'willingly.'"

Her gaze widened a fraction. "He told you about that?"

"He did. There are no secrets between us, Mia." Not now, at any rate.

She digested this for a few moments, then picked up her spoon and scooped up some pie. "I could promise you the world, then walk out of this café and do the exact opposite. You'd never know, because you're not wolf and will never be party to what happens in the compounds."

"Except I would. Remember my friend? The telepathic one? The gossip brigade in this town has nothing on her when it comes to information gathering." I took another sip of tea. "Of course, we could enforce the agreement mentally, but that could lead to bad karma, and I'd really rather make this a friendly arrangement."

Horror and perhaps a touch of fear flitted through her expression. She hastily scooped up more pie. "What happens to me if he does decide our relationship should renew?"

"Absolutely nothing. You and he would be welcome here anytime you wish."

She half laughed. "That would be rather awkward, wouldn't it?"

"No, because I'm also one half of the reservation witch team, so he and I will be working together on a regular basis."

She frowned. "Why on earth would the reservation need two witches?"

A smile tugged at my lips. This time, it actually did hold some amusement. "Because we have an ongoing demon and spirit infestation problem."

One eyebrow rose again. "Seriously?"

"Very."

"They didn't when I was last here."

"Lots of things have happened since you left, Mia." I paused. "Do you still have a common law husband?"

"I wouldn't have come back here if I did."

There was an edge in her voice that made me believe her, but nevertheless I reached out for Belle.

It's true, Belle said. *They split up not long after she returned to her pack.*

So she lost both the men in her life?

Yes. Belle paused. *Can't say which one she regrets more, though. She definitely cared for Aiden, but I'm not sensing any great degree of love.*

Caring can develop into love, given enough time together.

Belle didn't reply to that, but her emotions swirled down the link, a warm and caring telepathic hug that had me briefly blinking back tears. I dropped my gaze and drank some tea until I got them under control.

"If you know the story," she continued, anger evident, though I suspected it was aimed more at the situation she'd been forced into rather than at me. "Then you know I had very little control over all that."

Because her parents were at the bottom of the wolf rung, and she was bound to obey her alphas' ruling or see them suffer. "You could have told Aiden what was going on, Mia."

A smile twisted her lips. "A comment that shows how little you understand pack structure and life."

"No doubt." I studied her for a second. "So, do we have an agreement?"

She hesitated, and then nodded. "We do."

I held out my hand and quickly but silently raised a binding spell. "Shake to agree. But be warned, an agreement shaken on is an agreement that is best upheld when dealing with a witch."

She smiled. "As I said, I am no relationship breaker. I'm all too aware of the pain it causes."

Because her common law husband had another on the side, Belle said.

Damn it, Belle, I don't want to feel sorry for her. And yet there was a tiny piece of me that was starting to.

Probably because she isn't the ogre we'd painted in our minds.

No. In fact, her pack's alphas had treated her as badly as my father had me. Which wasn't news—Aiden had mentioned she'd been forced into it—but my reactions to the situation had been clouded by his obvious pain and hurt. I hadn't actually thought about what it must have been like for her.

Which didn't at all mean she was completely exonerated of guilt. She had a voice, and she'd been far enough away from her pack's influence to have said something. I might not understand pack politics, but I knew Aiden well enough now to know he would have confronted her alphas on her behalf.

"Do we have a deal?" I repeated.

She reached out and gripped my hand. The spell activated, a binding that would ensure she held to her word.

I might feel sorry for her, I might be inclined to believe her, but I wasn't a fool. If Aiden *did* break up with me, it wouldn't be because of any undue influence on her part.

"Deal," she said. "And may the best woman win."

"This isn't a game, Mia."

The amusement fell from her features. "Sorry, I didn't mean to be so glib."

I dismantled the silencing spell from around the table and then rose. "I'd better get back to work. Please feel free to stay and finish your coffee and pie."

"Thank you," she said. "It *is* rather good pie."

"Good coffee and cake is the reason this place is always so full."

That, and the thrilling prospect of a confrontation between rivals, apparently.

Belle squeezed my arm as I walked around the counter, but didn't say anything. Of course, she didn't need to. Her empathy and love washed through my mind, a wave that offered courage and strength.

I'd need both before the next few days were over.

Mia finished her coffee and pie and left about ten minutes later. The crowd quickly thinned out after that, leaving only a few stragglers left by the time closing time came around.

I was locking the door when my phone rang, the tone telling me it was Aiden. I sucked in a breath, gathering courage, and then answered it.

"Hey," I said. "Everything okay?"

"I've been at the hospital all day with Dillon. They told him yesterday he'll have a limp for life, and he's not coping well at the moment."

Tired frustration swirled through his voice, and my heart went out to him. "He's a teenager, Aiden. They're all about appearances at that age. He'll be fine in the long run."

"I hope you're right." A soft scraping came down the line, and I had a mental image of his rubbing a hand across his bristly chin. "Are you right to find your own way home tonight? My parents have demanded I make an appearance at some goddamn dinner they're throwing. Heaven only knows why."

To welcome Mia, I thought. To reintroduce her in the safe surroundings of the compound, where there was absolutely no hint or reminder of my presence. It was tempting, so very tempting, to warn him, but it wouldn't change anything and only serve to get Karleen more offside.

Maybe I needed to rethink letting Belle rain curses down on the bitch's head.

"Are you coming home afterward? Or will you stay up there the night?"

"I'll probably stay. It'll be safer than driving home when I'm bone tired."

I swallowed and found myself nodding, even though he wouldn't see the movement.

"Breakfast at the café, then? Or are you going straight back to the hospital?"

"Breakfast would be lovely." He paused. "I'll see you in the morning, hon."

He hung up before I could reply. I sucked in air, trying to control the thick rise of fear and hurt, anger and love, then turned and ran across the room, straight into Belle's waiting arms.

And sobbed for a relationship that hadn't yet ended.

I was of two minds as to whether I should stay at the café or go back to Aiden's, but in the end decided that if I was going to spend the night alone, it'd be better to do so in a place where there weren't so many happy memories to tear at my still fragile emotions.

Belle came out of her bedroom, an overnight bag slung over her shoulder. "Are you sure you don't want me to stay and keep you company?"

"Positive." I gestured at the extra-large slice of black forest cake sitting on my lap. "I have all the company I need right here on this plate."

A smile tugged at her lips, though it didn't really lift the concern swirling through her thoughts. "A mountain of chocolate cake *is* the perfect cure for a sore heart."

"Indeed." And it was a cure we'd both used more than a couple of times over the years—though I did have more of a tendency to fall for the wrong man than she did. "Can you remind Monty that if he gets that tracker spell working, he has to call me? If this bitch is capable of magic, it might take the three of us to bring her down."

"Is that precognition speaking? Or common old sense?"

"According to some, I haven't got a whole lot of the latter, so it has to be the former."

She laughed, but before she could say anything, a horn tooted outside. "That would be Monty."

"What, he's too lazy to get out of the car now?"

Her smile flashed. "He was given a friendly warning to stop parking in no-standing zones, so now he just keeps the engine running."

"He could go a little further down the road where parking *is* allowed and come get you like a gentleman, rather than just tooting the damn horn."

She laughed. "This is Monty, remember."

I smiled. "Is he in the Mustang?"

"From the sound of that rumble, yes."

"That explains it then." Monty wouldn't dare leave his precious pony parked out in the street where uncaring strangers could fling open their doors and dent it. Not unless he absolutely had to.

"Yes, I think he cares about that Mustang more than he will ever care about me."

"Oh, I wouldn't go that far."

A wry smile tugged at her lips. "I would. You haven't

witnessed him polishing her. He croons at her. It's seriously disturbing."

"Only if he doesn't croon at you as well."

"Also true."

She waggled a goodbye with her fingers, then disappeared down the stairs. A few seconds later, the front door slammed and thick silence fell. It was the sort of silence where bad thoughts lurked, ready to be picked and amplified. I'd already had one crying bout. I was not going to have another. Not until the end, and that wasn't here yet.

Enjoy what you have, while you can, I told myself fiercely. And then move on.

Except there was no moving on. Not for me. Not now.

I frowned at the thought, but whatever precognitive insight it had come from fled before I could pin it. I swore softly, put on some happy music, and then picked up the top book from the stack Belle had collected from our storage unit and read through it while munching on my ginormous bit of cake.

Time drifted, and the late afternoon moved on to night. The only thing I found in the book was a vague mention of something called a Baigujing, which was apparently a shape-shifting demoness with a fondness for eating flesh. It wasn't our spirit, but could have been related, if the side notes were to be believed. There was nothing on how to kill it, however, which was annoying.

I put the book down, then picked up my empty plate and walked over to the small kitchenette to wash it. As I filled up the kettle, my phone rang.

Aiden.

My heart leapt into my throat and, just for a second, I couldn't breathe. I dragged the phone out of my pocket and hit the answer button. "I wasn't expecting to hear from you tonight—is everything okay?"

"No. Where are you?"

The words were little more than a deep growl. He was angry. *Truly* angry. Obviously, the meeting with Mia had not gone well. And while a part of me wanted to dance in utter delight, I knew it was far too soon for that. Karleen had extended the invitation to Mia, which meant only she could rescind it.

"I'm at the café—"

"I'll be over to pick you up in five," he cut in brusquely.

"Where are we going?"

"Home."

With that, he hung up.

I stared at the phone and wondered just how far awry things had gone. And whether in the long run it would make any damn difference. If it wasn't Mia who broke us up, it would be someone else.

I shoved my phone back into my pocket, then turned and raced down the stairs to grab my coat and purse. I was waiting out the front when his truck pulled up.

He leaned across the seat to open the door for me, but didn't say anything. His aura was a turbulent mix of red and black—the former centered around his heart and the latter representing unresolved emotions and grief. It was the black that was dangerous—not physically, because there was no way in this world that Aiden would ever lash out at me with his fists, but rather emotionally. Hurt people hurt people, an old psychic had once told me. If I didn't step carefully, all that anger might unintentionally be unleashed on me.

He waited until I pulled on the seat belt and then took off, taking the corner so fast the tires squealed. For too many minutes, heavy silence reigned, but the wash of his anger continued to burn across my senses and my skin.

We were well out of Castle Rock when he finally slowed down. After a deep breath, he looked across to me, his blue eyes bright in the shadows of the night.

"Sorry. I didn't mean to be such an uncommunicative bastard, but my mother sprang a rather unexpected surprise on me this evening."

"I know."

His gaze sharpened. "You do? How?"

I half smiled, though tension rose, twisting my stomach into knots. "Remember the confrontation I had with her at your birthday party?"

He nodded but didn't say anything.

"Well, she told me then that she'd invited Mia—"

"Why the *fuck* didn't you say anything? I could have stopped her—"

"No, you couldn't have, and we both know it."

His breath hissed through clenched teeth. An admission I was right, even if he didn't come out and say it. "At least I would have been forewarned. Walking in there tonight and seeing her again ... well, it was a shock."

I couldn't help but note he hadn't said it was an *unpleasant* shock. He might be utterly furious about being caught so off guard, but all those unresolved feelings still swirled through his aura, and no doubt his mind, and who knew exactly where they would lead.

"I take it you walked out of the dinner?"

"Yes."

I hesitated. "You can't leave it there, Aiden."

He glanced at me sharply again. "Are you advising me to talk to her?"

"Oh, trust me, it's really the last thing I actually want you to do."

"Then why say something like that?"

"Because you've never really confronted what she did and what you felt for her, and you need to do both if you're to have any future—be it with her or with another wolf."

"I don't want that future. I want you."

My heart twisted. Ached. "Through sickness and in health, kids and old age?"

Silence.

He knew, like I knew, that he was thinking only about the present. His future lay with his pack, as their alpha, and he couldn't—wouldn't—jeopardize that.

We rode in silence for a while. As we swept into the outskirts of Argyle, I said softly, "Why didn't you tell me you'd taken time off work?"

He slowed for the roundabout. "It just slipped my mind. It doesn't mean anything."

"Would you have mentioned it if I had been a wolf?"

Again, silence.

Again, we both knew that the answer would have been yes. And no matter how much he cared for or wanted me, he would continue to compartmentalize our relationship as separate to his "wolf" life.

He drew in a deep breath and released it slowly. "I'm sorry. I should have said something."

"Yes. We did agree to the whole 'no more secrets' thing, remember?"

"We did—and yet you kept the whole Mia thing secret."

"Guilty as charged, but I just ... didn't want to upset your already strained relationship with your mother." Which was true enough, even if cowardice was in fact the real reason.

He flicked on the indicator and turned into the driveway that led around the lake to his house. "My mother can go to hell, as far as I'm concerned. I have no idea what she was thinking—"

"Oh, I think we both know *precisely* what she was thinking."

"Wanting you out of my life is no excuse for inviting back the woman I've already rejected."

He might have rejected her, but he hadn't entirely gotten over her. "She's your alpha *and* your mother. A rather deadly combination."

"That still doesn't excuse her behavior."

He pulled up in front of his house and turned off the headlights. Thunder cracked overhead, and the already heavy rain became an absolute torrent. Even though the door was only ten feet away, we were absolutely soaked before we got inside.

I stripped off my coat and slung it over the hook. "I think a nice hot shower is called for."

"Oh," he said, scooping me up into his arms. "I can think of a far better way to warm up."

I laughed. "You wouldn't be using sex to avoid any more discussions about a certain wolf, would you?"

"Discussions about that wolf are likely to kill my libido, not increase it. There's only one woman I want to think about and lose myself in right now, and she's right here in my arms."

"So that would be a yes, then."

"You can take that comment any way you please."

"And you, dear wolf, can take me any way you please."

He laughed, low and sexy, and a delicious heat stirred through my body. "Be sure that I will. Multiple times."

"Multiples are always good."

He laughed again, then raced up the stairs and got down to the serious business of lovemaking.

The wind rattled the windows, and the rain pelted against the tin roof, creating a deafening chorus of sound.

And yet, that wasn't what had woken me.

I frowned and flipped the sheet away from my face. Aiden stirred lightly at the movement; his arm slipped around my waist and pulled me just a little bit closer. I smiled, even as I wondered if he was subconsciously holding on to something he knew was already slipping away.

I ignored the stab of pain and reached for my phone to check the time. It was just after four, which meant we'd only been asleep for a couple of hours. Aiden had very definitely followed through with his "multiples" promise.

With a very contented smile, I scanned the shadows clinging to the room. There was nothing out of place, and nothing to hear other than the cacophony of the storm, and yet ... unease stirred.

Something was out there in the deeper darkness of the night.

Something foul.

I pulled away from Aiden's grip and climbed out of bed.

"Is something wrong?" he immediately asked.

"Maybe. I don't know." I walked across to the huge wall of glass and stared out into the storm. Though the windows were double glazed, a chill caressed my skin. I suspected its cause wasn't the cold that still seeped through the glass but rather the stirring of something unnatural. Something I could feel rather than see.

"That generally means yes." The bed squeaked lightly as he rose and padded across the room. He stopped behind me, his big body radiating heat, warming my spine and chasing away some of the cold. "Is it our killer?"

"I don't really know."

"But you think it's headed this way?"

I hesitated and reached out with my psi senses. They briefly snagged a sliver of darkness but were quickly spun away—whether by the wind or magic, I couldn't say, because the sensation was simply too far away.

"I can't tell." I crossed my arms and lightly rubbed them. "But given the specter has come after me before, it might be wise to get Monty out here."

"Why?" Aiden asked, surprise evident. "He surely won't be able to do anything more than you."

"Actually, in this case, he can. He gained an insight into our spirit's magic when we went after her yesterday morning and was working on using that to form a tracking spell. If she *is* out there, we might be able to find her."

"It would seem I missed a fair bit when I was sitting in the hospital."

"Your brother is more important than a hunt for a murderer, Aiden."

"Yes, but—"

"You're an alpha wolf *and* head ranger, and you hate not being on top of all things."

He laughed softly. "*That* is bitingly true. You want me to ring Monty?"

"Yes, though he isn't going to be happy about the hour."

"Tough. He's the reservation witch, not you." Aiden walked back to the bed to grab his phone and then made the call.

It almost rang out before Monty answered, and his voice

held a decidedly grumpy note. "Do you know what fucking time it is?"

"Well, yes, because I'm at the other end of the phone making the call," Aiden said dryly. "Do you want to get your ass out of bed and over to my place as soon as possible?"

"Has there been another murder?" Monty's tone showed a whole lot more interest.

"No, but Liz has a sense of darkness stirring and—"

"She's very rarely wrong about these things." There was a scuff of movement followed by a muttered curse. The latter had come from Belle, though the vague stirrings along the mental lines suggested she remained more asleep than awake. "How far away is it?"

"Far enough that I can't sense whether it's actually our skeleton spirit or something else," I said, raising my voice to ensure he could hear me.

"I'll be there in twenty," Monty said. "In the meantime, activate your muting spell, Liz. It'll stop this thing from sensing your presence if she is using your link to the wild magic to track you."

Something I should have thought about doing earlier. "She might not be here for me, Monty. It might be just a coincidence."

"It might, but it's not a risk we dare take. And please don't go after her until I get there. Belle won't be happy if something happens to you on my watch."

No, Belle silently muttered, *she definitely won't. So look after each other, please.*

Rest assured, I won't let anything happen to your man.

Well, good, because I've only just started playing with him, and I'm far from finished yet.

I think it's safe to say he will never be finished with you.

Will you just give it a rest?

Not until you admit the inevitable.

Never.

Not even when you're wearing white and walking down the aisle?

Even then.

I chuckled softly and walked back to Aiden. "I might grab a shower while we're waiting for Monty to arrive. I don't suppose you want to make the coffee?"

He snagged my fingers and drew me close. "I might even stretch my culinary skills to making some toast. I didn't have any dinner and I've expended a fair bit of energy since then."

"And I appreciated your effort. Multiple times."

I rose on my toes and kissed him, long and leisurely. Desire rose, a thick and heady scent that made my pulse race and body ache.

"We have at least twenty minutes before Monty gets here," he murmured eventually, his breath hot against my lips. "What say we make full use of it?"

"Tempting, but I need a coffee and a shower, and not necessarily in that order."

"You smell perfectly fine to me."

"You would say that, given it's your scent all over me."

His hand slipped down to my rump and pressed me against his erection. "What if I promised to be quick?"

"Tempting, but given the way my luck has been running of late, evil would strike just as we reached an interesting stage of proceedings."

He sighed. The sorrowful sound was spoiled by the glitter of amusement in his eyes. "My woman has a will of iron."

I wish that were true ... I forced a smile and kissed him

again. "No, she's just being cautious. You know, that thing you keep urging me to be."

He laughed and released me. "Never thought those words would come back and bite me."

I stepped back and pointed toward the door. "Begone, wolf. Your woman needs sustenance."

He made a flourishing bow. "Your wish is my command."

"I will remind you of that at an opportune time."

He laughed and headed out. By the time I'd taken a shower and gotten dressed, the rich aroma of coffee and toast rode the air. I quickly raised the muting spell Monty had taught me and then drew it back into my flesh. We knew it worked, because it had been tested against the best in the business—my father and ex.

Once I'd shoved on my boots, I headed out and clattered down the stairs, but stopped abruptly near the bottom step, my head snapping toward the wall of windows.

Evil was close.

Far too close.

Magic flickered across my fingertips, a repelling spell so fierce its sparks spun through the shadows, firefly bright. I scanned the wall of black beyond the windows, but I had no sense she was hunting us.

But she was hunting someone.

"Do you want vegemite or walnut toffee spread on your —" Aiden stopped abruptly. "She's out there?"

"Yes." I swallowed heavily and glanced at him. "How well do you know your neighbors?"

He frowned. "As well as anyone does these days. Why?"

"Is there a divorced single man among them?"

"I don't think they were married, but Jo and Mal

recently split up, and I think Mal is still living in their rental. It's the second house back from the main road."

"I think that's where our spirit might be heading."

"Meaning she hasn't attacked yet?"

"Not yet."

"Then let's go." He moved across to the gun safe in the corner and unlocked it. "You haven't got your backpack with you—will that be problematic?"

"Only in that I can't hit her with either holy water or my silver knife."

"Either require you getting entirely too close, in my opinion."

"In that, we agree. So I'll just cast a cage around her and hope it holds until Monty gets here."

"Will that actually work, given she's capable of magic?"

I shrugged. "There's only one way to find out."

"So much for being cautious," he muttered.

I smiled, despite the gathering tension. "Hard to be cautious when there's a life on the line."

"A truth I cannot deny. Lead the way." He must have seen my surprise, because he added, with a somewhat wry smile, "You'll sense this thing before me, and you're better equipped to handle it. I may be an alpha, but I'm also more than willing to cede the lead in a situation such as this. Doesn't mean I'm happy about it, of course."

"Oh, I think that goes without saying."

I pulled on my coat and headed outside. The wind hit hard, forcing me back several steps before I managed to catch my balance. I tugged the hood down to keep the rain out of my face and then went right, heading for the path that led around the lake.

Evil didn't need a path. She was coming straight across the water.

I clenched my fingers against the press of energy. The last thing I needed was for this thing to sense the presence of my regular magic now that I'd concealed the inner wild stuff.

I ran past several houses before cutting across the grass toward the man's rental. The place was shrouded in darkness, though that wasn't entirely surprising given the hour. I stepped onto the porch and strode toward the door. A sensor light clicked on, the sudden brightness making me blink rapidly.

"Is our specter close enough to see that?" Aiden asked.

"She'll probably see the glow, but I don't think she's close enough to actually see us. Too many trees along the shoreline." I motioned to the door. "You want to employ some muscle and force that open?"

"Why not just knock? Or magic it open?"

"Our spirit might sense the latter and, well, if I can smell the booze, surely you can."

His nostrils flared briefly, and his gaze narrowed. Though I could see the questions in his eyes about the sharpness of my olfactory senses, he didn't give them voice; he just stepped back, raised his foot, and kicked the door as hard as he could. It sprang open with little resistance, crashing back against the wall with enough noise to wake the dead.

But not, apparently, the drunk.

Mal lay on the sofa, one leg on the floor and his arms wrapped around a large bottle of Jack Daniels. If he'd gone through that entire thing tonight, he was damn lucky to be alive. Aside from the whole alcohol poisoning prospect, he was on his back and could have very easily choked on his own vomit.

"Bloody fool." Aiden plucked the empty bottle from the man's grasp, then quickly shifted him onto his side.

A staggeringly loud snore was the only response.

I shut the door as best I could, given the lock was broken, then walked down to the kitchen area. After a quick check through several cupboards, I found the salt container and raced upstairs, pouring a thin line along the edges of the bedroom and bathroom windows. Thankfully, the rental was smaller than Aiden's and only had the one bedroom up here. It at least meant there weren't as many avenues for our spirit to enter. *Not* that she'd shown any tendency so far to enter via windows—apparently all she had to do was knock on the front door, and her victims let her straight in.

Either her illusionary form was absolutely stunning, or her magic made her victims as horny as hell and willing to forgo all common sense.

I clattered back down the stairs. Aiden was on the phone, but hung up as I walked over to our target. He was still out to it.

"Monty is still ten or so minutes away. How do you want to play this?"

I hesitated. "I'm thinking this could be the perfect opportunity to attempt a trap of our own."

"With me as the bait, I take it?"

A smile tugged at my lips. "Well, you are a potential heartbreaker, so it's rather apt."

He snorted. "There will be no heartbreak for you when it comes to Mia, trust me on that."

Which wasn't a denial that heartache did lie in my future where he was concerned. "Let's get Mal upstairs, out of the way."

"Will he be safe up there?"

"I've laid salt along all the windows—"

"Will that be protection enough, given she's capable of magic? Salt doesn't stop witches, does it?"

"No, but she's a spirit capable of magic rather than a witch; salt will stop her, if only for the few seconds it would take to create a spell to get rid of it."

"And in those few minutes, we could have her."

I nodded. "I doubt she'll come in through the upstairs windows, though, and given what's been said about the awkwardness of her gait, it's unlikely she'll climb to the balcony."

"In this reservation, 'unlikely' isn't a word we should be putting faith in. We'll shove him in the shower—he'll be out of immediate sight, and if he vomits, it'll be easier to wash off."

I nodded, but my gaze was drawn to the darkness beyond the wall of windows. She was almost at the shoreline. We needed to hurry if we wanted to set our trap.

Aiden hauled Mal upright, then shifted his position so that his back was against the man's chest. After grabbing Mal's arms to hold him in place, Aiden bent and hauled him up. It very much looked like he was giving the unconscious man a piggyback.

We quickly went up the stairs and into the bathroom. Aiden sat him in the shower and propped him against the rear wall while I grabbed a couple of pillows to break his fall should he flop the wrong way. Thankfully, the shower was one of those large walk-in ones, and there weren't any large sheets of glass to fall against and smash.

"Right," Aiden said once Mal was secure. "What's the plan?"

I hesitated. "You take up position on the sofa. The minute you let her inside, I'll grab her."

"Things are rarely that simple. Not lately."

A truth that could apply to more than just the supernatural. "You're wearing your protection charm. You'll be all right."

The charm in question was little more than multiple strands of intertwined leather and copper worn around the neck. Each strand represented a different type of protection spell, and while the whole thing looked rather innocuous, it was probably the most powerful thing Belle and I had ever created. Only silver would have made it any stronger, but that wasn't really practical in a werewolf reservation, let alone for a werewolf to wear.

Warmth gleamed in his eyes. "It wasn't me I was worried about."

A statement that warmed my foolish heart. He turned and led the way back downstairs. While he walked over to the sofa and settled down, I went through the kitchen and into the small laundry room. It gave me a good line of sight down the entire length of the room but was far enough away that she shouldn't be able to see me. Unless, of course, she had eyes as sharp as a wolf.

I half closed the door, then hunkered down and reached out with my senses. Her presence was sharp and close, and she was heading straight for the door. I sucked in a breath, drawing Aiden's gaze, and held up two fingers.

He nodded, then crossed his arms, leaned back against the sofa, and pretended to sleep. My gaze went to the door. For several seconds, nothing happened. The rain continued to lash the night, and riverlets of water raced down the glass, providing a silvery curtain through which little could be seen.

Then a face appeared from the gloom. It was gaunt and white, with sunken eye sockets, sharp bony cheeks, and no hair. Though there was no discernable body, the light from the fire gleamed off what looked to be the upper part of a hip.

A *skeletal* hip.

Her face returned to the darkness, but her magic rose. I recognized the spell, though it wasn't one I'd used all that much, thanks to the fact my psi senses could generally do a better job of probing spaces. Threads of evil slipped into the room and gently spread out across the shadows, searching the room in a methodical manner until they reached the sofa and Aiden.

They immediately stopped.

Tension wound through me, and it was all I could do to remain still and not warn Aiden. But if I moved or did anything to counter the probe spell, she'd run. The only way I had any hope of catching her was to wait until she stepped into the room.

Two of the spell's threads unraveled from the mass and reached out, lightly touching Aiden's face. The charm reacted, instantly and violently smacking the probe away. There was a screech of fury, and the probing spell disintegrated. The dark presence that was our skeleton spirit fled.

I swore, leapt up, and raced for the door. Aiden was by my side in an instant. "Problem?"

"The charm reacted to her magic and scared her off."

"I can't say I'm sad about that."

"Me neither." Even if it wrecked our capture plans, it at least confirmed my magic would hold against an entity this strong.

I threw open the door, and the wind blasted in, chilling me to the core. "Stay here and protect Mal. I'll see if I can get close enough to throw a tracker at her."

"And if it's a trap?"

"I'll deal with it."

Aiden shoved my coat into my hand. "Please be careful."

"Always."

I thrust my arms into the coat's sleeves, zipped up the front, and headed out. I didn't bother drawing on the hood, simply because it restricted side vision. But the wind and rain was so fierce, it slapped long wet strands of hair across my face and made it almost impossible to see anyway.

But I didn't need to see to track our spirit.

I could feel her. Feel her power and her foulness.

She hadn't headed back to the lake, instead going right, toward the road. Perhaps she thought it'd be easier to lose me—or any magic I might send after her—in Argyle's more densely populated area.

I broke into a run, weaving a tracking spell around the fingers of one hand while sparks of energy danced around the other. The latter was purely defensive—if the bitch came at me, I was going to hit her with everything I could. I couldn't kill her with the inner wild magic simply because we had no idea just how connected it was to the reservation's magic. If there was a deeper connection than what was currently presumed, then using my inner wild magic to kill might forever stain the reservation's.

But stop her in her tracks? I sure as hell could do that.

Especially when the small but luminous threads of true wild magic were now visible. They were keeping pace with me but, rather weirdly, I had no sense that Katie had sent them. In fact, these particular threads seemed to have come from the bigger of the two wellsprings—the "wilder" one.

It was something that seemed to be happening more and more, and made me wonder if, in protecting the wellspring with my magic in those early months of our arrival—

well before Monty and Ashworth had gotten here—some sort of connection had formed.

Which should have been impossible, but in this reservation? Who knew?

Up ahead, streetlights shone, but they were little more than pale yellow spots that did little to lift the overall darkness. A figure moved across the outer reaches of one of those light spots and for the first time, I saw her—though it was undoubtedly an illusion rather than the reality, because she very much reminded me of the old-style movie stars from the forties and fifties: blonde and buxom.

She disappeared into the storm-clad darkness. I swung out onto the driveway and raced after her. She was now on the far side of the road, heading toward a construction site consisting of half-built two-story apartment houses.

I raced after her, splashing through the puddles and sending muddy water flying. As I crossed the road, lights swept around the long corner to my left, pinning me in sudden brightness.

A car, coming straight at me.

CHAPTER SEVEN

Panic surged, lending my feet wings as I raced for the safety of the road's edge. The twin beam of lights shifted abruptly, and I looked up. The car had slewed sideways and was now beginning a slow spin. The driver's face was a white blur, but I nevertheless recognized it.

Monty.

Fighting for control.

Failing.

He was going to hit me ...

I swore and leapt high in a desperate attempt to vault the oncoming car's nose. The jump was higher and longer than anything I'd ever done before, and was no doubt fueled not only by fear but also the changes the inner wild magic continued to make on my body. As I reached the arc of the leap and began to drop toward the ground, the car slid underneath me and continued to spin down the road. Relief surged, but it was short-lived; I landed hard and awkwardly, stumbling forward several steps before crashing onto my hands and knees.

That's when I felt it—a sphere of darkness, heading

straight at me. I flung up a hand and quickly raised a shielding spell. It flared through the rain-swept night, a thick round net that not only caught the sphere, but also sent it flying back.

A scream that was fury and surprise combined rent the air, then the force of her presence moved away once more.

I swore and scrambled upright. Heard a shout and looked around to see Monty running toward me. His car sat half on, half off the road several houses down, the engine off but headlights on, shining brightness into the front windows of the nearby house.

"You okay?" His face was ghost white. "I could have fucking—"

"Monty," I cut in fiercely, "she's close. Did you get the tracker going?"

He nodded and pulled out what looked to be a baseball-sized mass of inert threads. He made a motion with his hand, quickly activating the spell, and then tossed it into the air. It hovered for an instant, slowly turning around, and then shot forward. A tiny thread no thicker than fine cotton unspooled behind it, a shimmering guide for us to follow.

We ran into the construction site. The rain was now so fierce, rivers of water sluiced down the driveway, making the already muddy ground unstable, forcing us to slow down or end up facedown in the muck.

We slogged up the hill, past five of the half-built apartments and then around to the left, toward the small Portaloo and site office. The trail led us over to the fence that divided the construction site from the house behind it. Monty leapt up, swung one leg over the fence, then yelped and threw himself back, landing awkwardly.

I grabbed his arm, steadying him. "Why the hell—"

I stopped. Deep, fierce growls now filled the night, and

the fence shuddered under a barrage of weighty assaults. "Is that dog as large as it sounds?"

"Larger." Monty pulled away from my grip and gave me a nod of thanks. "We'll have to try the next house and hope there's not another psycho dog in that one."

I nodded and took the lead, warily leaping onto the fence that led into the neighboring yard, then whistling softly. Psycho dog immediately shifted position and tried to get through the fence between his property and this one, but no other dog responded.

Of course, he or she could just be lying in wait.

I wove a gentle repelling spell around my fingers, just in case, then threw a leg over the fence and leapt down.

Still nothing other than psycho dog.

Monty jumped down beside me, hissing slightly. "Hurt my ankle, it seems."

"Bad?"

"Nope. This way."

He moved forward. Though I suspected he was trying not to limp, his pain was obvious.

We moved around the side of the house, through a gate, and then up the drive. The tracker thread pulsed briefly, as if in response to Monty's reappearance.

As he hurried on after it, I said, "Has the tracker got a distance limit?"

"It'll spool out for about a kilometer," Monty said. "It'll stop after that and wait for me to catch up or recall it."

"And it's currently still spooling?"

He nodded and glanced around at me. "If you're about to suggest you run on without me, forget it. I'd rather lose the bitch than you."

"Well, obviously, but—"

I stopped abruptly. Darkness crawled my skin, and the night came alive.

It wasn't the weather. It was magic. Dark magic, coming straight at us.

This time, there was no time to shield. It was too fast, too close. I leapt at Monty, knocking him sideways and down. We hit the ground in a tangled mess of arms and legs, him on the bottom, me half on top. As he cursed and struggled to get back up, I growled, "Stay down."

He instantly stilled. I punched upwards with a clenched fist and called to the wild magic. So many strands responded, it briefly appeared as if the moon itself flew toward us. The thick ball gathered around my fist and then fell curtain-like across the two of us, covering us in a sheet of luminous power.

And not a moment too soon.

The sphere of dark magic hit the curtain and then spread out like a disease, covering the glowing threads with darkness. The force of the blow ricocheted through my body, and my arm briefly buckled, dragging the shield and the magic it was struggling to contain so close to my face that I could smell its foulness and taste the bitter rot of its creator.

And yet the sphere hadn't been designed to kill. It had been designed to stop.

More luminous threads of wild magic spun into the curtain, strengthening it, bolstering it. Bolstering me. I straightened my arm and forced the foul magic away from my face.

Then Monty's magic surged, attacking the dark spell, unravelling its threads and muting its force. Within seconds, there was nothing left but a few broken threads that the wild magic burned away.

I sucked in a deep breath and released the protective curtain. The luminous threads of wild magic disentangled themselves and moved away, undeterred and unaffected by the fierceness of the storm. I couldn't help but wish I was similarly unaffected, because right now, it felt like every bit of me was wet, cold, and aching.

I rolled away from Monty and sat up, my gaze sweeping the night, looking for the tracker's cotton-fine guide thread.

It was no longer visible.

Monty pushed into a sitting position with a deep groan. "Thank you for the save, but fuck, can you give me a little warning next time?"

"If evil ever bothers to give *me* a warning, next time I will."

I pushed upright, then winced as pain shot through my head. It felt as if there were dozens of tiny people inside my head gleefully shoving red-hot needles into my brain. I blinked back tears, offered Monty a hand, and quickly hauled him upright.

He swore, his face screwing up in pain. "Damn it, I really did damage my ankle when I fell off that fence."

"The ankle will heal. What about the tracker spell?"

"I do love all the cousinly concern you're showing." His gaze narrowed as he scanned the night. After a few seconds, he grimaced. "It lost momentum when we were attacked. It's hovering just beyond the kilometer limit."

"Meaning she's well past that?"

He nodded, raised his left hand, and made a "come here" motion. "At least we know the tracker works. If worse comes to worst, Tala or one of her team can drive me around the reservation tomorrow. You never know, we might get lucky."

"I think we both know how likely *that* is on this reservation."

"Yes, but it's still worth a shot. Miracles aren't exactly unknown in the place, either." The tracking sphere thudded into his hand. He tucked it into his coat and then added, "Can we take the long way back to the car? I don't think my ankle is up to climbing any more fences."

By the time we returned to his car, he was limping badly and the thick scent of sweat and pain swirled through the storm. He opened the door and then paused and glanced at me. "Do you want a lift back to Aiden's?"

"We're not at Aiden's. Our spirit's target was another single man in a nearby rental."

"Then I'll—"

"Do nothing more than get into your car and drive to the emergency department," I said. "You need that ankle checked out."

"But—"

"Argue, and I'll send Belle after you."

He rolled his eyes. "Fine. But I expect a full update on everything that happened before I got here over afternoon tea tomorrow." He paused, his expression lighting up. "Isn't it scone day tomorrow?"

"Yes, and yes, Belle will save you some if you happen to be out tracking rather than lounging around the café come afternoon teatime. Now go."

I stepped back out of his way. He slammed the car door closed, then drove off. After scrubbing a hand across my forehead and wishing the idiots in my head would just give it a rest, I trudged back to Mal's place.

Aiden met me at the door, a towel in one hand and a hot chocolate in the other.

"Oh, I think I love you." I wrapped my hands around

the mug and took a drink. It wouldn't do a whole lot to stop the tiny idiots in my head, but at least my fingers would thaw.

He smiled, but there was an odd light in his eyes, one that seemed almost wistful. "They do say the way to a woman's heart is through the provision of chocolate."

"And they would be right." Shame he wasn't really interested in said heart because it didn't come in the body of a wolf. I took another sip, then handed him back the mug and took the towel, drying my hair as best I could. "How's our victim?"

"Still unconscious. I've called an ambulance, just to be safe." He glanced at his watch. "They'll be here in ten if you want to head back home and grab a shower to warm up."

I shook my head. "I'll stay, just in case the bitch decides to circle back."

"Then at least get out of those wet clothes and go warm up near the fire. You're shivering so badly I can hear your knees knocking."

"You just want to get me naked."

"Always." He smiled, put the mug down, and then tugged off his sweater. "But in this case, I'd rather not keep you that way. The glory that is your body is mine, and only mine, to behold."

"I thought werewolves were exhibitionists?"

"In a pack situation, yes. Anywhere else? Not so much."

He handed me the woolen sweater. I walked across to the fire, boosted it with another log, then stripped off and laid my wet clothes in a soggy line across the hearth. The heat coming from the fire was fierce enough that they almost instantly began to steam. I couldn't help but wish I'd warm up that quickly. It felt like there was ice running through my veins and, despite Aiden's sweater, the shivering was growing.

He offered me the hot chocolate again. "I take it Monty's tracker didn't work?"

I took a drink then placed the mug down on the hearth and lifted his sweater to expose my butt and legs to the fire's heat. "It did, but it's limited distance-wise."

"And Monty? Where's he?"

"I sent him to the hospital. He sprained his ankle."

"That'll put a dampener on his movements."

I snorted. "We're talking about a man who chased a soucouyant through a forest on crutches."

"True enough." He glanced around at the faint sound of an approaching siren. "I'll go wave them in."

I'd started to thaw out a little by the time the paramedics walked in and followed Aiden up the stairs. I sipped my hot chocolate and listened to the soft conversation coming from the bathroom. The paramedics weren't able to get an intelligible answer from our drunk, so they simply did the full check of vitals and decided—given the amount of alcohol he'd consumed—that the best option was to take him to the hospital.

Once he was loaded into the back of the ambulance and whisked away, Aiden came back inside and asked, "Will he be safe at the hospital? Or will the spirit go after him there as well?"

"Given she kills during sex, he'll probably be safe, but I'll send Monty a text. Once his ankle has been checked, he can go place a protection spell on him or something."

Aiden nodded and pulled a long coat from the hook near the door. "You'd better borrow this. It's still bucketing down outside."

I banked the fire, dumped the empty mug into the sink,

and then quickly pulled on the coat. Aiden scooped up my wet clothes and, with one hand cupping my elbow, guided me back through the stormy darkness to his place.

It was way past five in the morning and far too late to go back to bed, given I had to be at the café by six-thirty, so we made a "proper" breakfast of bacon and eggs on toast and then both got dressed. He dropped me at the café and then went to the hospital. Whether he intended to visit Mal or not, he didn't say, but I suspected he would. He might have taken leave from his ranger duties, but I doubted he could ever let Tala completely take over.

The back door slammed as Belle arrived half an hour later. "How's Monty?" I called out.

"A minor sprain, though you'd think otherwise given the way he's carrying on. Men really do have no tolerance for pain. You want a coffee?"

"Always. And I'll bet you twenty he's playing up the injury to garner your sympathy."

She laughed. "Got it in one. Unfortunately, he picked the wrong woman for that sort of thing."

"Oh, I'm sure he knows that. And I'm just as sure that when it comes to hunting down our skeleton spirit, it won't in any way stop him."

She laughed again and started making our coffees. "He's already arranged to have Maggie ferry him and the tracker around."

Maggie was the receptionist and a ranger-in-training. As such, she got all the shittier jobs. "Has he forgotten it's scone day?"

"No, he has not, and I'm under strict orders to save him some. So of course, I won't. Best to set the obedience bar low at the very beginning of any relationship."

"I think the only expectation Monty has when it comes

to you is the fact you will eventually come around to seeing him as the catch he is."

She snorted. "So my mother keeps telling me. I ignore her as easily as I ignore you when it comes to comments like that."

Ignoring was a step up from denying. "Did he manage to visit last night's potential victim?"

"Yes. And he made the man a protection charm and warned him not to take it off unless he wanted to die."

"Was Mal sober enough to take him seriously?"

"Maybe. He did make some damn comment about it being better to die than to live without his heart for the rest of his life."

"Meaning *she* broke up with him?"

"Apparently he was a bit of a bludger."

"If she was the one who did the leaving, why would our hone-onna be going after him?"

"Who knows?" Belle walked into the kitchen with two coffee mugs and carefully slid mine across the kitchen's counter. "Maybe cheating men are actually rare in this reservation."

"I'd like to think that's true, but let's face it, it won't be."

She raised an eyebrow. "That's a rather cutting statement."

"But nevertheless true, if the recent article they did in the *Castle Rock Truth* is anything to go by."

Belle snorted. "And the *Truth* is so well known for its factual reporting of said truth."

I grinned. "Well, yes, but in a reservation this large, there'd have to be more than three men who have strayed and subsequently suffered the breakup of their relationship."

"On that, we can agree." She leaned a hip against the

counter. "How did last night go? Aside from being woken at an ungodly hour by our skeletal spirit, that is."

I grimaced. "As well as you might expect."

"So he didn't talk about Mia at all?"

"As little as possible, and then we got sidetracked by sex."

"Deliberately?"

"Yes." I drank some coffee. "He *will* talk to her. Eventually. He has to."

"Well, he actually doesn't."

I half smiled. "If he wants to move on with his life, he does."

"That man does *not* want to move on. He's rather content in the place he is right now."

"So he's said, several times, but we all know that won't last."

Belle sighed. "Sadly, no."

I ignored the wash of sadness and picked up my knife again. At least if the tears started to roll, I could blame the damn onions. "I take it you've warned Monty not to go after the hone-onna alone if he does happen to find her location?"

"Indeed I did."

"You think he'll actually listen?"

"Given I threatened a weeklong sexual drought if he didn't, I believe he will."

I laughed, and the conversation moved on to the more mundane business of café running. Last night's storm had continued unabated, so we didn't get many customers in during the morning, and the lunch hour "rush" consisted of ten people. The place was absolutely empty when the bell over the door chimed and Ashworth walked in.

He glanced around in surprise and then said, his Scottish brogue particularly heavy, "Has that alpha werewolf bitch chased all your customers away? Because I'm more than happy to throw a curse or two her way in retaliation if you'd like."

I laughed, walked over, and gave him a hug. I might not be able to confide in or even trust my own father, but Ashworth—and his partner, Eli—had quickly stepped into that breach. I really couldn't imagine my life without them now.

"It's the rain rather than the bitch, but I appreciate the offer. Would you like afternoon tea? We've a fresh batch of scones going to waste, and we've recently found a supplier who does clotted cream. Your opinion on whether it's worth the expense would be appreciated."

"Always willing to give an opinion, but you'd better make it tea for two. Eli is just parking the car."

I turned, tucked my arm through his, and escorted him over to their usual table. "Is this just a social visit? Or business?"

"A bit of both, actually."

"I'm not sure whether to be intrigued or concerned. Do you want coffee or tea today?"

"It's a coffee sort of day, I'm thinking."

"Then let me go grab everything, and I'll be right back."

Belle was already making their coffees, so I headed into the kitchen to plate up the freshly made scones, a couple of pots of jam, and the clotted cream.

When everything was on a couple of trays, we both headed over. Eli walked in just as we were placing everything on the table. He was almost the total opposite to Ashworth in looks; the latter was short and bald, with muddy silver eyes and very craggy features, whereas Eli was a tall, well-built, and very handsome man in his late sixties.

His thick salt-and-pepper hair was neatly cut, and his eyes were bright blue.

He dropped a kiss on my cheek, gave Belle a quick hug, and then dragged out a chair and sat down beside Ashworth. "You're spoiling us today—is there any particular reason?"

Belle sat down opposite him. "A desire for them not to end up in the bin."

"Well, in that case," Ashworth said, "you can wrap any unwanted ones up and we'll pop them in the freezer for a rainy day. I dare say there'll be plenty more of them over the next week or two."

"If we only get a week or two of this shittiness, I'll be ecstatic." I picked up a scone, cut it in half, and slathered it with jam and cream. "So, let's start with the business reason you're here."

"Heard on the grapevine we have a hone-onna in the reservation." Ashworth sliced open a scone and loaded it up. "Is she magic capable?"

I nodded. "She's attacked me a couple of times now."

Eli grimaced. "They do tend to go after the strongest witch in any zone they hunt in and, if the wild magic is taken into consideration, you're certainly that these days."

After years of being considered an underpowered, somewhat useless witch by my parents, it was still a little difficult to accept the opposite was now true. That I was, in fact, more powerful than Monty, Eli, and Ashworth, even if I didn't have the knowledge and skill to back it up. "Any idea why it would be hunting here?"

"No, and it's extremely rare for them to be in a place so sparsely populated." He shrugged. "Perhaps it was simply moving through and caught the scent of betrayal."

"Or it could have been brought here by either a curse or

a summoning," Ashworth added. "The latter is extremely rare, because they're hard spirits to summon, but it does happen."

I frowned. "Why on earth would anyone willingly call such a creature into being?"

"Anger and grief often override sane thinking," Eli said.

"A comment that would surely only apply to the very fragile of mind," Belle said.

"You'd be surprised, lass." Ashworth bit into his scone, and his expression dissolved into one of sheer bliss. "These are utterly divine. As is the cream."

"Have either of you come across one of them before?" Belle asked.

Eli nodded. "When I was younger, and up in Canberra."

There was something in the way he said "Canberra" that had my radar pinging. "Is Canberra the other reason you're both here today?"

"Yes," Ashworth said, "but let's concentrate on one thing at a time."

"Would that be eating the scones?" I said, watching in amusement as he all but inhaled the one he was holding and then reached for another.

"I *am* one of those rare multitalented male specimens," he said. "I can talk and eat at the same time."

"It's a true gift," Eli said, voice dry. "Just make sure you're not sitting opposite him when the conversation gets animated."

Belle immediately shifted her chair sideways. Ashworth scowled at her, though there was a twinkle in his eyes. "The spray zone isn't that bad, lass."

Eli raised an eyebrow but didn't otherwise dispute the statement.

"So why do hone-onnas go after the witch in their hunting area?" Belle asked. "Wouldn't it be more sensible to avoid us all?"

"And the younger ones generally do," Ashworth said. "But the older spirits who are capable of magic like to test their skills against those of the living."

"And the stronger the witch, the better," Eli added. "It's a means of relieving the boredom of their existence, is the common theory behind the practice."

I raised my eyebrows. "Surely they wouldn't be able to take down a highly skilled royal witch."

"That one in Canberra killed five high councilors before she was taken down," Eli said.

"And in the end, it wasn't the RWA or even the council's investigators who caught her," Ashworth added, "but rather the Black Lantern crew."

"Why would they have been involved?" I asked. "They track human criminals rather than supernatural, don't they?"

"As a general rule, yes," Ashworth said. "But the hone-onna responsible for the kills used black magic to entrap her prey. It was initially thought the deaths could have been the work of a dark sorcerer."

"That still doesn't explain why the Society was called in when the high council have their own investigation team."

"They do but, as I said, no one was sure what they were dealing with, so the council decided to employ all possible avenues of tracking the killer down."

"I would have thought the state she left her victims in would have clarified what you were dealing with," Belle said.

Eli glanced at her. "Many dark sorcerers gain power or favors from demons in return for a sacrifice, and not all of those demons require payment in the form of blood. There are many who prefer the energy of life, and it results in a corpse similar to that of the hone-onna's victims."

"The problem here," I said, "is the fact that I'm beginning to think that only one of the two attempts on me was meant to kill."

"Two?" Eli said. "I thought there were three attacks?"

"I don't believe the bomb spell was aimed at me. I think it was simply meant to erase any evidence of her presence."

"If that *is* true, then why hasn't she set them at the subsequent murders?" Belle asked.

"Maybe because we're now aware of her presence and there's little point." I shrugged and took a drink. "Something has definitely changed since she pushed the SUV down the canyon, though, because her spell last night was designed to stop rather than kill."

"Which wouldn't be all that surprising if she's come to the conclusion that you're the more powerful witch," Ashworth said. "Hone-onna are extremely intelligent—perhaps she has decided that caution is the best course forward."

"I'm not finding that statement overly comforting," Belle commented, voice dry.

Neither was I, even if instinct continued to insist she didn't actually want me dead. Mainly because I had a vague feeling there was a "yet" attached to it somewhere. "If a hone-onna is capable of killing high councilors, what hope have we got of capturing and killing one?"

"This one might not be as powerful as that one," Ashworth said.

"Given the encounters I've already had with her, she's right up there on the scale."

Eli grimaced. "That certainly cuts down our options."

"Monty believes it's a simple matter of finding her, trapping her, and then killing her as you would any old vampire," Belle said.

"Monty's still a little wet behind the ears when it comes to monster hunting," Ashworth said, amusement evident. "But he *is* right about the method of killing one."

"But if she *is* one of the old and powerful ones," Eli said, "then the only reason any of us would find her is if she wants to be found."

Alarm briefly crossed Belle's face. "Monty's gone out with a tracker spell attuned to her magic in an attempt to find her. Should we call him back?"

"Even if she does reveal her location to him, he should be safe enough. The lad may be green, but he's not stupid, even if he sometimes does play the fool." Ashworth paused, the amusement in his expression growing. "Don't tell him I said that, though. Don't want him thinking I'm mellowing."

Belle smiled. "Your secret is safe with us."

"Excellent." He picked up a third scone. "As are these, by the way."

"You won't be eating dinner at this rate," I said, amused.

Eli snorted. "A mountain of scones would never get between Ira and his dinner."

I laughed and took a drink. "How are we going to get rid of her if her magic is strong enough to conceal her presence from any of us?"

Eli hesitated. "There're three options, two of which would be far safer than the third."

"My vote's for the safe options," I said. "What are they?"

"If we are simply dealing with a curse, we find the person responsible and get her to recant it."

My eyebrows rose. "Do hone-onnas always answer the call of a curse?"

"It does depend on the situation, but the hone-onna are particularly attracted to curses placed on those who stray. That's why many believe they are the spirits of women who were similarly wronged."

"That is nonsense, of course," Ashworth said, "but such beliefs are often hard to counter with facts."

"If it is a curse, then the ex of the first victim is the most likely person to have placed it," Belle said. "The rangers would have her contact details."

"What if she's not responsible for placing the curse? Or even a summoning?" I asked.

"We lure her out with a juicy morsel, naturally."

"Me being the morsel, no doubt."

Ashworth nodded, but before he could reply, Belle said, "That doesn't sound like a sensible plan to me."

"And it's one that will depend on whether she actually still wants me dead," I commented. "As I've said, her actions last night suggest that might not be the case."

He grimaced. "Yes, but it has more chance of success than the third option."

"Which is?" I asked.

"If we *are* dealing with a summoning, we find the witch and get her to recant."

"The trouble being," Eli added, "that we're not sure it *is* a summoning, and no witch walking that edge would ever willingly admit—"

"We don't need them to," Belle said. "I'll just read her mind."

A smile tugged at Eli's lips. "Witches who summon dark spirits are very rarely without protections—be it magical or physical."

"So that leaves us where, exactly?" I asked.

"We'd need proof that the hone-onna was summoned here, and to get that we'd have to capture her and trace the leash back."

"Leash?"

"Any witch dealing with dark spirits would be well aware of the need to protect themselves from the creatures they summon. A leash is a means of preventing said spirits murdering them."

"If it does come down to an entrapment scenario and it *does* succeed," Belle asked, "how do we restrain the hone-onna, given she's magic capable and likely able to counter any spell we cast?"

"Anyone with enough power and knowledge can counter one spell. But spells combined? Unlikely," Ashworth said.

"'Unlikely' is one of those words that can't be trusted in this reservation," I commented.

Ashworth smiled. "Eli and I have both successfully countered this beastie—or ones similar to her—before. We'll be fine."

"And if we're not, I will come back to haunt you," Belle said.

Ashworth laughed. "I can think of worse prospects, lass."

"I'll ring Tala this afternoon, then, and see if she can arrange a meeting with the first victim's ex."

"Tala?" Ashworth's eyebrows rose. "Why not Aiden?"

"Because he's at the hospital with his brother and has handed control of the case over to her."

"Seriously?" Eli said in astonishment. "The alpha wolf has actually handed over control to someone *else*?"

I smiled. "In theory. I'm betting he's still keeping tabs on things."

"That's a bet none who know the man would ever take." Ashworth studied me for a second, his expression contemplative. I had a feeling he was seeing what few others would. "Everything okay with you two?"

I forced a smile. "Yes. But you know how it is with werewolves and their packs."

"Indeed," he said softly. "If you ever need to talk, we're here. Remember that."

I nodded and briefly glanced down at my coffee, desperately trying to control the sting of tears. "What was the personal stuff you came here to discuss?"

"Nice, if rather obvious, change of direction there, but I'll let it ride for now," he said. "My sister spelled several documents to me this morning. They concerned your father."

My pulse briefly stuttered and then leapt into a higher gear. His sister was none other than Sophie Kang, the Matriarch of the Black Lantern Society. "Let me guess—the case against him has been dropped."

"Quite the opposite, I'm afraid." Ashworth pulled a crisp white envelope from his pocket. An old-fashioned hot wax seal had been used to close it, rather than the regular sticky strips. He placed it on the table and slid it across to me. "That's a subpoena requesting your presence at the trial in a month's time."

CHAPTER EIGHT

I didn't reach for the subpoena. I just stared at it in ... revulsion? Fear? Dread?

Part of me wished I could ignore it. The other part wanted nothing more than to blast the thing with magic and send it to paper hell.

Neither option would make any difference to the events now set in motion, but the latter would have at least made me feel a little better.

I put my cup down and crossed my arms to hide the sudden trembling of my hands. "Why can't they cross-examine me remotely?"

"Sophie did try for that option, but your father's counsel insisted they be given the chance to question you face-to-face."

"Intimidate face-to-face, you mean," Belle muttered. "They're bastards. All of them."

"Most lawyers are," Eli said. "At least they are when they're in the courtroom defending their clients. To be honest, that's what they're paid the big money for."

"I take it then that the Lantern's lawyers will be doing

the exact same thing to Lawrence?" Belle said. "Or will his position on the high council offer him a consideration Liz will never get?"

"Oh, he'll be getting the full treatment, never worry about that." Ashworth's smile held an edge. "Of course, it's pretty obvious from the comments that have been made in recent weeks that your father believes you *won't* actually go through with the case. That, when push comes to shove, family loyalty will come to the fore and you'll ask for the proceedings to be dropped."

I snorted. "If he believes that, then he really doesn't know me at all well."

"And let's face it, he doesn't," Belle commented. "Even after you all but bested him and Clayton here in the reservation, it was pretty obvious he has no idea of your true strength—and I'm *not* talking about your magical strength."

"Ah, but you forget, nothing is more important than magical strength." Nothing except, perhaps, his own reputation. I returned my gaze to Ashworth and asked curiously, "If I did happen to ask the Society to drop the case—and I'm not—would they? They've already got the memory scan recording taken by their truth seeker and auditor. Even without me there in person, surely *that* would provide enough evidence for at least some sort of court ruling."

"In regular cases, yes. But this is the first time such a high-profile figure has been indicted for magically forcing an unwilling minor into marriage. In many respects, it will be a test case."

"Fabulous," I muttered. "The fate of future unwilling child brides now rests on my damn shoulders."

"Not really," Eli said. "Because even if your father is in the end acquitted, the mere fact it made the court will send a warning to others."

But would it stop them? Likely not. I took a deep breath that did nothing to calm the churning in my gut. "How long will I have to be in Canberra?"

"With Clayton and the priest now dead, the main testimony will come from your parents and yourself, so I can't imagine the trial will last too long. Certainly no longer than a week."

"Which is six days too long, if you ask me," I muttered.

"Eli and I will be there with you, lass," Ashworth said. "There's no way we would let you face this alone."

"And with all of us there, your damn father won't dare try anything," Belle said.

My gaze cut to hers. "I can't risk you being there, Belle."

Her silver eyes sparked dangerously. "You can't risk me *not* being there. I'm your damn familiar."

"Yes, and that's precisely why you have to remain here. I don't want another hostage situation."

"Lawrence isn't stupid," Eli said. "He wouldn't dare—"

"Everyone also thought Clayton wouldn't dare," I cut in. "And do you honestly think my father had absolutely no idea what Clayton intended? Because I have a coat-hanger-shaped bridge to sell you if you do."

"I have no doubt your father was well aware Clayton was unstable," Ashworth said. "But I doubt he expected the situation would dissolve as badly as it did."

"He knew Belle was in danger. Don't ever doubt that, Ashworth."

"I don't, but there is no way he would ever have expected Clayton to turn on *him*."

"That would be his natural arrogance rather than any sort of logical thinking," I said. "And you can damn well believe that if he *hadn't* been shot, he'd have used Clayton's kidnapping of Belle to his own advantage."

"Perhaps," Ashworth said. "It's a question the Society *will* be asking during the trial—and remember, threatening a familiar is a very serious offence."

"Possibly more so than forcing marriage," Eli said. "They've been happening for centuries and have an undercurrent of acceptance, even if it is against the law these days."

"Threatening familiars has underground acceptance too, and we all know it."

And that's the reason I have to come, Belle said. *You can't trust your father, and there's no guarantee he won't attempt to snatch me the minute you step into Canberra. Don't think he won't have people following your every movement.*

Yes, but you'll have Monty here, and there's no way known he'll ever allow anyone to hurt you.

The punch he'd landed on Clayton's jaw was proof enough of that.

She studied me for several seconds through narrowed eyes before growling, *You know this is a stupid move.*

My gut says otherwise. Please, Belle, don't argue with me on this. Don't make me force the issue. I need you here.

Need? Her eyebrows rose. *That sounds as if it's more than just a safety concern.*

I have nothing to base this on, and it may well just be the fear that, if you did step into Canberra, things might go ass up, but ... I hesitated. *Remember my suspicion that I will never be able to leave the reservation permanently?*

Yes, but that doesn't apply in this situation.

Doesn't it? I've never gone away from the reservation for more than a day or so.

Seven days isn't long. And you can make Katie aware that you'll be back.

It's not Katie I'm worried about. It's the wilder magic—the stuff she doesn't control. The stuff I was becoming more attached to.

Fair enough, but I still can't see how that in any way prevents me from accompanying you.

If you're here, the wild magic knows I'll be back.

The wild magic isn't sentient.

We can't ever be sure of that. Not now that Katie is a part of it.

Belle blew out a frustrated breath. *You're forgetting one thing—neither the wild magic nor Katie can actually do anything without you as their conduit.*

"I take it," Ashworth said, voice dry, "there's a somewhat heated telepathic conversation happening between you two."

"I'm just trying to talk sense into her," Belle said. "And she's throwing nonsense in response."

"Risking the stability of the wild magic is *not* nonsense," I growled. "I know the wellspring is protected by multiple layers of our combined spells, but given those same spells no longer prevent the threads of wild magic roaming the reservation, none of us can know what else they won't stop."

"There's never been a case of wild magic in and of itself becoming dangerous," Eli commented. "The danger usually comes from the dark entities who seek to corrupt its power."

"There's never been a witch born with wild magic infused in her DNA, either," I said. "So, unless that book you're transcribing has some concrete information about wellsprings and the wild magic's interaction with witches, we're all working on presumptions that may *never* have been true."

"*Have* you found anything of note in that book as yet?" Belle asked.

Eli shook his head. "There's nothing but a lot of nonsense about the creation of the world and the entities and powers that infused her with life and energy at the moment."

"And you can't skip ahead a chapter or two?" I asked.

"I can't risk missing a nugget hidden amongst the nonsense."

I grimaced. While I utterly understood the need for patience, I also desperately wanted to understand what was happening to me and just how far and deep the connection to the reservation's wellsprings and their magic could or would go.

Ashworth tapped the papers on the table. "You're arguing a moot point. You've both been subpoenaed."

"Why would Belle be—" I stopped. She'd been subpoenaed for the very reason I was trying to prevent her from going—she was my familiar. She could testify to my state of mind and my actions at the time. I took a deep breath and released it slowly. "I guess the choice has been taken from us."

"Yes. And let's just hope your fears about the wild magic don't bear fruit," Eli said.

"If they do, this reservation won't know what hit it."

Katie wouldn't allow anything bad to happen, Belle said. *She infused so she can protect those she loves, not harm them.*

Yes, but in doing so, I think she's given the wild magic some kind of sentience. That sentience seems to have attached itself to me. And yes, it's absolutely possible I'm overthinking things again and that nothing will happen if I leave ... but how often has my precognition been wrong of late?

But what can the wild magic do when you're also the conduit it needs to interact within this world?

I don't know, but I think it would be better if we never find out.

I glanced around as the bell above the door chimed merrily. An utterly drowned-looking Monty limped in. Though he was wearing a coat with a hood, obviously neither were up to the task of protecting him against a storm as fierce as the one currently being unleashed on the reservation.

"I thought Maggie was driving you around?" Belle said, amusement evident.

"She was." He tugged off his coat and hung it on the hook, then shrugged off his sweater. The shirt underneath had damp patches, and his jeans were so wet there were puddles forming around his feet. "But we went on a back road, and all the rain had the river crossing flooding. We got bogged."

"Then why didn't you magic the SUV out?" I asked.

"Because the only lift spell I know only works when I can actually see what I'm trying to lift. Which meant, of course, I had to get out of the car to apply the damn spell."

"Such a shame that you didn't pay more attention at school," Ashworth said, "because lift spells are something they teach at primary level."

"Not at mine they didn't." His gaze fell on the plate that now contained only scone crumbs. "I hope you two old buggers have left some scones for the rest of us."

"It would serve you right if we hadn't," Ashworth replied evenly. "You should know better than to go after this sort of spirit on your own, laddie."

I sipped my coffee to conceal my smile. Considering what he'd said earlier, it was obvious he was just needling Monty for the fun of it.

An opinion Eli obviously agreed with, because he

nudged Ashworth's shoulder with his own and said, "Enough."

Ashworth's smile flashed, but he didn't say anything else. Belle rose, squeezed past my chair, and then tucked her arm through Monty's. "Why don't you hobble on upstairs and grab a shower to warm up, and I'll go prepare some scones and a coffee for you."

"And clothes? Because I'm thinking no one in this room —other than you—wants to see me naked."

A smile twitched her lips. "What makes you think *I* want to see you naked?"

"Because we both know you adore this marvelously sculpted body of mine."

Belle snorted and patted Monty's arm. "Keep telling yourself that if it makes you feel better. Come along."

As she and Monty moved away, I returned my gaze to Ashworth. "I know I can't avoid going to Canberra, but I have no intention of staying anywhere near my family's compound."

Ashworth nodded. "Eli's already arranged for us to stay with his sister."

I raised my eyebrows. "Would this be the sister who enjoys your wine just a little too much every time she comes to visit you?"

"The same, and she's a teetotaler at home."

"She's also a high-profile judge," Ashworth said. "Your father won't mess with her."

I hoped he was right, but my father was arrogant enough to try anything—especially if the trial didn't go the way he expected it to.

I finished my coffee, collected the empty plates, and then rose. "I better get back to work. Would you like another coffee? Or more scones?"

A smile twitched Ashworth's lips. "I'd love to say yes to the latter, but I can feel Eli's frown without even looking at him."

"You're the one who was complaining about the waist of his jeans shrinking this morning," Eli said, voice mild. "But don't mind me."

"I'm telling you, I haven't put on any weight. It's the damn hot wash you put them through."

"To get rid of the grease you're always complaining about."

I snorted and left them to it. The remaining couple of hours went slowly. Monty stayed and helped out in the kitchen, cutting the vegetables we needed for tomorrow while Belle and I cleaned the café and set up for the next day.

"What are you doing tonight?" she asked.

I shrugged. "Not sure. You?"

"Monty has some movie he wants to watch. I'll probably work on getting some more of Gran's books into e-book format."

That raised my eyebrows. "You're still in the first blush of your relationship—why the hell aren't the two of you fucking like monkeys?"

"Who says we aren't?" came his comment from the kitchen.

She grinned. "Even monkeys have to take the occasional time out. You want to use the borrowed SUV to get back to Aiden's? Monty can drop me off tomorrow morning before he heads off for another round of unsuccessfully hunting the hone-onna."

"No need—I have the Suzi here if I decide to head back to his place."

"And *I* am deeply wounded by the implication my spell will amount to nothing," Monty said.

"You're the one who told me the odds were against it."

"Yes, but my wife-to-be should be showing a little more support."

"Ain't ever going to happen."

"You're obviously referring to the support factor, because our wedding is inevitable."

"Nothing is inevitable." But the sparkle in her eyes and her wide smile said otherwise. Her gaze returned to mine. "Are you sure you don't want me to stay here with you? I don't mind."

A smile tugged at my lips. "I'm fine. Take Monty home before his inattention ends in a knife wound."

"I'll have you know my knife skills have improved vastly," came his comment.

She shook her head in response and dropped a kiss on my cheek. "Just a reminder, don't go off anywhere alone, just in case this thing decides to come after you again."

I smiled. "I won't. Promise."

She harrumphed, then grabbed the keys, her purse, and Monty, and headed out. I locked up after them and then, after I finished the rest of the veg Monty had been cutting, headed upstairs to make myself a coffee and do some more reading. It was just going on seven when my phone rang; the tone told me it was Aiden.

I took a deep breath in an effort to calm the sudden acceleration of my pulse and hit the answer button. "Hey, how's your brother coping today?"

"A little better, but not out of the woods either physically or mentally yet."

"That's not surprising, Aiden. It's a hell of a thing he's going through right now."

"I know. It's just so frustrating that there's nothing much any of us can really do."

"You're there for him. That's the most important thing right now." I hesitated. "Are you coming home tonight?"

He sighed. "No. My parents wish to speak to me."

I closed my eyes briefly, fighting for control. Fighting to keep my voice even. "About your reaction to Mia's presence, I'm gathering?"

"Yes." His voice was grim. "I'm not sure how else they expected me to react, though."

I hesitated. It was tempting—damn tempting—to say nothing. Or better yet, to bad-mouth the bitch. But I couldn't. If I wanted this relationship to work out long-term, I had to accept his family would always come before me. Because of what I was. Because of what *he* was. That would never change, even if he did give up his dreams of being the pack's alpha for me.

"Is it possible your mother truly wasn't aware of your reasons for sending Mia home? Because from the little she's said to me, I don't think she was."

He snorted. "She's one of the pack's alphas. Nothing *ever* escapes her notice."

"Even so, I find it hard to believe she'd invite Mia back if she'd known that Mia was a participant—even if unwilling—in an insidious plan to funnel off some of the reservation's wealth. Your mother is many things, but I don't believe she'd risk your pack's security in any way, even to get rid of me."

He was silent for a long moment. "I'm told Mia visited the café yesterday. Why didn't you say anything?"

"It's not my place to say anything. I'm not pack, remember."

The slight intake of breath told me the barb hit home.

But all he said was, "I'm thinking her appearance at your café was no coincidence."

"No. But I also don't think she was aware that you and I are an item."

"You can't be that naive."

I smiled. "Belle checked, Aiden."

"Ah." He took a deep breath and released it slowly. "More of my mother's machinations, I take it?"

"I'm afraid so."

He made a low, angry sound. "She and I really are going to have words tonight."

"As I've said before, she's only doing what any concerned mother would."

Because concern *was* behind her actions—concern and fear. There was something in her past that had dramatically altered the way she dealt with witches, and I was positive it was the reason for her desperation to get me out of Aiden's life.

I might not like what she was doing or the way she was doing it, but there was a part of me that understood. And at least he had a mother who cared. The only thing mine cared about was not bringing the Marlowe name into disrepute.

Which, of course, was a totally unfair thought. Mom did care. It just wasn't the sort of caring I wanted. Wasn't the sort of caring Belle had.

"I'm *thirty*," he growled. "It's well past time she stopped interfering."

And she probably would, once I was out of the picture. "Will Mia be at the meeting tonight?"

"I fucking hope not. She's not pack, and she's certainly not family. She has no right or reason to be there."

At least that was one small mercy, even if it didn't solve

the bigger problem. "I presume you'll be back at the hospital tomorrow?"

"No, I'm resuming work."

"Really?" I said, surprised. "Tala is doing a perfectly fine job—"

"Of course she is," he cut in. "But it could be weeks before Dillon is in any shape to leave. I can't take that much time off work."

It was probably more a case of "won't," but I didn't say that. "Then I'll ask you my question rather than her."

"What question is that?"

"We need to talk to the first victim's ex, because we believe a curse might be the reason for the hone-onna's appearance in the res."

"When did you come to that conclusion? Tala never mentioned it."

So I'd been right—he might have taken leave but he certainly hadn't stepped away. Not fully.

"I've been talking to Ashworth and Eli."

"Scone day at the café, was it?" he said, amusement evident.

"Yes. But they also had to deliver a subpoena. The court case against my father is in a month."

"You won't be going up there alone—"

"No, I won't," I cut in. "Monty will remain here to help you with any magical problems that might arise, but everyone else will be travelling with me."

"And that includes me."

"There's nothing you can do up there, Aiden," I said, an edge in my voice. It was frustration, more than anger. This man wanted to be a part of my life and yet refused to make me a serious part of his. "You have the reservation and your family to worry about. That's enough."

"You and I—"

"Are just lovers, Aiden. You don't want or need anything more from me. You've cut a very distinct line in the sand between the two of us and your life in the pack, and you have no desire to change that ... do you?"

He didn't say anything. And probably never would. I sighed silently. Perhaps it wasn't Mia who would make or break our relationship after all. Perhaps the time in Canberra would put the whole thing in perspective and force some kind of decision.

Or not.

I had no doubt he'd be perfectly happy to continue on as we were until his werewolf mate eventually came along. Trouble was, Mia's presence had crystalized something in me, even if I'd been rather reluctant to admit or even confront it until now.

And that was the fact that I wasn't willing to just let things roll on.

I was sick of living in fear of things that might be.

Sick of the "what-ifs" and "when."

I loved this man with all my heart, but if he wasn't even willing to at least admit his own feelings, what was the point in staying?

"I've never been anything but honest with you, Liz," he said softly.

But you've never been honest with yourself, I wanted to reply. *You're well aware this thing between us stopped being a casual relationship months ago.*

It had developed into something that was good and rare. Something that was worth fighting for.

But he wasn't willing to fight. Not for me. Not for us.

Saying all that wouldn't get me anywhere, though, and it would possibly only anger him. And despite my new awareness, I wasn't ready yet to walk away. That time would come—and probably faster than either of us might want—but right now, I still wanted to hang on to a few last moments of joy.

"I know, and that's not what I'm saying," I said, the edge still there. "But this is family business—*my* family business—and, well, you know how that goes."

He snorted softly, but there was something in the sound that indicated the barb had hit home once again. "Fine. I'll ring Marian Letts—the first victim's wife—before I head over to the compound tonight. We'll go see her in the morning."

"Awesome. Thank you."

There was another long stretch of silence, and I suspected he was waiting for me to invite him to breakfast, as I usually did. And part of me wanted to. It really did. But the other part—the newly restive part—was playing hardball. He couldn't have everything his own way; if he actually wanted me to treat this relationship casually then I certainly would.

Eventually, he sighed and said, "Around nine suit?"

"Yes, fine."

"Sleep well."

As if I could, knowing he was confronting his family and in the same compound as Mia. "I will. You too."

He snorted again. "Unlikely."

And with that, he hung up.

I shoved my phone away, then stomped downstairs and raided the fridge for an overly large slice of cake.

It was much later in the evening when I felt the slight wisp of magic. It wasn't wild magic. It wasn't even dark magic.

It was witch magic.

Royal witch magic.

My heart skipped several beats and then raced.

Not only was there a royal witch on the street outside, watching the café, but it was a presence I'd felt here once before. That time, like this time, he or she stank of anger.

I rose and quickly made my way back down the stairs. The café was dark, and there was no moon to filter through the windows and lift the shadows. It didn't matter, because these days my night sight was wolf sharp.

My gaze went to the left side of the building. Magic shimmered, bright in the storm-lashed darkness of the lane between the two buildings. The thick weave of the spell's threads not only told me it was a concealing spell, but also that the person behind it was very, very powerful.

It couldn't be my father ... could it?

With subpoenas issued, would he really be so stupid as to make an appearance here in the reservation?

While the sensible part of my soul doubted it, there was something about the construction of that spell that echoed my father's magic.

I walked into the middle of the café and then said, as loudly as I could, "This is the second time you've stood out in that lane watching this place. Are you planning to come in this time and talk to me, or are you going to run again?"

For several seconds, there was no response. The figure behind the concealment didn't move, and neither did I.

Then the threads of the concealment spell parted a fraction; a hand appeared and motioned toward the doorway. It was a male rather than a female hand.

It being my father remained a distinct possibility.

With my heart hammering, I walked over to the front door and unlocked it. Then I stepped right back into the middle of the café. The spells around this place would protect me from anything this witch could throw at me, and if it *was* my father, he'd be aware of that. If he was coming in here, then, for the moment, he meant me no harm.

But if it *was* my father, there was no guarantee it would remain that way.

The bell chimed as the door opened and the invisible figure stepped inside. He closed the door behind him.

At the very least, he had manners.

I curled my fingers, hiding the energy that sparked across my fingertips. "And now that you're inside, are you going to reveal yourself? Or do you intend to keep your identity a big fat mystery?"

Again, there was no verbal response, but the concealment spell nevertheless disintegrated.

I'd been wrong in thinking it was my father but, in truth, it may well have been.

The man who stood in front of me was Julius Anthony Marlowe.

My fucking brother.

CHAPTER NINE

"How lovely to see you again, dear sister." His mellow tone was an echo of my father's and just as aristocratic sounding. "Especially after such a long time."

I crossed my arms in a vague effort not to reach out and smack the condescending smugness from his features. He had the same height and build as our father, but the structure of his face lacked the same sharpness. He was also nowhere near as lean; in fact, there was a very definite paunch developing.

But then, Juli had always been rather fond of the good life, even from a very young age.

"If it was so damn lovely to see me," I said mildly, "why the hell did you run the first time you came here?"

"Because I wasn't initially sure I had the right place or person. It wasn't until Father came back and mentioned that you had discovered a means of incorporating the wild magic into your spells that I realized—"

"The sister you'd declared useless and utterly unworthy of your attention, suddenly was?"

His silver eyes sparked, the fury I'd sensed earlier rising

briefly to the surface. But then, Juli had never appreciated people calling him on his bullshit.

"I never considered you useless, Lizzie. Your psi talents were, after all, responsible for tracking down our sister's killer when no one else could."

"I note that you didn't deny the whole 'unworthy' comment," I said, in dry amusement. "And let's not forget the fact that you and Father *did* hold me accountable for her death."

"Ah yes," he said, looking both uncomfortable and apologetic. Neither was real, of course. He was an accomplished actor, and well able to show whatever emotions were deemed appropriate for the occasion or situation. "We were perhaps a little hasty, but grief—"

"Had nothing to do with your reaction, Julius, and we both know it. You and Father were looking for someone to blame for her death, and I was, as usual, a handy scapegoat."

Because I'd done what he and Father and all the other high-flying royal councilors had failed to do—I'd found and then confronted the dark sorcerer responsible for a string of brutal, high-profile murders. I just hadn't done it in time to save Catherine's life—and that's what they couldn't forgive.

That and the fact that I'd lived while she hadn't.

"But hey," I continued blithely, "her death *did* at least have one benefit—you became Father's successor, something that would never have happened had she lived."

"That is a fucking shitty comment to make," he growled. "Aside from the fact I'm as worthy as she ever was, my place on the council had nothing to do with her dying."

It *was* a fucking shitty comment, but it was also the damn truth. Juli might be a powerful royal witch in his own right, but he'd never, ever been in Cat's class. Not in power, not in skill, and certainly not when it came to understanding the intricacies of spell development.

"I daresay you've said that often enough over the years to actually believe it."

His expression darkened, and he stepped toward me. Magic stirred around his fingers, though I had no idea what it was or what he intended. The spells protecting the café *and* me flared to life, and a moon-bright pulse of energy lit the room. It was a warning the wise would not ignore; Juli was many things, but he wasn't stupid.

He stopped abruptly, his silver gaze sweeping the room and the anger fading as swiftly as it had risen. "Father was right. Your use of the wild magic in the construction of your spells is quite impressive."

"It'd be even more impressive if I could actually control it," I said evenly. There was no way known I would ever confirm just how deep my connection and control over the wild magic was. Not to him, at any rate.

Of course, it probably wouldn't make any difference in the long run, as I'd already agreed to undergo a full magic audit ...

Would that agreement actually hold up in a court now, though? came Belle's comment. *Clayton did smash it when he came after me.*

Actually, no. The agreement concerned the annulment and the audit. It never mentioned Clayton leaving us alone.

Which was rather stupid move on our part.

I doubt it would have made a difference anyway.

True that. You want me over there? Juli always was a little afraid of my physical magnificence.

Nah, I'm fine. He can't hurt me physically or magically here in the café, and I'd rather keep you off his radar anyway.

I'll not only be on his radar but in his face if he does try anything.

A grin twitched my lips. *As much as I'd like to see that, if you wander over, Monty will, and he and Juli never did get along.*

That's because Monty has damn good judgment when it comes to people.

Of course. He chose you to be his wife, after all.

She did the mental equivalent of an eye roll. *Fine. Juli is all yours to deal with.*

"Of course you would have no idea on control," my brother was saying. "You're in a backwater town in the middle of goddamn nowhere. Who on earth would be able to teach you anything about the wild magic here?"

I raised an eyebrow and crossed my arms. "Who on earth would be able to teach me anything about the wild magic up in Canberra?"

"Our mother—"

"Knew so little it almost killed her when she was sent to restrain and protect a wellspring," I said. "I doubt she's learned anything since, because there are few enough books written about the subject and absolutely no scholars."

"Here in Australia, perhaps, but we're a young nation—"

"Actually, no, we're one of the oldest continuously inhabited nations in the world."

"I meant when it came to the presence of witches, magic, and their combined knowledge."

"And you think First Nations Peoples don't have any of that?"

He made a chopping motion with his hand, anger flickering through his expression once again before he got it under control. "That's not what I meant."

Amusement bubbled through me, but I pressed my lips together to hold it back. As much as I enjoyed needling him, I also didn't want to push him too far. Juli's anger was easier to trigger than our father's, but it was just as ugly.

Besides, he *was* bigger than me. Granted, with the wild-magic-induced changes to my body, I'd probably be his match strength wise, but I really didn't want to test that out.

"Look, say whatever the hell you came here to say, Julius, and then get the hell out of my home. You aren't welcome here."

Cool amusement crossed his face. "So much for sibling love—"

"Oh, I think we both know there was never any of that between the two of us."

"Fine." The vague amusement died, and his expression became hard. "Whether you like it or not, you're a part of our family, and it is extremely unbecoming to drag a family dispute into a courtroom."

"Oh, this is a whole lot more than a family dispute," I snapped back. "What he did to me was against the law, and I have no intention of letting him off the hook so easily."

"Your formal complaint has been investigated, and Father has been sanctioned—"

"By who, exactly? Not the high council, I know that for damn sure."

He waved a hand, as if it wasn't important. "The point, dear sister, is that there is no need to air our laundry in the very public setting of a court. The Black Lantern Society will drop the case if you request it."

I dug my nails into my palms to keep from lashing out at him magically. "I could. But I won't."

"Elizabeth, it is unbecoming for the Marlowe name to be dragged through the courts—"

"In case you haven't figured it out yet, I give exactly *zero* fucks about the Marlowe name. In fact, I legally changed my surname years ago, and I have no intention of ever changing it back." I paused and took a deep breath. It didn't help ease any of the inner anger. "Is that all you were sent here to say? Because if it was, feel free to turn around and get the hell out."

His expression darkened again. "I think you'll discover a name change means nothing. You will always be regarded as a Marlowe, and therefore a valuable asset to the family and those who wish a connection with us."

I laughed. Harshly. "Oh, so now I'm a valuable asset?"

He nonchalantly waved a hand around the room. "The spells here certainly speak to that."

"Then how is the unguided and undirected weaving of wild magic in any way useful to our family—or anyone else, for that matter—when it cannot be used beyond the confines of this reservation."

He frowned. "Whatever do you mean?"

"I don't have the control you and Father covet, Juli. The reservation's wellspring was unprotected for well over a year, and it seems to have garnered a vague kind of sentience that has nothing to do with me. Perhaps if you'd read the various reports sent up to the council from both Ashworth and Monty, you'd have saved yourself a trip and me the annoyance of your presence."

"The wild magic is not the sole reason for my being here." He reached into his pocket and drew out a long envelope.

It held an official court seal, just like the one Ashworth had slid across the table only hours before.

He offered it to me. I didn't take it. "What is that?"

"A subpoena."

"A second one? To the same court case or a different one?"

His smile was cold. "Different. Your inheritance is being challenged."

"Inheritance? What fucking inheritance?"

He laughed, but it was as cold as his expression. "What inheritance do you think? You were Clayton's wife—"

"No, I wasn't—the marriage was legally annulled before Clayton was murdered."

"A murder that very few of us believe you played no part in."

"He was alive when I left him."

"Which is *not* a denial that you took no part in his death."

"I did *not* kill the man, but you know what? I surely would have if I'd been given half the chance *and* an assurance of no legal blowback." I motioned to the envelope. "Why on earth would he have left me anything? I disappeared on our wedding night; he didn't have time to fuck me, let alone make a will."

He raised an eyebrow. It was a somehow mocking gesture. "Do you think our father was totally uncaring about your future?"

"Is that a trick question?"

He didn't look amused. "There was, of course, a prenuptial agreement in which your dowry—"

"My dowry?" I cut in, with a laugh. "What fucking dowry?"

"Your percentage of the Marlowe empire, of course."

"Yeah, like I was ever going to inherit even the smallest smidge of the so-called Marlowe empire."

"For the purposes of the agreement, you certainly were. In exchange, Clayton made you his main beneficiary on his death. The will was a part of the prenup agreement, so of course everything was made official before your actual marriage."

"And he never bothered to change said will in all the years I was missing?" I snorted. "I find that terribly hard to believe."

"Clayton was nothing if not stubborn. He could never believe that you—a mere snip of an underpowered witch—would ever outfox him for very long."

Now *that* I could utterly believe. "So why are you delivering the paperwork rather than Clayton's family or their lawyers?"

"Because I wished to see firsthand your spell skill, and because our families remain on good terms."

Of course they did. A squabble over a dead man's estate would never get in the way of old alliances. Like it or not, my family was one of the major powers in the ancient halls of the royal high court. No court case, successful or not, was likely to change that too much. Not when my brother and mother were also powerful figures in said court.

I reached out and took the subpoena. "When is the court case?"

"It will initially be mediation, and it's slated to start two days before the other case. We do not expect it'll take more than a day or so to sort out."

I raised my eyebrows. "That sounds as if agreements have already been made."

"There have been discussions, yes—"

"Without me? The main recipient of said estate?"

"You will of course be given final approval—"

"And I will, of course, require a full list of everything my inheritance entails before agreeing to anything you and Father might have negotiated on my behalf. I will also want a copy of said agreement so that my lawyer can go through it thoroughly."

"That is unnecessary—"

"Perhaps it is, but my days of trusting you lot are long, long gone."

He scowled, but he really had no choice and we both knew it. "Fine. I shall get the documents spelled down to you."

"Just make sure they're the real documents, not fakes designed to lull me into a false sense of security."

"We would not stoop so low—"

"Oh, we both know you *would* if it benefitted the family's position in any way." I motioned toward the door. "And now, feel free to make use of that; the sooner the better."

He stared at me for several long moments, then made a low, mocking bow, turned, and marched out. I locked the door behind him, then leaned back against it and closed my eyes.

Well, Belle said, *that was all unexpected.*

Understatement of the year, I believe.

Wonder how much of an inheritance we're talking about? Clayton was a very wealthy man, but I can't imagine he'd be foolish enough to sign his entire fortune over. Not even for the promise of a young and fertile wife.

My father has always coveted the residences Clayton owned in Yarralumla—they're opposite the golf course, and Father has long wanted to run a golf holiday resort there for the hideously wealthy.

Places in Yarralumla go for upwards of two million. I can imagine Clayton handing over one house for a nubile wife, but more than that? Unlikely.

He was desperate for heirs, remember. I mentally shrugged. *I guess we'll find out soon enough.*

It'd be nice if at least some of the money you inherit actually reaches our bank account. It'd certainly secure our future here.

Oh, I think it will. Juli was basically sent here to suss out the lay of the land on behalf of both parties. They now know I'm not going to be a legal pushover, so money will be on offer.

Well, you certainly deserve it.

We both do. Now stop talking to me and go play with your man.

She did the mental eye roll thing again. *He's still entranced by the movie.*

Belle, if you can't figure out a way of distracting him from said movie, I'll be very disappointed.

She laughed. *Enjoy your night.*

That was highly unlikely, but I bid her goodnight and then went and got myself another large slice of cake.

Aiden pulled up outside the café right on the dot of nine and leaned across the seat to open the passenger door. I jumped in, dumped my purse into the footwell, and then did up my belt. He didn't make any move to kiss me, which wasn't unusual when he was working, but it nevertheless left me on edge.

"I take it things didn't go well last night?"

He pulled back into the traffic and then glanced at me, eyebrows raised. "What makes you think that?"

I waved a hand up and down his length. "Dark countenance, tumultuous aura."

"Ah." He grimaced. "A few home truths were given and

received on both sides. It was a long night, and I'm not sure anything was really sorted."

"So your mother is still intent on interference?"

"My mother will never change. That much was made obvious."

In other words, the bitch remained determined to get rid of me. Which was a bit of a laugh when, for all her efforts, she wouldn't in the end be the reason we split.

"Anything happen on the Mia front?"

"My parents were told why I sent her packing and why I have absolutely no interest in renewing our relationship."

A statement that made my silly heart dance, but only briefly. If it wasn't Mia, it would be someone else. "And did your mother actually listen?"

"Yes." He glanced at me. "But she still believes we should at least talk—which is something you also rather weirdly insist on."

I half smiled. "And you know why."

He sighed. "I do *not* harbor any lingering feelings for the woman."

"And yet your aura does this weird emotional dance whenever you mention her."

"Because she betrayed my trust, and that's something I will never forget or forgive."

Which was something I could understand. "I take it she isn't being invited back for another family dinner?"

"Oh, she is. I gave ground on that point. Besides, it is ultimately better that our so-called heart-to-heart happens at the family residence. The last thing any of us need or want is to give the brigade more grist for their mill."

"So you won't be home again tonight?"

"Oh, I certainly fucking will be. There's only so many family 'heart-to-hearts' a man can take."

I once again quelled the rise of hope. Nothing had changed for us long-term, and it never would.

"Wouldn't it be better to simply get it all over and done with?"

"I am *not* spending another night without you in my arms. End of story, no arguments." He paused for a long moment. "Unless, of course, you would rather I sort this all out before you and I continue on."

"Continue on?" I couldn't help the bitter laugh that escaped. "That really does sum up our relationship, doesn't it?"

"You know I didn't mean it to sound so casual or uncaring." He reached across the seat, gripped my hand, and squeezed my fingers lightly. "Right now, I can't imagine my life without you in it."

"The modifier there being 'right now.'"

"Liz—"

"It's fine, Aiden, really. It's just that Mia's presence has made me confront a few basic facts I've been willfully ignoring." I glanced at him. "I suspect I'm not the only one guilty of that."

"If I'm guilty of anything, Liz, it's of enjoying my life as it is, for as long as it is, without worrying about the future."

"Which is all fine and dandy when there're no emotions involved, Aiden."

He took a deep breath and released it slowly. "I know. But this is neither the time nor the place—"

"Is there ever a perfect time and a place for such a discussion?" I asked mildly.

He grimaced. "In this particular case, I don't believe there will be. However, once we've caught our killer vampiric spirit and I've seen Mia on her way, we'll sit down and discuss us. Openly and honestly, and see where we go from there. Okay?"

I knew where exactly we'd go, but all I did was nod. Continuing on blithely wasn't going to work for us anymore, and he had to know that, even if he didn't want to acknowledge it.

"Okay." I glanced out the window but not out of any interest in the passing scenery. I didn't want him to see the heartbreak and anger in my eyes—though he'd undoubtedly smell the latter and wonder at its cause. "Did you tell Marian Letts *why* we were coming to see her?"

"No, just that I needed to talk to her." He glanced at me, a weight I felt rather than saw. "I figured if she was responsible for the curse, it would forewarn her."

"Good idea, though unless she's a witch—"

"She's not."

"Then she definitely couldn't have placed the curse herself. She'd have gone to a practitioner who specializes in such things."

"And are they hard to find?"

I shrugged. "In large city centers, no. Out here, in the country? Probably. Curses are considered a gray area for witchcraft, and it's far easier to track down the caster of a curse gone awry in a less-populated area."

"Do they go awry very often?"

I hesitated. "Anytime a demon or a dark spirit is involved in a curse, there's always a high probability of things going awry. If the hone-onna *was* brought here by a curse Marian had placed on her ex, then the practitioner behind it failed to set all the necessary parameters, and that has allowed our spirit to go after *all* cheating men."

He grunted. "So once we get a name, Monty should be able to contact the RWA and get the witch's location?"

"If she's in the area, yes. If it was done in Melbourne, he'll probably have to ask the state witch council to track him or her down."

"That could take longer than we have."

"It would depend on whether that particular witch is on their radar."

"Meaning state councils keep track of curse givers?"

"They keep track of all witches who flirt around with the edges of darker magics. It's a very slippery slope to traverse, and darkness has ensnared more than one overconfident witch over the centuries."

He glanced at me. "Have you ever done a dark spell?"

"Once." I shivered at the memory even though I had no lingering regrets. That spell had saved Belle's life. "I felt unclean afterward."

"Did it hold a cost?"

"All magic holds a cost, Aiden."

"You know what I meant."

I half smiled, though it held little warmth. "I had to destroy something extremely precious, so I guess it did."

And while Belle might have paid *that* particular cost, it remained to be seen what price I'd eventually pay. While the spell lay more in the gray zone than the black, it had required blood. Worse still, it had come with a warning that invoking the spell would make the caster more susceptible to the darker forces of this world.

Which might well explain the hone-onna's current fixation on me.

We turned off the main highway a few kilometers out of Castle Rock and then stopped in front of a cute, white miner's cottage. There was no car sitting under the small carport to the right of the cottage.

I undid my seat belt and grabbed my purse. "She is expecting us, isn't she?"

He nodded. "Her car is at the mechanic's down the road."

I climbed out of the truck and then followed him over to the front door. There was no yard, which meant there was about three feet, if that, between the footpath and the door. "But something had to have drawn the hone-onna here. According to Ashworth, it's rare for them to be hunting in a place like this. They prefer major city centers."

He rang the doorbell. A soft bell chimed deeper within the old house and, after a few seconds, footsteps approached. The woman who opened the door was short, with elfin features, sharp blue eyes, and short red hair. She was also human, rather than wolf, and her scent spoke of pregnancy ...

I blinked. Not just at the fact that pregnancy had a scent, but also at the fact I smelled *and* recognized it.

"Ranger O'Connor, and right on time too." She stepped back and waved us in. "Would you and your friend like a cup of tea? I just boiled the kettle."

"That would be lovely, thank you, Marian," Aiden said. "This is Liz Grace. She's working—"

"At the café with the amazing cakes," Marian said. "My friends keep saying we should go there."

I smiled. "I'd have to agree with your friends, but then I would, given I own the café."

"Indeed you would," she said with a laugh. "Head on down to the kitchen—it's at the end of the hall."

Aiden led the way, his steps quieter than mine on the old wooden floors. The wild magic might be strengthening my senses, but it certainly wasn't altering the way I moved.

Grace might be my last name, but it really didn't play any part in my overall physical repertoire.

The kitchen had been built in what was basically a lean-to attached to the back of the house. It was a small but perfectly formed galley kitchen, with enough space for one person to comfortably work, as well as an area big enough to hold a square, four-person table. Marian motioned us to sit and then brought over a tray holding a large teapot and three cups.

After pouring the tea and handing us the cups, she said, "Now, what is this all about? Have you discovered who did me a huge favor by killing the bastard I once called husband?"

Aiden hesitated. "Not yet, though we do have several leads we're following up. One of them is a bit out there, and it's the reason we're here this morning."

She raised a pale eyebrow. "Now *that* sounds intriguing."

There was no change in the flow of pink through her aura—which generally indicated a gentle, peaceful nature—and nothing to suggest she had anything to hide in her expression. If Marian had paid for a witch to place a curse on her ex, then she didn't consider it in any way a legal problem.

And it generally wasn't unless it resulted in a death.

"Ms. Grace is here this morning in her capacity of assistant reservation witch—"

"Ha!" Marian cut in, her eyes smiling. "That would explain the much sought-after nature of your cakes—you sprinkle them with a little bit of magic."

I smiled. "I wish that were possible. It'd save us a whole lot of hard work."

"I guess it would." She leaned back in her chair, her

expression open and unworried. "So why would a reservation witch be involved in a murder investigation?"

Aiden glanced at me, and then said, "It would appear that something non-human was responsible for the murder of your husband."

"Ex. And it surely couldn't have been a werewolf—you lot couldn't do that to a body."

"You saw his body?" I asked, surprised.

Her gaze returned to me. "Had to ID it. I must admit, I did think there was something rather odd about the severe state of his dehydration."

"It wasn't dehydration, and it wasn't a werewolf," I said. "He was attacked by what we believe was a vampire. Of sorts."

She raised her eyebrows. "Wasn't Hale killed during the day?"

"Yes. This particular being isn't as restricted as a regular vampire."

"Huh." She took a sip of tea. "What do you wish to know?"

I hesitated. "Did you seek out a witch to place a curse on your ex?"

She laughed, though her amusement abruptly died when she realized the question was serious. "No, I did not. Although, I have to admit, if the thought *had* actually occurred to me, I probably would have. I've certainly cursed him many a time over the last few months, but that, I'm afraid, is as far as it went."

Which meant this trip was a dead-end information-wise. Unless, of course, she was a latent talent. Plenty of humans could lay claim to a witch ancestor—it was part of the reason why Belle and I had successfully pretended to be half-bloods for so long—but most were incapable of magic.

In the few who could spell, it generally took some kind of trauma or stress to bring the ability to the fore—often with disastrous results.

But there was no hint of magic in Marian's aura and absolutely no evidence that she was, in any way, a latent talent.

So if she didn't place the curse and Hale *was* the first person killed, did that by necessity mean we were dealing with a summoning? Or was the hone-onna's presence here simply a matter of bad luck? Had she, perhaps, simply been passing through at the exact same time as Marian had been physically rather than magically cursing her ex?

"Would there be anyone in your immediate circle who could have placed such a curse?" Aiden asked. "A family member or friend, perhaps?"

Marian was shaking her head even before he'd finished the question. "There's just me and Bonny here in the reservation. My family lives interstate."

"Bonny being the dog," Aiden said, with a glance at me.

I smiled. "Dogs are utterly loyal to their humans, but it's rare for them to get involved in curses. Cats, on the other hand, are extremely untrustworthy when it comes to such matters."

"I take it your familiar isn't a cat then?"

"No, thank God."

She laughed and drank some more of her coffee. "If a curse *is* responsible for calling Hale's killer here, could it have been placed by his lover?"

I hesitated. "Maybe, although it'd be extremely unusual."

Mainly because revenge spirits generally weren't drawn to women involved in the act of betrayal."

"Hale was a smooth operator. I don't believe his bit on

the side knew I existed until the fatal evening I answered his phone. Her shock was too raw—too real."

"Do you know anything about her?" Aiden asked.

Red flickered briefly through her aura's gentle pink. "No, and I think it best it remain that way. I still have his phone here, though, if you'd like it. It's not in great condition, because I threw it at the wall multiple times, but you might be able to resurrect the database and get the list of his contacts. She's there, though knowing him he probably has her listed under a false ID."

"If we could have the phone, that would be great," Aiden said.

"Hang on a sec, then."

She briefly disappeared down the hall but wasn't gone all that long. When she'd said the phone wasn't in great condition, she'd actually been understating it. The casing was cracked in multiple places and the glass screen so spiderwebbed I doubted anything would be visible even if the phone still worked.

Aiden pulled a small plastic bag out of his pocket and motioned her to drop it in. "Do you want this returned with the rest of his effects?"

"No. I've plenty of other things of his to destroy should the urge take me. But thank you for asking."

He finished his tea and then rose. "We'll be in contact if we have any further questions."

She nodded and led us back to the front door. "You know, there is a part of me that hopes you never catch the thing behind these murders. The world in general is a much nicer place without men like my ex."

"Problem being," I said, "is that sometimes the innocent get hurt."

"That's the way of the world in general, I think." She

shrugged and closed the door once we were through.

I walked over to the truck and climbed in. Once Aiden had done a U-turn, I asked, "Can werewolves smell pregnancy?"

He glanced at me, eyebrows raised. "That's an extremely odd question—you're not pregnant, are you?"

I snorted. "Heaven forbid. I was just curious."

He turned onto the highway and headed back to Castle Rock. "I take it you smelled hers?"

I nodded. "My olfactory senses have been sharpening for a while, but I wasn't expecting something as personal as pregnancy to have a smell."

"It's the hormonal changes a pregnant woman's body goes through that you're smelling."

"Does that mean a pregnancy is obvious from the point of conception?"

"No. It generally happens from about three months on."

"I've never actually thought about it, but I'm guessing that means you're also sensitive to menstrual cycles? I can't imagine that would be pleasant on a day-to-day basis."

A smile tugged the corner of his lips. "You learn at a very young age to basically turn off certain scents. I'm well aware of your cycle and can generally tell a few days out when it'll happen, but that's only because we live together."

"Huh." I studied the street ahead for a moment. "Do you think Marian is aware she's pregnant?"

"I think when she stopped menstruating it'd have been pretty obvious."

"There are women who continue to menstruate all the way through their pregnancy."

"Then their past selves must have done something pretty shitty to be stuck with *that*. But yes, she knows." He glanced at me again. "Why the curiosity?"

I shrugged. "Just found it odd that she didn't seem fazed by the fact that, with her husband dead and no family here, she hasn't anything in the way of a support system."

"Some women don't need all that. I can't imagine you ever would."

"Except I have more help and support here than I ever would have up in Canberra. Between Belle, Monty, Ashworth, and Eli, I'll never have to worry about a sitter for my daughter when she pops along."

"Daughter?" His eyebrows rose. "Not a son?"

"Nope. Not first up, at any rate."

He glanced at me. There was something in the blue of his eyes that spoke of longing, and it made me angry and sad all at the same time.

"So says your psychic self?"

"Multiple times."

"Huh." He paused for a long moment. "I don't suppose those same dreams gave you any idea who the father will be?"

"No, but what does it matter to you if they did?"

"That's unfair, Liz."

"Why, when sooner or later we'll both move on to other partners?"

"Moving on doesn't mean we can't remain friends. Moving on doesn't mean I will stop caring about you. Moving on doesn't mean I will *ever* cast you from my life." He glanced at me, his gaze fierce. "I'd hope that you feel the same way."

I sighed. "Of course I do."

But hope was a fickle lover at the best of times, and I wasn't entirely sure I had the strength to keep him as a close friend, to see him happy with another woman, day in and day out.

But maybe that was fear speaking. I'd seen that blonde-haired little girl, after all, and if she wasn't Aiden's, she had to be someone else's. Which meant I was absolutely destined to find happiness in the future, even if my present was falling to pieces.

Silence fell, but it was haunted by what-ifs and far from comfortable. At least for me.

As we neared the café, his phone rang sharply. He pressed the switch on the steering to answer it and then said, "I take it there's a problem?"

"There certainly is" came Monty's reply. "We've got ourselves another goddamn body, and this time it's a woman."

Aiden swore and briefly scrubbed a hand across his eyes. "Where are you?"

Monty gave us an address and then added, "Maggie's already called in Ciara and notified Tala."

"Brilliant. It'll take us about ten minutes to get there."

"Us? Lizzie's with you?"

"Yes. Aiden out."

He flicked on the lights and siren then did a tire-squealing U-turn and headed toward Louton. Thankfully, there wasn't that much traffic on the road, and we got there in eight minutes. Only one ranger vehicle sat out the front of the old brick house, which meant neither Tala nor Ciara had arrived as yet. Police tape had been rolled out around the front of the building, though; Maggie, being her usual efficient self.

Aiden stopped behind her SUV, and we both climbed out. Monty appeared in the front door, kitted out with crime scene booties and gloves. His expression was pale and grim, which didn't bode well for what had happened inside.

Aiden held the tape up so I could go under and then

followed me through. "Are we dealing with the same MO, Monty?"

"No. This time the victim wasn't murdered during sex, and she very obviously fought back. It's all a bit of a mess."

I frowned. "Why would the hone-onna change tack this late into the game? That doesn't make any sense, given what we know about them."

"Which isn't a whole lot, let's be honest here." Monty handed us both a pair of booties and some gloves. "Maggie says the victim is Candice Taylor. She's thirty-five, single, and a vet nurse who worked over in Colban Falls."

"Where did the murder happen?"

"In the living room. Straight ahead and then to the left."

I followed Aiden down the narrow, somewhat cluttered hallway into a surprisingly large and bright room. Maggie was taking a photo of what appeared to be a raw piece of meat but glanced up as we all walked in. "This one is bloody nasty, boss."

As I stopped beside Aiden, a thick wall of terror, agony, and fury slapped across my senses, tearing a gasp from my throat. I automatically sucked in a breath, only to find it filled with blood and death and horror. My knees buckled, and I would have fallen had Aiden not grabbed me.

"Fuck. Sorry, I should have mentioned the violence," Monty said. "If the psychic vibes are that bad, maybe it would be better—"

"I'm fine. I just need a minute."

"We can cope without your sensory input," Aiden growled. "You don't need to put yourself through—"

"I'm *fine*." I pulled away from his grip and shored up my mental shields. It helped, even if it didn't completely shut out the psychic waves. I ignored them as best I could and studied the room. The victim's emotions were a tangled weave that floated through the room, but now that I was aware of them, I could for the most part hold them at bay. It was the random bits of flesh and limbs scattered all over the floor and furniture, and blood sprayed across the nearby furniture and walls, that weren't so easily ignored. When Monty had said it was all a bit of a mess, he'd definitely been understating the situation.

"I take it the rest of her body is elsewhere?" Aiden asked.

Maggie nodded. "In the kitchen. I suspect she was going for a knife. She didn't make it."

"Is there any evidence the hone-onna made any attempt to feed on Ms. Taylor the same way as she had the others?" I asked.

"Hard to be positive without a proper postmortem, but I'd have to say no. All the body parts are fully fleshed." Maggie paused and frowned. "It's almost as if we're dealing with an entirely different creature."

"That's always possible in this damn reservation." Aiden said, his tone grim.

"Except," Monty said, "that the neighbor who reported the attack gave us a description of the woman who entered just before the screaming started, and it matches the report we got of the woman who entered Kyle Mason's house."

"Then why the violence this time and not the others?" Aiden said. "Why tear this woman apart and not the men?"

Monty shrugged. "It could be something as simple as the sex of the victims—maybe our spirit simply isn't into women. Or maybe it's the fact that this victim fought back."

"All reasonable explanations," I said. "But it doesn't explain the anger lingering in the air. It's the hone-onna's rather than Ms. Taylor's, and I doubt it's a result of our victim fighting back."

Aiden's gaze swept the room before returning to mine. "But why would a revenge spirit be angrier at a woman than a man? Betrayal is betrayal, no matter what the sex of the person committing it."

"As the old saying goes, it takes two to tango. What if Candice Taylor was the clandestine lover of one of our victims?"

"If that's true, all the mistresses of all our victims could be on her hit list." Monty glanced at Aiden. "Do we know the names of the women the other victims were seeing?"

"In Kyle's case yes, but the affair happened off reservation and several years ago, so isn't likely to be a problem here," Aiden said. "We're still checking phone records of the other victims and calling possible contacts."

"I have to say," Monty said, amusement evident, "if someone called me out of the blue and asked whether I was fucking so-and-so, my reaction would be automatic and less than pleasant."

A smile twitched my lips. "Except no one would ever cold call you with such a question, because you're well aware what Belle would do to your nuts if you ever did dare cheat."

His smile flashed. "True, but also a totally unnecessary warning. When you have found perfection, there is no need to go elsewhere."

"You," Aiden muttered, "are nauseatingly romantic at times."

Monty patted him on the shoulder. "Yes, and you should try it sometime."

Aiden rolled his eyes but didn't say anything as his phone rang. He tugged it out of his pocket, glanced at the screen, and then walked out of the room. Personal call, if his aura was anything to go by.

I did my best to ignore the stupid rise of anxiety and studied the door on the other side of the living room. It obviously led into the kitchen, because the twisted weave of emotions were still emanating from it. What was odd, though, was the fact that the fury appeared to override the victim's agony, and that really shouldn't have been the case, given how brutally she'd died.

"Maggie," I said, "are we okay to go into the kitchen?"

She glanced up. "If you're careful not to disturb or step in any evidence, yes, but are you sure you really want to? Things are much, much worse in there."

"I know, I just ..." I stopped and waved a hand. "Something feels odd, that's all."

She nodded. "Okay, but can I suggest you go in through the hall entrance? There's less chance of stepping in gore."

I tried to ignore the images that rose and silently motioned Monty to lead the way. He limped down the hall and stopped at the last door on the left. Instead of ushering me in, though, he placed an arm across to prevent me from entering. "Are you really sure you want to do this? It's a rather nasty dismemberment, so I'd imagine the emotional waves will be pretty full on."

"I can already feel them." Thankfully, the anger continued to drown them out. I just had to hope it remained that way, because the underlying wash of Ms. Taylor's final moments suggested their full impact would be harrowing and all consuming. "But I really have no choice, Monty. Instinct is saying there's something here to be found."

"Damn." He grimaced and removed his arm. "Can I at least suggest that you do not, under any circumstances, breathe deep? That could prove deadly given your strengthening olfactory sense."

I nodded and motioned him on. At first glance, the

kitchen didn't look all that bad. Well, compared to the living room, at any rate. There were several arterial sprays across the far wall and blood splatters on both the kitchen counter and the canisters sitting on top of it, but there was no immediate evidence of dismemberment.

I could smell it, though. Smell the flesh and the blood even as pain and terror briefly pulsed across my senses. The epicenter lay out of sight on the other side of the kitchen counter, close to the door between the kitchen and the living room. I had absolutely no desire to step any closer to that counter. No desire to see the bloody, fragmented remains of humanity beyond it.

The waves of fury weren't emanating from that area though, but rather from the left. I scanned the rest of the room. Beyond the rectangular kitchen table was a glass sliding door that led out into a small pergola area.

A dark smudge on the sliding door's handle caught my attention. It was blood, though how my nose could be certain of that when the entire room reeked of the stuff, I have no idea.

"Monty, did you or Maggie check out the back yard?"

"Not as yet—why?"

"Because our hone-onna exited through that door—and she left some blood behind on the handle."

"It's probably the victim's. Given the brutality of the kill, she must have been covered in blood and gore."

"It's not the victim's," I said. "It's hers."

"Even if it is, a smudge isn't going to be of much use, spell wise." He paused. "Unless, of course, there's more out in the yard. Come along."

"I can't imagine our hone-onna would carelessly leave handy pools of blood lying about," I said, following him around the table. "She's magic capable, so she'll be well aware of just how much blood it takes to set a spell."

"Still worth a shot," Monty said.

It was, but not because of the blood. The caress of anger had sharpened closer to the door, and it seemed to be centered outside rather than in. Whatever had angered the hone-onna, it had nothing to do with this victim fighting for her life.

Monty took out his phone and took a photo of the smudge, then carefully slid the door open, using the top edge of the handle and keeping his fingers well away from the bloody smear. I stepped out after him and raised my face, drawing in deep breaths of fresh air to chase the foulness from my lungs.

"There's another spot here," Monty said. "Looks like she was running for the fence."

I walked over, squatted beside the droplet, and lightly pressed a finger into it. It was tacky and hummed with power and purpose. The anger that had led me out here might have dissipated in the open air, but it still burned through her blood. Which was decidedly odd.

Unless, of course, anger was a part of her DNA.

Do spirits even have DNA? Came Belle's question.

Don't know, I replied. *But if we ever find more than snippets about this thing in your gran's books, maybe we'd have an answer.*

I rose and scanned the grass between the fence and us. There was a tiny smudge of black that could have been dirt as much as blood on one of the rocks that lined the garden border, but little else. I'd put money on the fact that there'd be another smudge on the top of the fence, though.

"Anything useful?" Monty asked.

"Not really. But I don't think the placement of these

blood drops is accidental."

He raised his eyebrows. "Why would she deliberately leave a bloody trail?"

"Well, she has tried to kill me twice now. This might be the beginning of a third attempt."

"It's a pretty damn lame attempt if it is. There was no guarantee that you or even I would step out onto the patio and find these spots."

"Uncertainty could be part of the game."

"I'm sensing a 'but' in that reply."

"That's because I don't think this is a game. I think it's deliberate."

"On that, we agree."

I glanced at him, surprised. "You do?"

He waved a hand at the blood on the rock. "Aside from the fact it's doubtful our victim had the time or the skill to injure our spirit this seriously, she's too clever to leave an obvious trail like this. She wants us to follow. What we need to be wary of is the why."

"I'm not feeling anything in the way of magic."

"Doesn't mean it won't be there at the end of this trail if it does happen to be a trap."

"It isn't."

"So says your gut?"

"Gut reinforced by second sight, yes."

I stepped onto the next rock and peered along the top of the fence. As I'd suspected, there was more blood here, and it was no mere smudge this time. She'd wanted to ensure we actually saw it.

"I don't think we should be climbing over another fence," Monty said. "Especially if your gut is wrong."

"You're the one who is constantly telling me I need to trust my instincts more." I glanced around as he hobbled over. "But I agree in part—you definitely shouldn't be climbing any more fences. Not with that ankle."

"It's fine."

"It's not. Too much walking—or in this case, fence jumping—will see you in that brace for weeks longer. Is that what you really want?"

"If it means you not going on alone after this thing, then yes." He clambered up onto another rock, his balance somewhat precarious as he peered over the top of the fence into the next yard. "I'm not seeing a dog."

"That's because there's only a cat, and it's three feet further along the fence in the bushes to your right." Aiden strode across the yard and leapt up onto the rock on the other side of me. "What are we looking for?"

"We were following a trail of blood. It led us to the fence."

"The creature isn't in that yard. Nothing nasty is. There's a kid shrieking in the house, though, and I think it needs to be checked out."

"The hone-onna hasn't shown any inclination to hurt kids," I said. "In fact, she went out of her way to protect Jack when she murdered his dad."

"I know, but I've been a ranger a long time now, and every instinct I have is suggesting we need to get inside and check that kid. Especially if our spirit did head that way."

He didn't wait for our response; he simply leapt over the fence. I stepped onto the fence railing and followed him over, as did the ever determined, not-to-be-left-behind Monty. I raised my eyebrows at him. He merely grinned and motioned me on.

There were two more spots of blood; a spatter on the grass midway between the fence and the house, and another close to the steps that led up to the back door. There was no blood on either the door or the handle, but the kid was still screaming inside, and it was rather odd no one was making any attempt to calm him down. Especially when he sounded far too young to be left alone.

"Oh God," Monty murmured. "I hope the hone-onna hasn't done a two-for-one deal on victims."

"I don't think she has," I said. "Her blood might be on the bottom step, but I have no sense that she lingered here or even went inside."

And there were no further blood spots to be seen, either on the path that led around the edge of the house or on any of the nearby shrubs. And given the regularity of the drops that had led us here, there should have been.

I returned my gaze to the back door. "She wanted us to come here. Because of the kid."

Monty blinked. "That's a bit of a jump."

"Not really. Not given her efforts to protect Jack. It might also explain why the anger got stronger the deeper we went into the house—she was hearing the upset kid."

Monty's expression was one of disbelief. "It'd be extremely unusual for a dark spirit to be in any way concerned about human life, young or not."

"And yet dark spirits do breed, and they certainly do raise offspring. Who knows, maybe this one lost a child somewhere in the past and now holds a soft spot for them."

"You two can discuss the finer points of all that at a later time," Aiden said. "We need to get inside. Now."

He drew his gun, then padded up the steps and pressed his hand against the door. It opened. Magic briefly shimmered.

"Well, that's interesting," Monty said.

Aiden glanced at him. "What is?"

"There's a protection spell in place across the doorway."

"Would it have stopped the hone-onna from entering?"

"No, but her entering would have shredded it. It's intact." He paused, gaze narrowing. "It's also not wrapped around the entire house; just across this doorway and, from the faint echoes I'm getting, the front one."

"Can you dismantle it?"

Monty immediately did. I touched Aiden's arm and said, "I'll take the front door and meet you inside. Just give me a couple of minutes to get around there."

He nodded and glanced briefly at his watch. I ran around the corner of the house and followed the concrete path toward an old wooden gate. There were no further droplets of blood and no indication our spirit had climbed through any of the windows along this side of the house—but one of them *was* open, and there was an old wooden box sitting under it.

Our spirit might not have climbed inside, but someone definitely had.

I unlatched the gate, made my way through an empty carport, then stopped at the end of the house and peered around. Agapanthuses lined the path that led up to a covered concrete porch. The screen door was open, but I couldn't see the main door from where I was standing.

I headed for the porch, ducking under each of the windows in an effort not to be seen. Though I was absolutely certain the hone-onna wasn't here, someone with bad intent definitely *was*.

I quietly bounded up the steps, then pressed back against the wall and peered around. The front door was closed, so I leaned forward and pressed my fingers against it. Magic stirred against my fingertips, its touch clean and pure. It wasn't immediately obvious who it had been designed to protect the homeowner against, and though I could have found out with a little time and effort, I was growing more certain time was the one thing I didn't have a whole lot of. Not if I wanted to stop the bad thing that was about to happen.

I reached for the door handle. It was locked, but a quick spell soon fixed that without disturbing or deactivating the protection spell.

I pressed the door open and warily stepped inside. The carpeted hall wasn't very long and there were two rooms running off it, both on the right side of the house. The overwrought kid's desperate, frightened screams might dominate the airwaves, but they didn't erase scents. There were two people in the room with him and neither appeared to be making any effort to comfort him. One of them stank of fear; the other was all anger. If not for those two scents and the sharp rasp of breathing, it would have been easy to believe that the kid had been left alone.

Unease ratcheted up several notches, and energy unfurled around my fingertips, ready to be unleashed. But as much as I wanted to rush toward the kid's room, caution was needed. One room lay between us, and this might yet be a trap.

I carefully opened the first door. It was a large bedroom —probably the master—though it didn't have an en suite and there were a couple of freestanding wardrobes instead of built-ins. The bed was neatly made, and there was nothing to indicate a problem.

Relief stirred but just as quickly died. As I quietly moved down to the next room, I briefly considered waiting for Aiden and Monty. But I just as quickly dismissed the idea. Time was of the essence. I was certain of that if nothing else.

I called on more energy and glanced down as it rolled

around my right hand and formed a thick ball—one that could be thrown as a weapon or shield. I just had to hope it would be enough to protect the kid and stop whatever the hell was going on inside the room.

I carefully peered around the doorway. The first thing I saw was the little boy. He was standing in his cot, his face tear streaked and bright red, his arms raised and reaching desperately for his mother. She stood to the left of the door, her hands clenched by her sides and her breathing so fierce her whole body shook with it. Sweat beaded her pale skin, and she stank of fear and horror.

I only had to look right to realize why.

Standing on the other side of the room was the second person I'd sensed. He was tall, broad, and muscular, his physique that of a bodybuilder or weightlifter. His expression was cold and his pupils were pinpoints, suggesting he was either drug- or alcohol-fueled.

But *that* wasn't the worst of it.

At the end of one outstretched hand was a gun. I knew enough about them now to see that the safety was off. As Aiden had once said to me, "red and you're dead."

"Jim, please," the woman said, her voice low and shaky. "Please, we can work this out. You can't do this. You don't want to do this."

I clenched my fists to hold back the magic pulsing furiously around my fingers. I wanted to unleash it, wanted to intervene, but I had no idea if my magic would ever be faster than a finger already resting on the trigger.

If I made one wrong move, someone could end up dead.

For several seconds, the man didn't reply. Then, with a low, incomprehensible growl of fury, he fired.

Not at the woman.

At the little boy.

CHAPTER TEN

"No!" I screamed, and threw the sphere of energy.

It hurtled across the room and flung itself over the child a heartbeat before the bullet hit. It flared fiercely, bending briefly to absorb the impact energy before rebounding. The bullet dropped harmlessly to the floor.

The man swung around to face me and suddenly all I could see was the gun barrel pointed straight at my face. Anger burned through my limbs, and without thought, I flung out a hand, spooling energy from my fingertips in the form of a rope. His finger twitched on the trigger at the same time as my rope ripped the weapon up and then out of his hands. The bullet meant for me smashed into the ceiling instead, and plaster dust rained down. I flung the gun away, then, as a look of sheer surprise crossed his twisted, ugly features, I launched forward, hitting the floor and twisting around in one smooth fast motion. My boot struck his shin hard enough to knock him off his feet and land him on his butt. He cursed, but nevertheless scrambled upright, his fists clenching and unclenching as he lunged toward me.

I pushed back and raised a hand, but before I could

unleash another bolt of energy, a gruff voice said, "Drop low."

I immediately pressed flat against the carpet, felt the wind of a leap high above me, saw Aiden land and lash out with a clenched fist, burying it deep in the stranger's solar plexus. As the man gasped and doubled over, Aiden followed with an elbow to the head. The stranger dropped hard and didn't move.

The woman made a garbled sobbing sort of sound and ran for her child. I quickly dismantled the shield so she could pick him up, then pushed into a sitting position.

Aiden squatted in front of me, his gaze sweeping my length and coming up relieved. "You're okay."

It was a statement rather than a question, and I smiled. "Yes, and so is the kid, thank God."

"Yes."

He rose, offered me a hand, and then hauled me upright.

"Where's Monty?" I asked.

"Calling in reinforcements and an ambulance." He brushed a finger down my cheek, as if in reassurance that I really was okay, and then turned to the woman. "Are you okay, Mrs. Lloyd?"

"Yes, but only thanks to the timely intervention of your witch, Aiden. If not for her—" She shuddered and hugged her son tighter. "Thank you. Thank you both."

He nodded. "I'll move your husband out of the room and send the paramedics in when the ambulance gets here, just to make sure you're both okay. I'm afraid we will need a statement from you."

She nodded and continued to make soft, soothing noises. The little boy *had* calmed down, though he continued to make hiccupping sounds that spoke of his distress.

Aiden pulled a zip-tie from his pocket, lashed the stranger's wrists together, and then roughly hauled him from the room. I started to follow, then spotted the gun and moved across to pick it up.

"I can never repay what you've done for us," Mrs. Lloyd said. "If you hadn't intervened, if you hadn't thrown that spell when you did, Robbie would be dead, just as that bastard wanted."

"You're able to see magic?" I said, surprised. There was certainly nothing in her aura or her energy output to suggest she was a witch of any kind, and we were generally the only ones who could see spell threads.

Fear and panic flashed through her expression and she said, the words tumbling out so quickly they practically ran into each other, "No, God *no*, I'm not a witch or anything like that."

Which very much suggested that magic—or perhaps the suspicion of it—had in some way been responsible for what happened here today.

"I'm not implying you are, but just so you know, there *is* nothing wrong with being a witch or even magic sensitive. And they stopped burning us eons ago."

She blinked, and then half laughed, though it came out more of a sob. "Not in Jim's family, they didn't."

"Ah. I'm sorry." And I couldn't help wishing that I'd been a whole lot more brutal on the bastard; maybe it would have given him some inkling of what it meant to terrorize a *real* witch.

"No, *no*, I'm sorry. I didn't mean to react so badly. It's just habit born out of necessity." She shrugged and kissed her son's forehead. "What I do isn't magic, even if his family considered it so. It's more a psychic ability—I can see energy, good and bad. In fact, it's the sole reason I was even in Robbie's room—I felt something very dark move past the house. If I hadn't come in to check on my son, goodness knows what Jim might have done."

Jim would have done exactly what he'd tried to do there at the end, and then would probably have tried to kill her for good measure.

"That darkness you sensed passing by the house," I said. "I don't suppose you have any idea which direction it was going?"

"It went through the side gate and was headed in a north-westerly direction. Beyond that, no. Sorry." She hesitated. "Is that why you came in here? Because you were tracking that dark energy?"

"Yes, though it was your son's screaming that brought us into the house. It didn't sound right."

"Then I thank the stars and good fortune darkness decided to walk past my house at that precise moment."

I didn't believe the stars or good fortune had *anything* to do with it. I really did believe that the hone-onna had sensed what was going on and had deliberately led us there.

Which was a weird thing to think about a creature of death, but a definite indicator that maternal instincts weren't restricted to flesh-and-blood beings.

Two medics came into the room, so I said goodbye and followed the sound of Monty's voice down the hall and into the kitchen.

He'd been talking on the phone, but hung up as I entered. His gaze swept me critically and came up ... puzzled. "You're looking surprisingly well, considering."

I frowned at him. "Considering what?"

"Considering the force behind that bolt of energy you

unleashed—you do know it was pure wild magic, don't you?"

"It's a part of my soul, Monty, so these days it's a given that it'll appear in any spell or energy I cast." I walked over to the sink, then grabbed a cup and filled it up. The adrenaline of the moment was fading, leaving my throat parched and a deepening ache in my head. I had painkillers in my bag, but my bag was still in the truck. Water would have to do for the moment.

"It wasn't your personal wild magic. It was the real deal."

My gaze shot across to his. "Don't be ridiculous—there has to be threads of the stuff nearby for that to happen, and there isn't."

But even as I said that, a soft glimmer caught my eye. A tiny thread of wild magic, lazily circling around the room, as if waiting for something.

Or some*one*.

Me, to be precise.

I held out a hand, and it immediately responded, wrapping lightly around my wrist. My skin tingled with power and awareness.

That awareness scared me, because it wasn't coming from Katie. This thread of wildness wasn't from her wellspring, but rather the main one.

Which could only mean it wasn't her soul, her spirit, creating the growing cognizance in the main wellspring's wild magic.

It was *mine*.

And it was all thanks to the magic in my DNA; it was forging an ever-deepening connection with the larger wellspring.

No wonder my psi senses had been warning that I'd

never truly be able to leave this place. It wasn't, as I'd been thinking, because I was Katie's conduit to the people she loved, but the fact that, like her, I was becoming irrevocably linked to a wellspring. Perhaps not forever—not unless I wished it, an inner voice whispered, and I didn't—but for as long as I lived, this place was now both my home and my prison. Leaving might have been possible in the earlier days of our arrival, but it wasn't now.

"Liz, what's wrong? You look ... well, you look as if you've seen a ghost," Monty said. "You've certainly gone as pale as one."

"Sorry, just the aftereffect of using that much power." I waved a dismissive hand. "I'll be fine."

His gaze narrowed, no doubt suspecting there was more to the story than what I was saying, but Aiden came back into the room, so he didn't push the matter.

Because we both know Monty has every intention of harassing me with his questions later this evening came Belle's comment. *I'm not sure I see the point of keeping your silence now.*

I don't want to worry Aiden.

Bull. Besides, regardless of what might happen with you two in the future, you're still currently in a very caring relationship with that man. He deserves to know.

Yes, and I will tell him. Eventually.

She harrumphed. The sound echoed loudly through my brain, making me wince.

"I take it," Monty said, "that Belle is currently conversing with you and isn't entirely happy."

"Yes indeed, and no, you have no need to know." I glanced at Aiden. "Where's Jim?"

"The husband? Jaz is escorting him to the station and will take a statement when he's conscious."

"You might want to get the medics to check him out. I think he was high on something."

"Already made the call. They'll meet Jaz at the station." He dug into his pocket and held out his truck keys. "You two might as well head home. There's nothing more you can do here or over at Ms. Taylor's."

Monty frowned. "You sure you don't want me to stay, just in case she returns?"

"How likely is it that she will?"

"Not very, but that doesn't mean she won't."

A smile tugged Aiden's lips. "Then your time might be better spent trying to track this thing down."

"Yeah, because that's been a success so far." He pushed away from the counter and offered me the crook of his elbow. "Shall we go hunting, dear cousin?"

"Only if Belle doesn't need me at the café—"

And she doesn't.

"It appears that I am indeed free."

I linked my arm through his, and we headed out the back door. I pulled free at the bottom step and bent to press a finger against the blood smear. It had well and truly dried, and the pulse of energy and life had long left it. I nevertheless called to a sliver of the inner wild magic and sent it into the smear, searching for a connection, a reason, or simply some sense of the monster that had cared enough to save the child.

All I got was an odd sense of dread. Her next kill would be far worse than anything we'd seen so far. And this time, it wouldn't be a stranger who died. It would be someone we knew.

Unless we stopped her.

I glanced up sharply at Monty. "She's already on the hunt."

He frowned. "That makes no sense, given she's only just killed."

"Killed, not fed."

"You think the next victim will be a feeding?"

"No, I think it'll be a frenzy. We need to find her, and fast."

"All we've got is my tracker, and that'll only work if we're in her vicinity."

"I know, but we have to try. If intuition is right, her next victim is someone we know."

Alarm crossed his features. "Someone close?"

I hesitated. "I don't know, and in the end, that's neither here nor there in the scheme of things."

"True." He motioned me forward. "Let's go."

We made our way back over the fence and then through Ms. Taylor's yard. There were a couple more ranger vehicles sitting out the front of the house now, suggesting that Tala and Ciara had arrived. Monty headed over to Maggie's SUV to grab his backpack and the tracker, while I climbed into Aiden's truck, then leaned over to grab my bag and fish out some painkillers. I didn't have any water, so I simply chewed and swallowed them. Not my favorite thing to do, but better than putting up with a headache.

"Where to?" I asked, once Monty was in the truck and had his seat belt on.

"You tell me. You're the one who communed with the blood spot."

"I only got a warning of danger, not a damn location."

"And you really should work on that. I mean, what good is a psychic talent that doesn't provide much in the way of usable information?"

I lightly slapped his arm, then put the truck into gear and headed back toward Castle Rock, though for no particular reason other than the fact it seemed to be the general direction our hone-onna had been heading.

We were on the outskirts of town when the tracker came to life.

"Well, fuck me," Monty said. "The damn thing found something."

I snorted. "I love how your certainty that a spell will work becomes surprise when the thing actually does."

"Well, it was created from a vague memory of a long-ago lesson, so in reality, there was only ever a fifty-fifty chance of it working. Keep going on this road for a bit."

We swept around several corners, turned right at a set of traffic lights, and continued on, quickly moving through Castle Rock and onto the highway.

"Next right," he said.

I slowed and turned. "Isn't this one of the roads that eventually leads up to the O'Connor compound?"

"I think so, but I couldn't imagine she'd go after a werewolf. They're a whole lot tougher to fool than a human. Besides, werewolves mate for life." He paused. "When they actually do commit to a partner, that is."

I smiled, even as my stupid heart ached. "I knew what you meant."

"Good." He motioned to the crossroad up ahead. "Keep on this road."

There was no traffic coming in either direction, so I accelerated through the intersection. The tracker's pulse continued to grow stronger, suggesting we were getting closer. "Aside from the O'Connor compound, is much else up this way?"

"Grazing lands and orchards, mostly." He glanced at me. "Why?"

"If I'm wrong and she's not hunting, then it's an odd

place for her to be. I can't imagine a pine forest would provide much in the way of comfortable cover."

"She's a dark spirit. They don't need comfortable. Left ahead."

I turned. "We're talking about a spirit that normally hunts in major cities. I can't imagine she'd want to be hiding out in the open."

"You're applying human sensibilities to an inhuman creature," he said, clearly amused. "But that aside, her movements aren't restricted by daylight, and her magic affords her the resemblance of normality. In reality, she could take up residence in the busiest hotel, and most people would be none the wiser."

"Would she risk that though? If she's aware of my presence, then she'd have to be aware there are four other witches in the reservation."

"Yes, but the reservation is large. The chances of one of us coming across her by accident are rather low, and she'd be aware of that, too. We're not dealing with a dumb spirit here."

No, we were dealing with one who saved children.

Which doesn't mean she can be allowed to rampage through the reservation unchecked, Belle said. *It only takes a sideways step to go from killing cheaters to wiping out the innocent.*

I know. I suppose I just didn't expect a dark spirit to react in such a caring manner to a human child, and now I can't help viewing her in a slightly different light.

It's not really surprising that there are differing levels of evil within the spirit world. They aren't all the same, just as witches and humans aren't. She paused. *Hell, that statement might also apply to demons.*

No one will ever convince me demons have a soft side.

And yet, until today, we both thought the same about dark spirits.

The large pine plantation where Byron—one of the rangers—had recently been murdered soon came into sight. I slowed and, without Monty needing to tell me, turned into the dusty road that ran between two orderly rows of pines.

"If we keep on following this track through the plantation, we'll end up on the mountain and the outskirts of the O'Connor compound," I said. "We can't go in there, Monty. Not without permission."

"I know, but hopefully she's doing nothing more than just tracking through their territory, and we'll be able to catch her again on the other side." He shrugged. "I can't see any reason for her to be hunting in the compound, given married wolves don't stray."

"You can't make such a blanket statement when there are always outliers. Hell, take Mia as an example—" Horror surged, and my gaze snapped to Monty. "Fuck, you don't think *Mia* could be the target, do you?"

"Why on earth would she be a target?"

"Well, she technically *did* cheat—she had a common-law husband when she became engaged to Aiden."

"True, but she appeared in the reservation *after* the kills started," Monty said, "She shouldn't have been included in the scope of the spell."

"Except we don't know yet who created the spell or what its parameters were. Hell, the caster might not have set any limitations at all—it would certainly explain why the hone-onna is going after both the cheater *and* the lover."

"There's no indication as yet that Ms. Taylor *was* the lover of one of the victims. For all we know, she's married, cheating on her husband, and we're simply dealing with an equal opportunity killer."

"*We* might not know, but that doesn't mean the witch behind the hone-onna doesn't," I said. "She has to be using some kind of magic to locate her targets, so why couldn't the same spell uncover whomever they were cheating with?"

"If we *do* work on that theory, Aiden could be a target as well."

I blinked and, for a second, couldn't breathe. I gulped and then said, "We can't discount that possibility, even if he was an unknowing participant in the betrayal."

While the charm he wore had already protected him from this spirit, now that she knew it was there, it wouldn't take her too long to defuse it. "You'd better warn him. We need him to contact Mia anyway."

Monty grabbed his phone and hit the call button. It rang several times before Aiden said, "I take it there's a problem?"

"There could well be—do you know where Mia is?"

"No—why?"

Sharp concern rode his question, and something twisted inside. Which was stupid. Even if he didn't love her, he certainly wouldn't want to see her hurt or murdered.

"Because," Monty replied, "we've tracked the hone-onna up to the Mount Alexander pine plantation. We believe she's heading for the compound."

He didn't ask why we believed Mia could be the next target. He would have made the connection as easily as we had. "Give me a few minutes to get permission for you to enter, then I'll contact Mia."

He immediately hung up. Monty tucked the phone between his legs and picked up the tracker again. The closer we got to the compound, the stronger its pulse became.

I might have wanted Mia out of Aiden's life, but not like this.

We came to a T-intersection, and I braked. If we went left, we'd end up in the O'Connor compound; going right would take us on a loop around the plantation and then back into Castle Rock.

The tracker was of course indicating to the left.

I was more than willing to risk going up there without permission if we were given no other choice, but I also knew the O'Connors *would* come down on us hard. If they *did*—if they delayed us for even a few minutes—it could have disastrous results. Not just for Mia but also for the longer-term relationship between the witches and the pack. For that same reason, we couldn't use magic to clear a path through their ranks, not even in an effort to save a life.

But sometimes the quickest way to achieve a much-desired goal was by the slowest method available. Or so Belle's mom used to say back in the day, when Belle and I were impatient teenagers wanting things done *now* rather than later.

It was a memory that made me smile. At least we'd be able to go visit Belle's parents while we were up in Canberra, and that alone might make the whole trip worthwhile.

No might about it came Belle's comment. *In fact, I've already contacted Mom. She's invited the four of us for dinner the night we arrive in Canberra.*

We haven't even booked the flights yet.

We don't need to. The Black Lantern Society has taken care of all that sort of stuff. Ashworth forwarded me the tickets about an hour ago.

I frowned. *Why would they be paying for it?*

We're key witnesses to the case being brought against your dad, so why shouldn't they? She shrugged mentally. *But maybe they simply want to make sure we actually get on the plane.*

I do believe that's the reason Ashworth and Eli are coming with us. They want to ensure we get there in one piece.

That sounds ominous—intuition? Or did I miss something when Juli appeared at the café?

Not intuition, and you didn't miss anything. But let's be honest here—Juli's sudden appearance was nothing more than a vague attempt at intimidation.

Very vague indeed. Her amusement swam down the mental line. *He was never as good as your father at that sort of thing. He's too soft to be scary.*

He doesn't have to be scary when he's got the magical nous to back up any threat he makes.

So have you, now. Remember that.

Except we're not exactly sure whether my personal wild magic will be functional outside the confines of the reservation. Without it, I remain an underpowered witch.

You can't say that with any certainty, given the way your psi abilities are morphing. But I can't imagine why the inner wildness wouldn't be available—it's part of your damn DNA.

A part that was inactive until I entered this reservation and came into contact with its unprotected wellspring.

That's not exactly true. There was some leaching over to me—it was in the erectile dysfunction spell I unleashed on Clayton, remember.

Monty's phone rang sharply, making me jump. He hit the answer button and quickly said, "Do we have permission to go in?"

"If necessary, but Mia's currently on the way out of the compound. Do you want her to turn back?"

"No," I said quickly. "The hone-onna is between us and her—she'll get to Mia before we ever could."

"Except this time, she's in a wolf compound. Even a dark spirit as deadly as this one will have her hands full dealing with a pack of werewolves ready and willing to protect one of their own."

"Oh, come on, Aiden," Monty said, with a surprising amount of annoyance running through his voice, "you've dealt with enough supernatural entities by now to recognize the stupidity of that statement."

"It's not—"

"Aiden," he cut in again. "The tracker is indicating the hone-onna is moving toward the residential hub—are you really willing to risk the lives of all those you care about on the off chance the hone-onna won't cut a bloody swath through the pack to get to Mia?"

"Of course not, but—"

"Guys," I cut in sharply, "can we argue over who'd provide the better protection *after* we actually save Mia from the hone-onna?"

"What do you want her to do, if not return back to the hub?" came Aiden's curt response.

"She needs to hightail it out of the compound and meet up with us," Monty said.

"She's on the main exit road, which will take her onto the Faraday-Sutton Grange Road. If you're at the pine plantation's crossroad, it'll take you roughly ten minutes to reach Faraday."

I immediately took off; a wave of dust and stones bloomed behind us as I sped down the rough old road.

"We'll meet up with her somewhere along that road then," Monty said. "But there's one more thing, Aiden. We think you'll probably have to go into protective isolation with her—"

"No," he cut in bluntly.

"Aiden," I said, "you know it's absolutely the last thing I want, but I really don't think we have any other option right now."

"There's always another option," he growled, "but that's something you and I can discuss once she's safe. Keep the line open. I'll keep relaying her position."

"Stubborn fucking man," I muttered, my gaze on the road and my grip so tight on the wheel my knuckles gleamed white.

"Something you were well aware of before we ever got into a relationship" came Aiden's curt reply.

"Yes, but that doesn't mean it's any less annoying in a situation like this."

He laughed, though it was a slightly brittle sound. "The same can be said in return, my darling witch."

I didn't reply, though I wanted to. How could he use an endearment like that and yet be utterly unwilling to admit the depths of his emotions? Emotions I could see in his eyes and his aura?

I flexed my fingers in an effort to release the frustrated anger. Right now, it was better for everyone—but especially for Monty, who was holding onto the grab handle in a white-knuckled manner—that I fully concentrated on driving.

Aiden kept us updated on Mia's position, his voice tense and filled with muted, angry frustration. But then, he was an alpha, and it was part of their makeup to protect those they cared about. But this situation, just like that of his brother, was not something he could control or fix, and that grated.

The tracker's pulse remained bright and steady, an indication that our dark spirit was moving in roughly the same direction we were. It wasn't a direct confirmation Mia was her target; in fact, it could have just as easily confirmed *we* were.

She might have guided me to a kid in danger, but that didn't mean she'd given up on testing her magic against the "strongest" witch in the reservation.

I glanced at Monty and murmured, "We need to be careful. She could be out to trap us rather than Mia."

"I came to that conclusion several minutes ago." He raised an eyebrow, amusement evident. "You're a bit slow today."

"I've only had one coffee so far," I said, voice dry, "so I'll blame it on the lack of caffeine."

"Right," Aiden said, "she's just swung onto Faraday Road. How far away are you from the other end?"

I glanced at the GPS screen. "Two minutes? We've just hit Harmony Way."

"Put the siren on and floor it," he said. "Is the hone-onna still tracking her?"

"Unclear," Monty said.

"What the hell does that mean?"

"Exactly what I said," Monty growled back. "Don't get all antsy at me, wolf man."

I glanced at Monty in surprise, eyebrows raised. "What the hell has Belle been feeding you for breakfast?"

He grinned, though there was an angry light in his eyes that belied the mirth. "Bullshit intolerance pills."

"That doesn't explain this." I waved a hand toward the phone.

"Maybe bullshit is the wrong term, then. Maybe it's the lack of courage I can't abide."

"The line *is* open, Monty," Aiden noted, voice dry.

"Oh, I know, but if my cousin won't call out your bullshit, I'm legally obliged to."

"What the *fuck* are you on about now?"

"Calling her darling but refusing to commit? That's cowardice in my book, Aiden. And don't give me the whole 'she's not wolf' bullshit, because we both know—"

"Can we please concentrate on the hone-onna?" I said, even though I wanted to roundly cheer every single word Monty had said. "Aiden, where's Mia?"

"About a kilometer away from the Harmony Way intersection." He paused. "A car has appeared behind her."

A car? Why would the hone-onna be using a car, given the speed with which she could move? I briefly hit the brake to take off some speed, then wrenched the truck left into Faraday Road, leaving a trail of black tire smoke behind me.

A silver car appeared on the road up ahead, headlights gleaming brightly as it approached at speed. There was no sign of a car behind her. Either it had turned off or the hone-onna was now using magic to conceal it.

"That has to be Mia," Monty said.

"And the other car?" came Aiden's question.

"Not currently visible," I said. "But the hone-onna is still closing in."

"We'll pull over," Monty added. "Tell Mia to stop opposite us and jump into the back of the truck."

"Will do."

I moved the truck onto the road's gravel shoulder but braked too quickly, sending us into a brief sideways slide before I brought it back under control. Dust plumed around the vehicle, then fell away.

Monty peered through the windscreen. "I'm not seeing anything to indicate a concealing spell is being used."

"No, but the tracker is still reacting, so she's somewhere up ahead."

"Maybe she's just passing through. Maybe we're overreacting."

"Maybe."

He glanced at me. "But you don't think so?"

"Not given the premonition that someone I know would die."

"You don't know Mia."

"On a deep and personal level, no. But I have met her, and that may well be enough. Remember, my psi talents aren't always specific." I paused. "Right now, I'm just hoping that I haven't read this whole thing wrong."

"You did say the dead person would be someone 'we' know, and that implies you and I aren't her targets."

"Unless this is one of those rare occasions my talents get it wrong."

He returned his gaze to the road. "Let's hope not. I'm really not in the mood to die today."

The silver car was now throwing up a cloud of dust as Mia edged onto the shoulder in readiness to stop.

It was in that cloud that the outline of a second vehicle became visible. It was close to the tail of Mia's car.

Too close.

"Oh fuck," Monty said. "The bitch is going to ram her."

"Yes, she damn well is."

I scrambled out of the truck and hurled a ball of sheer energy at the dusty, semi-transparent vehicle ... just as it plowed into the back of Mia's, sending it sliding sideways over the embankment and down into the water-filled trench.

My bolt hit and punched the second car high into the air. It tipped over end-to-end several times then crashed heavily onto its roof and spun slowly down the road, well past us.

"Monty, see to Mia," I yelled and ran back to the other car.

Though there was no immediate sense of evil emanating from the upside-down car, I nevertheless wrapped a cage spell around my fingertips. While I had nothing on hand that could in any way kill a spirit as strong as the hone-onna, Ashworth and Eli were only a phone call away. All I had to do was keep her contained.

The second car had come to halt sideways across the road. There was no movement inside, and for a moment, I wondered if she'd escaped us.

Then the back window shattered, and a spell that was little more than a mess of twisting threads of black foulness speared out and arrowed straight at me.

I didn't need the charm at my neck burning to life to know that mass intended me no good. I slid to a halt, threw up my hands, and quickly wove a shielding spell—one that was interlaced with inner wild magic. The pulsing screen of silver and gold flared out in front of me, and the dark threads reacted instantly, sweeping to the left in an obvious attempt to get around the shield and attack from behind. I shifted with it, keeping the shield between us as I studied the threads, looking for a weak spot in the hone-onna's magic.

There wasn't one.

The bitch was *strong*.

An ominous prickle went down my neck.

The bitch was also *behind* me.

CHAPTER ELEVEN

I dropped low and lashed out with one booted foot. Heard a sharp crack and saw the pale glimmer of a bone shard flying. The hone-onna screamed—a sound that was fury and pain combined—and then fled, her steps light but weirdly arrhythmic. I twisted around. Her form was shifting, changing, *disappearing*.

I thrust to my feet to go after her, then yelped as something lashed my cheek, leaving it stinging and burning. I swore, spun around, and saw a dark thread snapping back toward me. I thrust the shield between us and caught the end of the whip before it could strike my cheek a second time. The damn thing hit the shield so hard it forced me back a step before I caught my balance and resisted. Rather than withdrawing, the end of the whip crawled across the shield's network of gold and silver threads, a deadly worm of power seeking a weakness to exploit. It wouldn't find any, but I nevertheless pushed a fraction more energy into the shield and incinerated the fucker. Then I flung the whole damn shield toward the rotating mass of foreboding black and wrapped it around the dark threads, utterly encompassing them in a shining orb of silver and gold. As the two magics fought for dominance, I turned and charged after the hone-onna. She was no longer visible, but the taint of her darkness rode the air, a scent I could follow as easily as a wolf could prey.

I was very aware it might be a trap—or, at the very least, a means of separating me from Monty and Mia—but it wasn't like I had many other options. If I didn't take this chance and try to snare her, she'd continue to have the upper hand and more people would die.

I leapt across the water-filled ditch that ran along the side of the road and raced through the plowed field. My steps were fast and sure—fueled by adrenaline or perhaps even the wild magic that was changing my body—but the distance between us remained static.

I rather suspected that was deliberate on her part.

The cage spell remained around my left hand, but a sudden burst of caution had me weaving a repelling spell around my right.

If the first failed, I sure as hell would need the second.

I leapt over a rock, landed awkwardly on the soggy soil, and threw out my arms to catch my balance. My fingers brushed against something that was gossamer soft and sticky. For an instant I thought it was a spider's web floating by on the breeze, but it was too late in the season for spiders to be ballooning.

Another web brushed by; I caught the tail of it in my fingertips, and my psychometry flared to life, whispering all manner of dark secrets.

These webs weren't natural.

They were born of magic.

Dark magic.

Her magic.

And once again they'd been designed to trap and hold rather than kill.

But why? Granted, it might be easier to test your skills against the strongest witch in the area if said witch was your captive, but that hardly made for good competition. But that wasn't her intention here. Death was.

Just not *my* death.

Which wasn't to say that if either the dark mess of magic or these gossamer webs had succeeded in grabbing me, she'd have released me, but for the moment, she simply wanted me out of the way so she could go after her assigned target.

Mia.

I swore, spun around, and ran like hell back across the field. As my feet flew, I dragged out my phone and called Monty. He didn't immediately answer, and I cursed him a dozen different ways before he eventually did.

"Sorry, it was a bit involved getting Mia out of the car. Where are you?"

"In the other field. The hone-onna is looping around and coming back for Mia, and she'll kill you if you get in her way."

"Well, I sure as fuck won't get *out* of her way."

"I know, and I'm not asking you to, just—"

The rest of the sentence was lost to a scream. A woman's scream. Mia's.

"Monty?" I yelled. "What the hell is going on?"

He didn't reply, but his magic surged, a fierce wave that burned my skin. It wasn't a spell I knew, and it felt darker than anything he'd ever crafted before. It was a spell meant to destroy rather than protect and something he'd use only as a last resort.

I swore and reached for more speed, but I was never

going to get there in time, and I knew it. I flung out a hand and called to the wild magic, praying like hell that the luminous thread I'd noticed earlier had remained close.

It had.

As it wrapped around my wrist, other threads came in, filling the air with their presence and their power. Their force energized me, making me feel I could run as fast as any wolf. Making me feel like I could fly.

Another scream.

Another surge of magic. Monty's again, but weaker than before.

All but flying over the ground wasn't going to cut it. If I didn't do something right *now*, what I'd foreseen would come true.

I conjured a picture of Monty and Mia in my mind and then imagined a net of pure power around them, protecting them as my shield had protected me. I directed the image at the moonbeams that spun around me and then unleashed them.

Their response was so damn powerful that I was blown off my feet and ended up butt down in soggy soil. Pain shimmied up my spine, and a gasp escaped, but I nevertheless scrambled upright and chased after the moonbeams. I was never going to catch them, of course, but that didn't really matter as long as the spell did its job and protected the two people ahead.

My heart now raced so damn hard, it felt ready to tear out of my chest, but I wasn't sure whether it was fear, exertion, or the cost of casting the magic. Sweat beaded my skin, and each breath was a harsh rasp that raked my lungs. My vision was going in and out of focus, and energy seemed to be trickling away from my limbs so fast that I was beginning to shake.

The moonbeams, I realized abruptly. They were still connected to me, and were drawing down on my physical strength rather than that of the distant wellspring.

I unleashed the luminous sliver at my wrist. As it floated away, the draining sensation eased. My heart still raced too damn fast, and my lungs continued to burn, but both were more likely a result of my desperate flight across the field rather than the drain of the wild magic.

I scrambled up the embankment, digging my fingers into the soft soil to prevent slipping back. I had no idea whether my magic had been unleashed in time to protect Monty and Mia. For all I knew, they could be—

A fierce, unholy scream cut the thought dead.

If the hone-onna was venting her displeasure, that surely meant the shield had worked. Relief surged, even though I had no idea yet if Monty and Mia were okay or injured or worse ...

I reached the asphalt, pushed upright, and ran across to the other side of the road. Mia's car was now on its roof rather than its side, and one of the rear tires had melted. I couldn't see the hone-onna or even Mia, but Monty stood on the far side of the upturned vehicle, unleashed magic burning all around his body.

Between him and the hidden spirit stood my moonbeam net. It had encased not just him but the entire car, and it was flexing and humming under a barrage of darker magic.

I might not be able to see our dark spirit, but she was definitely still here somewhere.

I slid to a halt, sending stones flying as I scanned the area through narrowed eyes. After a second, I caught an odd blurring in the air—it was the hone-onna's concealment spell, briefly blotting out her immediate surrounds as she shifted position.

I unleashed the cage spell. She screamed in response and cast a spell of her own—one designed to destroy. It wasn't cast at me but rather my spell. The two hit and exploded with enough force to briefly rock the car.

The blur that was the dark spirit moved again, this time running away rather than toward us. While I doubted it was another attempt to lure me away, I wasn't about to give chase.

"Liz," Monty shouted, "release your net! I can't spell through it."

I immediately did so. As the delicate fragments unwound and floated away, Monty unleashed his spell. It wasn't a tracker; it was too dark, too dangerous, to be something so simple.

It tumbled across the field after the hone-onna and disappeared into distant trees.

"Did that hit?" I asked.

"Don't think so." He turned, his gaze briefly sweeping me and coming up relieved. His face was smudged with dirt, and blood trickled down the left side, but otherwise he looked okay. "That was a pretty impressive spell you unleashed—I'm kinda surprised you're still upright."

"So am I, to be honest. Where's Mia? She okay?"

"I'm here and also upright." She stood up from behind the car next to Monty, her hair a bird's nest of mud and glass, and a multitude of small cuts over her face. "I wouldn't mind an explanation as to what the hell just happened, though."

"Later." Monty lightly cupped her arm and led her around the upturned car. "Right now, we all need to get the hell out of here before that bitch returns."

"What bitch?" Mia said, frustration evident. "I didn't see anything or anyone. The damn tire exploded just before the car flipped onto its roof, and then you appeared to help me out."

"So Aiden didn't give you an explanation when he was talking to you?" I asked.

"No, he just said I was in danger and that I was to meet you and Monty along this road. But then, he's never big on explaining *anything*."

"Isn't that the goddamn truth." I reached down, grabbed her hand, and hauled her up the incline, then repeated the process for Monty. "I need to check the other car before we go anywhere."

"Why?" he said.

"On the off chance our dark spirit wasn't driving herself."

"Dark spirit?" Mia's expression was bemused.

"Yeah. You chose a hell of a time to reenter Aiden's life, let me tell you." Monty's gaze returned to mine. "I'll reverse the truck back. That way, we can nudge the car off the road if there's no one in it."

"As long as you're careful not to scratch the truck in the process," I said. "He will get annoyed if you do."

Monty grinned. "I would say boys and their toys, but you'd no doubt throw a jibe about the Mustang in my face."

"I certainly would, cousin dearest."

He laughed, caught Mia's elbow, and guided her over to the truck. I jogged back to the other upturned vehicle. The idiots with the hot pokers chose that moment to get busy in my head again, but I'd already taken one lot of painkillers, and there wasn't a whole lot more I could do until I got back to the café. And, to be honest, if the headache was the only side effect of casting the moonbeams, I'd count myself damn lucky.

The top of the driver-side door had been partially

crushed in the flip over, and as a result, the window had popped out and shattered. I kicked the glass aside, then knelt to peer inside. An unconscious woman was slumped in the driver seat.

She was a wolf rather than a human, and a member of the O'Connor pack, if her hair and scent were anything to go by. Which certainly explained how the hone-onna had gotten through the reservation's gates unchallenged.

I reached in and carefully pressed a couple of fingers against her neck. Her pulse was a little thready, but otherwise strong. She'd been knocked out, but seemed to have escaped serious injury. Which didn't, of course, mean there weren't multiple internal injuries. I turned off the engine and then sat back on my heels and studied the rest of the car. There was no sign of fuel leakage and nothing to suggest the car was likely to catch fire or explode. While hanging upside down wouldn't be pleasant—I knew *that* from personal experience—I also knew it was far safer for her to remain where she was until help got here—as long as her vital signs were monitored and the situation didn't change in any way, of course.

I pulled out my phone, called in an ambulance, and then rang Aiden. His line was busy—maybe he was still connected to Monty's phone—so I tried Tala instead.

It didn't even have a chance to ring before she was on the line and asking, "Lizzie—is everyone okay?"

"Yes, but we've got an unconscious woman in the other car. I've called an ambulance, but I need a ranger up here ASAP. Monty and I can't hang around, just in case the hone-onna decides to come back for another go at Mia."

"Mac is already on the—" The rest of Tala's comment was cut off as Aiden growled, "Are you all right?"

"For the most part, yes."

"Which no doubt means you're bruised, bleeding, or close to exhaustion."

"Only one of those three is correct," I said, a smile twitching my lips.

He sighed. It was a sound that was both relieved and frustrated. "Where are you taking Mia?"

I hesitated. "I'm not actually sure. This thing is damn strong, Aiden."

"Stronger than four witches combined?"

"Possibly." I glanced up as the wail of a siren bit through the silence. An SUV appeared in the distance, red and blue lights flashing. "Mac's almost here. I'll call again when we find a safe house."

"Okay." He paused. "Is Mac going to be safe out there alone?"

"I think so. This thing isn't going after randoms, Aiden. It has specific targets, and it doesn't appear to be deviating."

"Is that why you think I'm also in danger? Because she appears to be going after both parties involved in the extra-marital activities?"

"Yes."

He grunted. "Then let's hope the charm you made stops this thing, because there's no way known I'm getting locked up with Mia."

"Why? Don't you trust yourself not to fall back in love with her?"

It was out before I could stop it, and I winced. He'd already said he could never forgive someone who'd so readily betrayed his trust, and I had no right—and no reason—to doubt that.

But sometimes the inner green demon popped up before I could stomp her back down.

He made a low rumbly sound that had the tiny hairs on

the back of my neck rising. "Even suggesting *that* is offensive, Liz."

I sighed. "I know, and I'm sorry. It's just—" I waved a hand, though he couldn't see it. "This whole situation is just getting to me."

"Which is why we need to talk."

"But will it actually achieve anything?" I didn't give him a chance to answer that, but rushed on to add, "Look, Mac is here. I'll call later."

And then I hung up.

He didn't call back. He probably knew I wouldn't answer.

I touched the unconscious woman's neck again, just to be sure nothing had changed, then glanced around as Aiden's truck pulled to a halt a few meters away.

Monty jumped out and walked over. "There *is* a driver, I take it?"

I nodded. "An O'Connor wolf. I don't think she's badly hurt—not by the hone-onna, at any rate."

Monty squatted and peered in through the window. "There are a few minor threads of magic caught in her hair, but they're the remnants of a control spell rather than anything more serious."

"That's what I figured." I pushed to my feet. "Do you want to keep an eye on her while I hunt around for a bit of bone?"

"Bone?"

"It came off the hone-onna's leg when I kicked her. If I can find it, I might be able to use my psychometry to find her."

"It would certainly be a whole lot faster than my spell."

"If it works. No guarantee that it will."

"No guarantee that it won't, either."

"True that."

I walked back to the spot where I'd been attacked and then tried to remember the direction the shard had speared off to. After a moment, I headed to the edge of the road, slid down the slope, and then paused again, drawing in the air, searching for the scent of darkness. I didn't find it, but I did find the smell of blood. It was only faint, but it was nevertheless noticeable—at least to my newly sharpened olfactory sense.

I followed my nose several yards to the right and then bent. Caught in the spiky branch of a scotch thistle was a bloody bit of bone. I grabbed a tissue from my pocket and carefully retrieved it. Even though there was no direct contact between the bone and my skin, my psychometry talent once again stirred to life. There were secrets to be mined from this bit of bone.

I hesitated, then tightened my grip around it. The tissue made for a slightly fuzzy connection, but I wasn't overly worried about that given what I was dealing with. For all I knew, the hone-onna might have deliberately shed this bit of bone in the hope that I'd pick it up. Maybe she wanted to use it to find me just as I did her.

And yet it wasn't a location that rose, but rather the image of a woman. She had crimson hair, silver eyes that gleamed with power, and a mark that ran down her face and ended in an odd sort of hook near her mouth.

For one horrible instant, I thought it was a maker's mark, which would have meant she was either a dark sorcerer or the apprentice of one. But the image shifted—sharpened—and it became clear that it was just an ill-healed scar. She had three more near her collarbone, though they resembled the slashes of a large cat. Or maybe a disgruntled spirit.

This, I suspected, was the witch who'd called the hone-onna into the reservation. I had no idea if she was a full-blood royal witch or not, but she was definitely someone who'd been well trained. She might not be a dark sorcerer, per se, but she was definitely walking that line.

What the shard of bone wasn't telling me was whether someone had paid to unleash vengeance, or if she too was a woman betrayed.

I pulled another tissue from my pocket, wrapped it around the bone fragment to provide more of a buffer between it and me, then carefully placed the bundle in the breast pocket of my coat and scrambled back up the hill.

Mac had pulled up in front of the upturned car and was now walking toward Monty.

"The ambulance is only a few minutes behind me," he said. "Are we dealing with any serious injuries?"

"The driver is unconscious, but there're no obvious external injuries," Monty replied. "The hone-onna has left the area, so you should be safe. Unless, of course, you're married and cheating on your partner."

"A wolf stupid enough to stray is a wolf who'd be nutless pretty damn quick." A smile tugged at Mac's lips. "I'm under strict orders not to delay you two, so you'd better go."

I nodded and retreated to Aiden's truck, climbing into the passenger side while Monty jumped into the driver seat. With the upturned car blocking the road, we had to head in the opposite direction for a couple of klicks to find a road that would take us back to Castle Rock.

"Any luck?" Monty asked.

"Yes indeed. But a quick scan provided expected results. It appears our hone-onna—"

"Okay, I think I've been extremely patient about all

this," Mia cut in. "But really, what the hell is going on? And what the fuck is a hone-onna?"

"It's a dark spirit," Monty said. "It's been called into the reservation to hunt and kill those who break their marriage vows and have an affair."

"Then why the hell is it coming after me? I was never married."

"In most Australian States, a de facto couple holds many of the same rights as a married couple," I said.

"Many isn't all."

"Semantics generally don't matter to dark spirits."

"So the thing that hit my car and sent me into that ditch was the dark spirit?"

"A dark spirit in a car, yes" Monty said.

"But how is it possible to make an entire car *invisible*?"

"She was using magic to conceal it."

"Huh." She paused. "So, what happens next?"

"Well, first up," Monty said, "We're going to the hospital to get you checked over."

"I've already told you—I shifted shape, and I'm perfectly fine."

"That may well be true," I said, "but we've learned the hard way it's always better to be safe than sorry after such an accident."

"So speaks a witch with no real understanding of wolf physiology."

"That witch," Monty growled, "just saved your goddamn life, so cut the patronizing crap."

"And I've also been in a serious relationship with Aiden for over six months now," I added. "So I actually have a pretty good idea about all things wolf."

"You could never—" She bit the rest of the sentence off and sighed. "Sorry, I don't mean to sound ungrateful or patronizing. But it's not easy to walk into a situation that's totally the opposite of what I'd been told to expect. I can only imagine how difficult this all is for you, Liz. In fact, had the situation been reversed, I'm not entirely sure I would have been as understanding and as compassionate."

"Oh, trust me," I murmured, "I'm a little bit surprised by it all myself."

She half laughed. "What happens once the hospital gives me the all-clear then?"

"We'll take you and Aiden into protective custody," Monty said.

"Oh, I can just imagine his response to *that*."

Her voice was droll, and I couldn't help smiling. "It doesn't take any imagination at all, trust me."

"If this spirit is so bad," she said. "Why didn't you just kill it when it was attacking us? I take it that's what was happening when you had me crouching down beside the car."

"Because," Monty said, "she's not only cunning, but probably stronger magically than either of us."

Which was true only as long as I didn't call on the wild magic. But given my growing connection to the wellspring, using it to do anything more than capture the hone-onna was absolutely out of the question. The last thing we wanted or needed was death forever staining the purity of the wild magic.

"Well," Mia muttered, "that doesn't fill me with a whole lot of hope."

"Luckily for you," I said, "we're not the only witches on the reservation."

Monty glanced at me. "You might want to check with Ashworth and Eli first before you start dobbing them in for protection detail."

"I will, but do you honestly think they'd refuse, given the situation?"

He raised his eyebrows, amusement evident. He knew I wasn't talking about the hone-onna's attacks but rather Mia herself. Questions would be asked, both subtly and not.

"But even if they're unable to help," I continued, "we still need to talk to them. It was a dark witch who unleashed this hell on us. A *royal* dark witch."

Monty's gaze snapped to mine again. "Seriously?"

I nodded. "I know the council has a register of witches who stray into the dark side of magic, and Ashworth has the connections to arrange a search ASAP."

"That might take more time than we have, but definitely worth a shot." He pulled into the hospital parking lot and stopped. "We'll head in. Do you want to contact Ashworth?"

I nodded, waited until they were safely inside the Emergency Department, and then did so.

"It's far too early in the afternoon for you to be ringing about an excess of cake," he said, tone amused, "so that obviously means there's a problem. Are we talking big or small?"

"Both," I said with a smile.

"Then you'd better hit me with the smaller one first while I sit down for the other."

I laughed. "Monty and I just rescued Mia from the hone-onna, and we were wondering if you and Eli could protect her and Aiden for a few days."

"Mia *and* Aiden? You're not setting yourself up for heartbreak much, are you?"

"Aiden swears he would never resume their relationship, and I believe him."

"Which was a neat sideways step on the heartbreak comment."

"And you know why."

He sighed. "I do. But I am at heart a romantic soul who keeps hoping this one will turn out."

"All good romances eventually do," I said, keeping my voice deliberately light. "But there's always a black moment, when the whole thing goes to shit, and there's never a guarantee that things will work out."

And sometimes, in the books that were often called romances but were actually love stories, a happy ending definitely *wasn't* on the cards. Ever.

Despite all my psi skills, I had absolutely no idea whether my story would in the end be a romance or a love story.

"What's the second request?" Ashworth said.

"I managed to pick up a bit of the hone-onna's bone—"

"Did you now," he cut in. "That *is* interesting."

I frowned. "Why?"

"Because the hone-onna is a spirit—"

"A skeleton spirit, which means they do have bones."

"A technicality, and one that is actually up for debate. I've been reading up on them, and there are many who believe their skeletal presence is no more real than the other forms they can project."

"They're real enough to have sex—just ask their victims. And I can absolutely confirm that they do have bones, because when I kicked her leg, it was definitely solid and she definitely yelped."

"Just because they can attain a form doesn't mean they can maintain it permanently," he said. "And let's be honest here, a mere kick should not have caused a piece of bone to shear off like that. If it did, then it's because she wished it. I take it you now possess said bone?"

"I do, but why would she deliberately lose a chunk of leg? Surely she couldn't track me through it?"

"With dark spirits, one never knows, but it is unlikely. Did you get any reaction when you touched it?"

"I did, and that's the other reason I'm ringing. I saw a woman I suspect is the witch who called the hone-onna into our lives."

"And that is again very interesting."

"Because?"

"Because it suggests she might not be a willing participant in this hunt."

"A summoning is by its very nature a means of bending a dark spirit or a demon to your will. Doesn't that imply most aren't willing participants?"

"It depends on the practitioner and the words used in the summoning spell. Those who wish a longer life would never deign to treat spirits or demons as anything less than equals."

"I'm betting there's plenty of sorcerers who wouldn't agree with that statement."

"And most of them end up dead."

Like the one who'd killed my sister and who almost succeeded in taking my life. Though his body had never been found, plenty of his blood had. The high council had eventually declared that the demons he'd trafficked with had taken advantage of his weakened state and torn him apart.

My psi dreams had been telling me for years this wasn't true, but then, my psi dreams also tended to be overly dramatic.

"Even if the hone-onna *is* an unwilling participant in the hunt, why would she be showing me the witch? Why wouldn't she just go about her bloody business and then move on?"

"It is not unknown for witches who tread the dark path to be so twisted by the magic they call into being that their ability to think logically deserts them."

"Which is a roundabout way of saying ... what?"

He laughed. "It could be that this witch has decided there is no end game. Perhaps she has decided that all cheaters must pay, not just the person the hone-onna was summoned to hunt."

A chill went through me. That certainly appeared to be what was happening now. "But surely the longer the witch holds the hone-onna's leash, the greater the chances of her slipping up? No witch can hold a spell—or a spirit—for long. It'll sap your strength and eventually kill."

I knew *that* from the few times Belle had summoned dark spirits.

"If she used her own magic, yes. But if she uses blood magic, then no. All she'd have to do is refresh the sacrifice, and the spirit remains on the leash."

"How hard would it be to find her circle?"

"On a scale of one to ten, it'd be fifteen."

I laughed. "If I send you a description, would you be able to arrange a search through the high council's dark witch register and see if she's there?"

"Of course, but there is a strong possibility she won't be. Few witches strong enough to summon such a spirit would be caught in a backwater such as this."

"You moved into this backwater, remember."

"Because I'm close to retirement and people I care about happen to live here."

"Not to mention the lure of unforgettable cakes and scones."

He laughed. "There *are* a couple of witches who sneak in ahead of them, but only by a smidge."

"I'm sure Monty will be pleased to hear that."

"You know well enough who I mean, lass. But enough of this guff—why do you think the summoner remains here? Did you get more than just an image when you picked up the bone?"

"No, but she's got the coloring of a royal witch, and she's around my age."

"That doesn't explain why you believe—"

"It does," I cut in, "if the hone-onna saw me from a distance and thought I was the witch who'd summoned her."

"Possible, but the leash really should have told her you were not holding the other end."

"What if the leash is tied to the altar rather than the witch?"

"Again possible."

"It would not only explain the rollover, but also why she'd run from Monty and me rather than magically combatting us. If she'd believed I was the one holding her leash, she wouldn't have dared risk a direct attack."

"Spirits can attack aplenty if they get desperate or angry enough."

"This one isn't desperate. She's just furious."

"Which makes her all the more dangerous, lass."

"All dark spirits are dangerous, but I think this one is willing to negotiate."

He snorted. "It's never wise to negotiate one on one with darkness, because it rarely ends well. That's why the leashes are employed."

"This one saved a kid, Ashworth. A *human* kid. I'm

willing to bet that she'd be happy to leave this reservation in exchange for her freedom."

He was silent for a second. "While I never advocate allowing darkness to walk free, perhaps in this case it might be worth investigating."

"It's a better option than trying to track and kill the hone-onna."

"I think you'll find the witch won't be any easier to take down."

"Yeah, but at least she's human."

"Which won't give us any edge. Not if we're dealing with a full-blood royal witch gone rogue." He paused, and then added in a sterner tone, "And if we *are*, you are not to hunt her alone. It might well take the four of us to cage her."

"There's one problem in that statement—we can't risk leaving Mia or Aiden unattended."

"Don't you mean unprotected?"

I grimaced at the slip of the tongue. It seemed that for all my protestations of trust, there was some inner—probably green—streak that didn't. Or maybe I just didn't trust fate not to throw another spanner in the works. "Of course I do."

He chuckled softly. "This place is safe enough from the likes of a hone-onna on a short-term basis. But I'd nevertheless advise against any attempt to read that bone here. As much as I'd be interested in seeing the results firsthand, it might well draw us to the attention of the hone-onna *and* the royal witch."

"I wasn't intending to." Our café was the safest place in the entire reservation when it came to dealing with—or even seeking—spirits of any kind, thanks to the protections around it *and* the reading room. And the latter had been specifically designed with darker forces—no matter what type—in mind.

"Good." He paused. "How exactly are you going to convince Aiden to remain here? Because we both know what his instinctive response will be."

"I've broached the subject, and he did refuse. But his only other choice is to stay at the café, and I really don't want to risk drawing the hone-onna there."

"A statement I rather suspect is both the truth and a lie," Ashworth commented.

The man was too canny for my own good sometimes. I sighed. "There're already too many good memories of him and me there, Ashworth. I don't need any more battering my senses if our relationship goes ass up."

"A point *I* can understand, but one I doubt he will. The man has a deep aversion to confronting the emotional side of life."

"Only with non-werewolves," I muttered, then quickly added, "I'm not sure when we'll get there—Mia was involved in a car rollover, so we're currently at the hospital getting her checked out."

"That's no problem, as neither of us are going anywhere."

"Thanks, Ashworth."

He bid me goodbye and hung up. I shoved the phone away then opened the glove compartment and raided the stash of chocolate and energy bars Aiden kept there specifically for me. A couple of Picnic bars at least toned down the idiots in my head but didn't do much against the growing wave of tiredness. I locked the doors, then grabbed my coat, balled it up, and propped it against the window to use as a pillow. I was asleep within minutes.

A sharp rapping on the window startled me awake

hours later. A squeak of surprise escaped, and I sat bolt upright, blinking rapidly for several seconds while my mind scrambled to shake sleep and start functioning.

"Sorry," Aiden said from the driver side of the truck. "Didn't mean to frighten you."

I leaned across and unlocked the door. "Then you shouldn't have pounded the window so damn hard."

"I very lightly tapped a fingernail. That's hardly pounding." He jumped in, then leaned across the center console, wrapped a hand around my neck, and held me still while he kissed me very, very thoroughly. "You taste like chocolate."

"I raided the stash."

"Then I shall restock tomorrow." His gaze scanned mine. "How's that headache?"

I raised an eyebrow. "How do you know I have a headache?"

"Your eyes get bloodshot when things are bad. Did you take anything stronger than Panadol?"

"Didn't have anything stronger."

"Then I'll add that to the stash." He pulled back. "I've been in to see Mia. They're still waiting for the final clearance from the doctors, but they shouldn't be much longer. Have you decided where she's going?"

"Not just her—"

"I will *not* go into hiding—"

"It's not hiding, and if it were anyone else in your team, you'd be demanding they stop being childish and just do it."

Annoyance flashed through his expression. He did *not* like being called out. "True."

"And it might not be for very long anyway," I added. "We've got a fragment of bone from the hone-onna—"

"How the hell did you get that?"

"I kicked her."

"That must have been a hell of a kick."

"Ashworth seems to think the fracture was deliberate."

"Why on earth would she deliberately break off a bit of limb?"

"That is the million-dollar question." I shrugged. "Anyway, it's possible we can use it to track either the witch responsible for the curse or the hone-onna herself. But to do either, I need to know you're safe."

He blew out a breath. "Fine. Twenty-four hours, then. No more."

I leaned forward and kissed him. "Thank you."

He rolled his eyes. "It was either give in or have you nag me for the next twenty-four hours."

"Very true."

He snorted. "So where are we spending our time in protective custody? The café? It's the safest spot around here, isn't it?"

"It is," I said, and repeated the earlier half-lie I'd told Ashworth. "You'll both be staying with Ashworth and Eli."

"Where he can keep an eye and ear on Mia and me and report back?" he asked, his mild tone at odds with the deepening annoyance.

"You know Ashworth would never do something like that."

"I know of no such thing. Ashworth basically considers you the granddaughter he never had, and he'll certainly have something to say about anyone who hurts you."

I raised my eyebrows. "Which won't happen in this particular case because you and Mia are finished, are you not?"

"We are." His gaze searched mine. "You know I'd never lie about something like that, don't you?"

"I do." And I did. But Mia wasn't the real problem here;

she was just a flesh-and-blood representation of it. "Has the team had a chance to talk to the other exes yet?"

"A rather unsubtle change of direction there, Liz."

"I'm not in the mood for deep and meaningful tonight."

He looked ready to argue, but in the end, simply said, "Yes. All swear they went nowhere near a witch."

"And none of them were witches themselves?"

"Not that I know of, but you lot can magic away those tells, can't you?"

I nodded. "Did any of them have a nasty scar down the side of their face?"

"No." He frowned. "Why?"

"Because when I picked up the bit of bone from the hone-onna's leg, I saw the image of a witch who is probably responsible for her presence here in the reservation. From a distance, she looks like me."

"And is that why the hone-onna attacked you?"

"Possibly. We're going to use the bit of bone in an attempt to track the witch."

"How? It's from the hone-onna, not the witch."

"Yes, but if the witch I saw is responsible for the hone-onna's presence here in the reservation, then she'll have some kind of controlling leash around her creature. If I can make a connection with the hone-onna, I might be able to trace that leash back to the witch's location."

"That's a few too many ifs for my liking."

"And mine, but we have to try, otherwise more people are going to die."

He did not look happy but didn't offer any more arguments either. Perhaps he knew the futility. "I take it you're going to attempt that after you drop us off at Ashworth's?"

I hesitated and then shook my head. "I've a booming headache, so it's probably better to wait until the morning."

"And if the hone-onna—or the witch who controls her—doesn't give you that option?"

"We'll deal with it." I paused. "How's your brother? Any improvement since yesterday?"

"If you don't want to talk about it, just say so, Liz. Don't change the goddamn subject like that."

I sighed. "Aiden, what else did you want me to say? You know we can't predict what will happen. You know we'll be as well prepared as we possibly can be. And we're both well aware that your annoyance stems not from my changing the subject but the fact that you can't be there, despite knowing full well your presence at the reading attempt could well endanger us all."

A muscle ticked in his cheek for several long seconds, then he looked away. "You're right, of course. But it's natural for a wolf to protect their pack—"

"I'm not pack," I cut in softly. "And never will be."

"You're in a relationship with me," he growled. "That makes you part of *my* pack."

"But only peripherally. And only when it doesn't involve your 'real' pack."

"Neither fact negates the truth of what I said. Damn it, Liz, you know how I feel about you."

"Yes, but I'm beginning to wonder if the same can be said about you."

"What the hell is that supposed to mean?"

"You know what it means." I glanced around at the sound of footsteps and saw Monty and Mia walking toward us. "I think we'd better finish this discussion at a better time."

"As you've noted, is there ever going to be a better time? I get the feeling you're now intent on avoiding it."

"And you would be right, but only because I'd rather get through this disaster before I embark on another."

"We're hardly a disaster, Liz. Quite the opposite, in fact."

"Your mother would disagree."

"My mother can take a long jump off a very short pier. As I keep telling you, she doesn't control my life."

"While in the end that might be true, pack life and expectations always will."

"I cannot change what I am."

"I'm not asking you to."

"Then what the hell are you asking?"

"Nothing." Everything. I forced a smile and glanced around as Monty opened the door for Mia and she climbed into the back seat. "You okay?"

"I said I would be." Her nostrils flared and her gaze narrowed. "I'm sensing a little tension in the air here."

"That's natural, given what we're dealing with." I switched my gaze to Monty as he climbed into the other side of the truck. "Ashworth has given the all clear for his place to be used as a refuge."

"Ah," Mia murmured. "That would no doubt explain the tension. Our alpha is displeased."

"Over more than just this situation." Aiden fired up the truck and reversed out. The headlights came on automatically, casting the evening shadows from the road. "But I meant what I said earlier, Mia."

"Oh, on that I'm left with no doubt." Her voice was dry. "Especially given your mother rescinded her invitation this morning. Courtesy and good manners appear to be seriously lacking amongst the O'Connor pack alphas."

"Perhaps we just don't enjoy being played."

"I wasn't the one playing games; not this time."

"I'm aware of that."

"And yet you're still bitterly angry at me. Why is that, Aiden? Is my presence forcing you to confront the realities you've been side-stepping?"

I sucked in a breath. Mia wasn't exactly holding back, but I could understand why, given the situation she'd found herself in. Granted, if she'd understood *anything* at all about Aiden she would have known he'd have never issued that invitation or rescinded his rejection of her, but I guess they'd both been a lot younger when they'd been together. How many of us really understood relationships in our early twenties? Hell, I didn't understand them *now*.

"I'm not side-stepping anything." His voice was only a fraction above a growl. "And I'll kindly ask that you keep your opinions on situations you don't understand to yourself."

Mia snorted. "And there, in one sentence, is the alpha ostrich in full display."

Never in a million years would I have thought the wolf who'd once held his heart would be fighting on the same side as me. Although in truth, she wasn't so much supporting me as pushing him to face his responsibilities both to the pack and his parents.

Silence fell, though it was a far from comfortable one. Ashworth and Eli were in for a fun twenty-four hours if the current wash of emotions was anything to go by.

Aiden pulled up in front of Ashworth's cute cottage but left the engine running. "I take it you and Monty aren't coming in?"

I shook my head. "I need to go home and rest. We'll do the reading on the bone in the morning."

"Let me know how it goes."

He opened the door and jumped out before I could

answer and without a kiss goodbye. Part of me wondered if it'd simply slipped his mind, or if Mia's presence—the fact that she was a wolf, even if not from his pack—was the problem. He'd never been one for overt public displays, and I'd always put that down to his nature and professionalism. But what if it was neither? What if it was, in fact, due more to my humanity? I wasn't pack, so therefore public displays of affection were considered ... unwarranted. You couldn't publicly claim what you had no intention of keeping.

Mia climbed out of the truck and followed Aiden through the gate and onto the covered porch. Ashworth opened the door as they approached and then stepped to one side and bid them enter. He gave me a wave and a thumbs-up. Aiden was right about one thing—nothing untoward would be happening under Ashworth's watchful eye. Not even an argument.

Monty reclaimed the driver seat and, after waiting for some traffic to pass, turned around and headed back to the café. "What time do you want us there for the reading in the morning?"

I hesitated. "Sevenish? That'll still give us plenty of time to get the café ready if the reading turns out to be a bust."

He nodded. "You're not going after this thing alone—you do realize that, don't you?"

I couldn't help a chuckle. "I've already had that particular lecture from Ashworth. Besides, I'm not that stupid."

"I know, but there's nevertheless a reckless streak in you, and if something happened overnight, you'd be out investigating immediately rather than waiting for the rest of us."

I raised my eyebrows. "What makes you think something will happen overnight?"

"Because something always does when you least expect it in this place."

"Well, I'll be praying to any god that's listening that is *not* the case. I need my beauty sleep." Devilment stirred, and a smile twitched my lips. "Not that you'd know much about *that* of late."

"A truth I cannot deny," he said. "And long may it continue."

I snorted and unclipped the seat belt as he pulled up in front of the café. "You coming in?"

He shook his head. "Got a message as we were leaving the hospital—Belle's cooking tea as we speak."

"Then I'll see you both in the morning. But please, do be careful with Aiden's truck."

"Have no fear—I shall treat it as gently as I treat the Mustang."

I snorted, grabbed my gear, and climbed out. After waving goodbye, I pulled out my keys and opened the front door.

But as I stepped over the threshold, I felt it.

Darkness. Death.

And once again, it was behind me.

CHAPTER TWELVE

I curled my fingers against the instinctive surge of energy and turned around. Neither she nor her magic could reach me in this place; it had withstood the assaults of two of the strongest witches in Canberra. No matter how powerful she was, she wouldn't succeed where my father and Clayton had failed.

With the bright flow of the spell threads that were protecting the café standing between the spirit and me, I calmly scanned the shadow-infested street.

While I didn't immediately see her, the caress of darkness seemed to be coming from the small lane on the other side of the road. I studied the old two-story building directly opposite; it was currently empty and up for sale, but there was no indication anyone or anything had breached its boundaries, either physically or magically. A quick check on the funeral director's that lay on the other side of the small lane came up with the exact same result.

Which meant she was somewhere in the lane itself, out of immediate sight.

There was no way known I was going to step out and

hunt her down, however. Monty might be right about that streak of recklessness, but the streak of self-preservation was definitely stronger right now.

"I know you're out there." I only raised my voice a fraction. The evening was quiet, and I had no doubt she'd hear me. "What do you want?"

For several seconds, there was no response. Then a cool whispery voice said, "Freedom."

I narrowed my gaze and stared at the darkness gathering in the lane. After a moment, I spotted a brief flicker of magic. It was the tail end of a rather powerful concealment spell. Part of me couldn't help but wonder if that flicker had been deliberate.

"From what? The witch who leashes you?"

"Yes."

"And you want my help?"

"Yes."

"Then why did you try to kill me?"

"Thought you her."

Meaning my instincts had been spot-on. "So, this witch who looks like me—she's in the reservation?"

"Yes."

"Where?"

"Cannot say. Leash prevents."

The reply was accompanied by a fierce wave of anger at the lack of free will and her inability to refuse the kill order.

To be honest, there was a part of me that could totally sympathize with that anger, especially given my own history when it came to free will. But that was a very dangerous voice to listen to in a situation like this.

"And you wish to be free of this leash?"

"Yes. Hates being forced."

Killing on her own terms was obviously okay. But then,

she *was* a dark spirit—that's what they did. "I was under the impression that dark spirits such as yourself were attracted to curses and summonings that involved those who stray. Why is this any different?"

"This more. This never ends."

I frowned. "How long have you been leashed?"

"Months."

Which meant the witch had been using the hone-onna to kill cheaters well before they'd ever ventured into this reservation. It also meant she was definitely using blood to strengthen her magic—there was no other way she could keep the leash strong enough to contain the hone-onna over such a long period of time.

And all *that*, by necessity, meant her altar had to be located within the reservation but away from the compounds—wolves could catch the scent of blood from miles away.

"If we hunt this witch down and destroy your leash, what guarantee do we have that you won't remain in this place and keep killing?"

"Not comfortable here. Too open."

"Which doesn't answer the question."

"Would trust if did?"

To be honest, no, but it was at least worth a shot. "We will kill you if you don't leave."

"A challenge? Like. But death? Not ready for final darkness yet."

Which wasn't an agreement to leave, but might be as close as we got. "Do you know where the witch keeps her circle?"

"In hills."

"Which hills? There're a hell of a lot of them in this place."

"Near hot springs. More cannot say. Leash prevents."

The witch had certainly woven a whole network of rules and compliances into her spell. But again, I guess that wasn't surprising, given what she was attempting to control long-term. "Do you intend to kill her if we do manage to remove the leash?"

"If lives past removal, yes."

Did that mean the leash was somehow tied to the witch's life force? I knew it was theoretically possible, but I hadn't ever heard of anyone actually doing it—especially when they were also using blood magic.

Monty's looped around and is now standing at the other end of the lane came Belle's thought. *How do you want to play this?*

I don't think we should be playing it any way. I think we should just let her be and concentrate on the witch who holds the leash. Otherwise, these killings won't stop.

At the very least, we need to be able to track her. If we can't stop her until we find the witch, then we can at least prevent her kills.

Nice theory. Not sure it'll work.

"Know other witch close," the hone-onna said. "Attack me, will respond."

"If you want our help," I said bluntly, "we need to stop the killings."

"Cannot. Not in control."

"You control the way in which you kill, do you not?"

"Sometimes. Witch intervenes."

"When it's a woman?" I guessed.

"Yes."

That would definitely explain why Ms. Taylor had been utterly torn apart but the men had not. "Why does your witch want the women treated differently?"

"Once betrayed."

Which at least confirmed what we'd been presuming. "Here?"

"No. Another reservation."

"Meaning she was betrayed by a wolf?"

"Yes."

My confusion deepened. "Then why come here? Especially when none of those killed were werewolves?"

"First was."

Meaning there was another kill out there? One we hadn't found? Crap. "Where did that happen?"

"Won't find. Destroyed."

Obviously not by a spell bomb, then, because someone would surely have reported the explosion to the rangers. But if her very first victim *had* been a werewolf, why had no one been reported missing? Given pack mentality, that was definitely unusual.

"Look, we need to stop the killing. If we place a tracker on you and follow your movements, we can protect your targets."

"No track. Won't allow."

She wouldn't? Or the witch wouldn't? I suspected the answer was a bit of both. This spirit may hate being leashed and controlled, but she wasn't against the actual killing.

"Then I cannot help you."

As I stepped back and started to close the door, she said, "Use bone. Will lower magic when sent on hunt. You read."

I hesitated. Psychically connecting with a dark spirit would undoubtedly hold more than a handful of dangers ... but if I was inside the reading room whenever I made the attempt, those dangers would at least be muted. It also meant I pretty much had to keep the damn bone on me twenty-four seven so I could be ready to track her movement at short notice.

"Won't the connection between you and it fade over time?"

"Not human. Spirit. Won't."

"Will it help me track the witch?"

"No. I go now."

And with that, she disappeared. Totally and utterly. There wasn't even a hint or surge of magic.

Well, fuck, Belle said. *If she can do that, she's far stronger than we've been presuming.*

I reached into my coat pocket, drew out the tissue-wrapped bit of bone, and unwrapped it. It felt warm and oddly heavy against my palm, but I wasn't getting any distinct images from it this time. I wasn't even getting anything to suggest I'd be able to track her. It wasn't dead; it was just inert.

I wrapped it up again. *Is Monty coming back here or continuing home?*

Home. The rump roast is just about ready to serve.

A roast? You're spoiling him.

Amusement rippled down the mental line. *No, just ensuring he has plenty of red meat to keep his strength up.*

Oh, I don't think there's any danger of his libido faltering anytime soon.

Probably not, but it never hurts to be safe. Go rest. You need it.

I will. I closed and locked the front door. *It's probably pointless coming in too early tomorrow now. It appears we're not going to be able to track the hone-onna until she actually wishes it.*

Cool, she said, and mentally signed off.

I blew out a breath and then headed into the kitchen to

grab something out of the fridge for dinner. There was nothing that really excited my taste buds, so I grabbed a bit of scotch fillet steak to cook and then slapped it onto a bit of well-buttered toast, poured on some tomato sauce, and put another slice of toast on top. Heaven on a stick ... or in this case, in between bread.

Once I'd made a coffee to go with it, I headed toward the stairs. But as I passed the reading room, instinct stirred. If I could locate the hone-onna through the bit of bone, then it was more than possible she could use it to track me. And, in fact, probably had, given her well-timed appearance just as I was entering the café.

If she could do that, it was possible the witch who held her leash might also be able to. While I had no idea how closely she was paying attention to the hone-onna's movements, I really didn't want the bitch tracking me down here. Though, in truth, it might be all too late to be worrying about that.

Even so, I headed into the reading room. After placing a minor alarm spell around the bone sliver so I'd know if it activated, I tucked it safely in one of the storage boxes hidden behind the bookcase. Then I went upstairs to eat and watch some mindless TV before heading to bed.

But once again, I dreamed of that blonde-haired little girl with eyes the same glorious color as Aiden's. Her presence was so damn real, so damn close, that it felt like I could reach out and touch her.

It seemed my dreams were really determined to mess with my head.

The first thing I did the following morning was go into the reading room to check on the bone sliver. It remained warm to the touch, but I wasn't getting anything in the way of location or images. I hesitated, and then tucked it back into the box. While the hone-onna had suggested keeping it on me, she was a dark spirit and I wasn't about to fully trust her, even if instinct was suggesting that she wasn't intent on killing me.

At least not yet.

We opened the café at eight and had a fairly steady flow of customers throughout the morning, which made a nice change after the last few days. I continued to check the bone throughout the day, just in case the alarm spell wasn't working, but the stupid thing remained inert.

At least it did right up until closing time.

The images that hit the minute the fragment touched my skin were so fast and furious I simply let them reel through my mind and hoped like hell that I could remember them all later. *A circle. A stone altar. Several large hares slaughtered by a knife that gleamed with a silvery-blue fire. Blood dripping onto a heavily stained altar, energizing the words of a spell that sang through the air and vibrated with power.*

It was a call to action. A call to kill. And the hone-onna was already responding, even if against her will.

But the flow of images hadn't finished with me yet, and what I saw next chilled me to the core.

A woman with a slender build, dark hair, and green eyes. A woman who was very heavily pregnant.

The witch was upping the ante.

The images pulled away from the woman, revealing the house in which she lived, then the number, and then finally the street.

Monty's two minutes away came Belle's comment. *You have time to get there.*

That's debatable, given Woodbury is twenty minutes out of Castle Rock. I picked up our backpack and added extra charms, potions, and holy water. I had no idea if any of them would deter so strong a spirit, but if our magic failed, they were better than nothing.

It will depend on how fast she moves and whether she's in the Woodbury area, Belle said. *But from the rush of anger in those images, I can't see her hurrying.*

She may not have a choice when it comes to timing. The witch seemed pretty determined the kill happen this afternoon.

Which means the witch must be scouting the locations before she sends her creature in, Belle said. *How else would she know all that detail?*

She must also be using some form of spell to hunt transgressors down. She couldn't possibly find these people any other way.

Well, PIs are well experienced in this sort of thing, but it wouldn't make sense for her to be employing one.

Not when she's killing the victims once she uncovers them. I slung the pack over my shoulder and strode out of the reading room. "Can you ring Tala and tell her what's going on? Warn her not to come near the place until we give the all clear."

"Will do." She hesitated. "Be careful, won't you?"

"She wants my help, Belle. She won't hurt me."

"Yeah, but I'm betting the witch who holds her leash won't feel the same."

"Probably not." I unlocked and opened the door. "When you're on the line to Tala, could you also ask her to give us a list of all the mineral springs in the area?"

"I'm thinking there will be more than a few of those, given that's what this area is famous for."

"Undoubtedly, but we can discount any that are near the compounds. This witch has had her altar set up for some time, so it's obviously in a fairly remote location."

Otherwise, the wolves would definitely have caught its scent. There was too much old blood staining the stone for the smell not to be obvious.

"Will do."

Aiden's truck came skidding around the corner, the lights and siren on. A smile tugged at my lips. "I think your boyfriend might be living out his childhood dreams right now."

"There's no might about it." Amusement flowed through the mental lines. "Don't let him hurt himself. You know how he gets."

"He has every intention of marrying you. He's not going to do anything daft, trust me on that."

She snorted and pushed me out the door. "Go. If you need anything, I'm here."

The truck slid to a stop, but Monty didn't lean across to open the door as Aiden usually did. But then, I was family, not the woman he wanted to marry. I jumped in, threw the pack into the footwell, and then clipped on the seat belt.

He immediately took off. "I did a search on the address. The owner is a Mrs. Joanna Rankin."

He raised his voice to be sure I heard him over the screaming siren, but it wasn't really necessary. Not these days.

"She's married? That surprises me."

"Why? Women might not cheat as often as men, but it does happen."

"I know, but she's pregnant—"

"Belle didn't mention that," he cut in brusquely.

"Because it doesn't make a difference in the scheme of things."

"I know, but still—" He stopped, took a deep breath, and then released it slowly, as if to counter his anger. "How far away is the hone-onna from her target?"

I fished the tissue-wrapped bit of bone out of my pocket. Again the images hit, but this time they were little more than a blur. She was moving at speed through a forest, but more than that, I really couldn't say. Mostly, I suspected, because the sheer weight of her anger was blocking the signal.

She might be a dark spirit, she might be a creature who killed, but she nevertheless had her boundaries—a point she would not go past.

Children, be they born or not, were her line in the sand.

"Lizzie?" Monty said, voice soft but wary.

I jumped and blinked. "Sorry. Just trying to sort through the images."

"Anything useful."

"She's moving fast but not as fast as she did last night. She's attempting to give us time to get there."

"Because of the half-baked agreement she made with us?"

"Because she doesn't want to murder an unborn child."

He swore. Several times. "We really have to stop this bitch."

The bitch he was talking about this time was the witch, not the hone-onna. "Yes. But the reservation is a big place, and she's had more than enough time to set up her defenses."

"You can't set the wild magic on an investigative hunt? That'd surely be the easiest way to at least find her altar, and it's something she wouldn't be expecting or guarded against."

I hesitated. I hadn't actually thought of doing that, and it might be worthwhile trying. And yet, at the same time, it was also dangerous. "The last thing we need is this witch thinking the wild magic is, in any way, controllable."

Especially when we had a second wellspring that no one as yet knew about.

"Even a witch powerful enough to control a dark spirit over the length of time this one apparently has isn't getting through the protections that now ring the wellspring."

It wasn't the main wellspring that I was worried about. While Katie and the soul of her witch husband did protect the second wellspring, neither had been tested yet. Not in any way. I really wanted to keep it that way.

"One thread," Monty said. "That's not dangerous, and it's unlikely to catch the witch's attention."

"I can try." Albeit reluctantly.

But he was right—it would be the quickest and easiest way to find the witch. Even if Tala came through with a small list of mineral springs, it would still take more hours than we could afford to check all of them.

The truck skidded right onto the highway that would lead us down to Woodbury. I wrapped my hand around the grab handle so tightly that my knuckles were white but, in truth, Monty was an excellent driver, even if he wasn't overly familiar with the truck.

I regularly checked the bone, especially once we drew close to the woman's address. The hone-onna was now following the winding path of a tree-shrouded river, giving us time but drawing inexorably closer.

We were cutting it fine. Real fine.

The victim's house lay in a street close to the football

field, which itself was too damn close to the river the hone-onna followed.

Monty swung left, the tires screaming and the big truck wobbling unsettlingly before he got it back under control and then sped on. There was a T-intersection up ahead, but he didn't slow. He just did another of those unsettling turns onto a rough old dirt road. Dust and dirt plumed behind us as we sped on.

The bone's pulsing increased. "She's close, Monty."

"How close?"

"Like, if I looked out the window, I might see the whites of her eyes close."

He didn't look up at the rearview mirror, and I certainly didn't want to.

"Then get a protection spell ready now, because I may not have time to construct one before she hits. Just make sure you weave in an exception for my magic this time, otherwise I won't be able to respond."

I nodded and started weaving a heavy-duty protection spell. By necessity that meant weaving in threads of personal wild magic, but I resisted the impulse to reach for the real stuff. If the witch connected to her creature in order to watch the kill—and I rather suspected she would, given her anger focused more on the women involved in the extramarital activities than the men—she'd see the threads of my inner wild magic. I just had to hope they were different enough from the reservation's that she wouldn't connect the two.

Monty hauled the truck right onto a stone driveway then accelerated toward the white weatherboard house perched on stumps tall enough to allow a car to park underneath.

He stopped in front of the stairs, threw the truck into

park, and then scrambled out without bothering to turn it off. I grabbed my pack and followed, bounding up the steps two at a time after him. He didn't knock on the front door or announce his presence in a calm manner; he just blasted it open with magic and yelled, "Mrs. Rankin, are you in the house? I'm Monty Ashworth, the reservation's witch. I believe your life is in danger, and we need you to leave with us immediately."

"What on earth are you talking about?" came the startled comment from the far end of the house. "Get out of my house before I call the rangers."

"The rangers are already on the way, Mrs. Rankin."

As he ran down the hall, the bone in my left hand pulsed, and images rose. We were out of time. The hone-onna was on the dirt road and only seconds away.

"Monty, get her in here now! I can't protect the whole house."

There was a squawk, a stream of curses, then the sharp rap of dual footsteps coming back down the hallway. As Monty appeared, dragging the heavily pregnant woman behind him, I unleashed my spell. It rolled swiftly through the room, covering not only all the doors and windows but also the floor and the ceiling in a net of pulsing power. I immediately activated it, then swung the pack around and pulled out the salt and holy water. I tossed the former to Monty, then slammed and locked the front door and popped the cork on the first bottle of holy water. Once I'd poured half of it in an unbroken line across the threshold, I raced over to the nearby window to repeat the process.

The hone-onna hit before I could get there. The sheer force of her attack sent me staggering sideways, but I somehow remained upright and pushed more energy into the netting. Another magical blow. A gasp escaped, and I dropped to my knees even as Monty's energy surged.

The threads of his spell flew over my head and pierced my protective netting. The hone-onna screamed, and her magic surged anew, the spell one I didn't immediately recognize. It hit Monty's caging spell, and the two exploded. As the broken threads of magic drifted past the window, he swore and quickly weaved a repelling spell—one so powerful it lit up the room.

The hone-onna continued to hit my protection net. Each blow hit like an invisible fist, making my body quiver and jerk. My net pulsed rapidly in response, but it held, even if the ache in my brain was getting steadily worse.

I ignored it all the best I could and, through slightly narrowed eyes, watched and repeated the spell Monty was creating. My version, however, was reinforced by my inner wild magic. It was a beast of a thing, and if it actually hit, it would fling her right across the reservation.

But that's exactly what we needed if we were to have any chance of getting Mrs. Rankin to safety.

Monty cast his spell. As it pierced my netting and speared toward the hone-onna, I cast my duplicate, keeping it close to the tail of Monty's in the vague hope she wouldn't immediately notice it.

The hone-onna screamed and flung another counter-spell. Once again, the two spells hit and then exploded, the blowback strong enough that the little ornaments on the nearby shelving unit shook. But the debris of those two spells hid mine, and it sped on through and hit the hone-onna square in the chest. For a second, nothing happened, but just as I started wondering if I'd done something wrong in the construction of it, there was small *whoomph*, and the hone-onna started screaming. It was a sound that became ever more distant. Despite those screams, despite the fury so evident in them, there was an odd wash of ... not really relief, but perhaps satisfaction ... coming from the bone fragment. A response from the hone-onna rather than the witch who controlled her, I suspected.

Monty sucked in a breath then ran over to me. "You okay?"

I nodded and clasped the hand he offered me, letting him help me up. "The force of her attack just caught me by surprise."

"Speaking of surprise," Mrs. Rankin said, "someone care to tell me what the fuck is going on? What was that thing outside? It sounded like a wild boar."

"Oh, it's *far* worse than a wild boar, and it will be back." Monty's voice was grim. "Do you want to pack a bag with enough clothes to last a few days? We need to get you out of here."

"I'm not going anywhere with you fucking two until you tell who you are and what is going on."

"Mrs. Rankin," I said, rather impatiently. "You're in danger. There's a witch out there in the reservation currently hunting down and killing everyone who's had an extramarital affair. You're on her list, and that means you either leave with us now or you stay here and wait for that fucking creature to come back and kill you."

Her face paled. "But I haven't—"

"Don't bother with denial, because it won't wash," Monty said. "We believe she's using a spell of some kind to track everyone who has strayed."

The woman swallowed. "But it happened nearly two years ago! My husband and I have reconciled—"

"The witch apparently doesn't care about small details

like that." I cocked my head for a second, listening. "The rangers are almost here. I'll go out and meet them."

"I thought you told them not to come in until we contacted them?" Monty said.

Belle mentally cleared her throat. *I rang and gave them the all clear. Saves time.*

I repeated that to Monty, then dismantled my protection net. The hone-onna had been tossed far enough away not to worry about now, and the—admittedly vague—input I was still receiving through the bone fragment suggested the witch wasn't close. Which in some ways surprised me. Given the serious hate-on she had for her female victims, I would have thought she'd want to witness the destruction firsthand rather than through the lens of her creature.

We are dealing with a witch both canny and strong enough to summon and control a dark spirit, Belle said. *She'd be aware of our presence in the reservation and wouldn't want to put herself in a situation where we could sense her.*

"So you really are connected to the rangers?" Mrs. Rankin was saying, her gaze moving between us.

"Yes," Monty said, with just a touch of impatience. "Now please, go get a bag ready."

She hesitated and then obeyed. Monty followed me out onto the front veranda. "Where are we going to stash her? Ashworth's?"

"He hasn't got any spare beds left, and given she looked ready to pop, a sofa isn't going to be optimal."

"We both know Aiden would give up his bed for her. Hell, Ashworth and Eli probably would, too."

"I know, it's just—" I paused and shrugged. "Holding too many eggs in one basket might just be a little too tempting for our witch."

"Then she has to stay at either your place or mine."

"The café is probably the better option. I can't imagine you or Belle wanting an intruder right now."

"We're not rabbits," he said, amused. "We can skip a night or two."

Speak for yourself came Belle's droll comment.

He laughed, so she'd obviously broadcast that wide. Which meant—given we were a fair way out of Castle Rock—her telepathic range was increasing when it came to reaching the minds of other people.

It could be another consequence of us using that restrictor spell and merging to battle the Empusa, she said. *If it is, it's one I'm not going to grumble about.*

No, if only because it'd make things a whole lot easier when it came to making emergency contact with Monty or the rangers.

The siren drew closer. I ran down the steps and over to the gate. A ranger SUV appeared around the corner, spraying dust and stones behind them in much the same manner we had not too long ago. I stepped out, waved them down, and then waited near the fence.

The SUV pulled to a halt, and Tala climbed out. Her gaze swept me, and relief crossed her expression. "Good to see you're all in one piece. Did the spirit attack?"

"Yes, but she was too powerful to kill. We resorted to tossing her to the other side of the reservation."

Tala laughed. "That'll work. At least for a little while, anyway."

I nodded. "We're going to place Mrs. Rankin into protective custody at the café. She should be safe enough there until we catch the witch behind this thing."

"What about her husband?"

"Unless he's strayed—and from what Mrs. Rankin has said, he didn't—he should be safe from retribution."

"Even so, we'll go grab him and shove him somewhere safe."

"We do need to keep the two separate, just in case the witch decides in the heat of the moment she has something against spouses that forgive." I turned and led the way toward the house. Tala fell in step beside me. "Did you manage to get a list of mineral springs for us?"

She tugged a folded bit of paper from her back pocket and handed it to me. "I pulled it from the Central Vic Mineral Springs GMA plan. Best I could do at short notice."

"GMA?"

"Sorry, groundwater management area."

"Ah. Thanks."

I unfolded it. It was a map of the entire reservation and detailed not only mineral springs, but also waterways and lakes. It didn't give precise locations, but I could probably use the wild magic for that once we were closer. The majority of the springs ringed Argyle and Rayburn Springs, which was unsurprising, but there was a smaller cluster between Woodbury and Campbell's Creek, and another up near the Marin compound in Maldoon.

"Any good?" she asked.

"Yes. It cuts down the search area, and that's the main thing right now." I folded the map back up. "Have there been any reports of missing wolves in the last week or so?"

She frowned. "No, why?"

"I was told that the *very* first victim was actually a werewolf. Apparently, his body was destroyed."

"Where? And who told you this?"

"She wouldn't say where—she being the hone-onna."

Incredulousness crossed Tala's expression. "You were speaking to her? And didn't kill her?"

"Trust me, if I could have, I would have."

Tala grunted, her expression a mix of disbelief and frustration. "And you trust she's telling the truth?"

"I do."

"Then we'll investigate."

Mrs. Rankin stepped out onto the porch, tugging a suitcase behind her. Monty locked the front door, then took the case and one-handedly helped her down the stairs.

"I'd better go talk to her," Tala said, and immediately jogged over.

Monty threw the suitcase in the back of the truck, then walked over to me.

I handed him the map. "I can send the wild magic into the Argyle area to check out the situation there—it'll be quicker, given how many springs are clustered around that area. But we should be able to do the rest."

He nodded and glanced at his watch. "By the time we get her back to the café and settled in, it'll probably be getting too late. The springs near Maldoon are probably the closest to Castle Rock, but it'll take twenty minutes to get there. There's too many old mines in that area to be clambering around in the dark."

"There are too many to be clambering around in daytime, too." The damn things were often difficult to see, especially if they were shafts that went straight down, rather than tunnels that ran diagonally into the hills.

He smiled. "This is why we take a ranger with us. They can lead the way and fall in first."

"I heard that," Tala said. "And if I fall in, I'm not going alone."

Monty laughed. “Wise move, actually. I can cast a spell and magic us out of there.”

“Good to know. What time do you want to meet tomorrow morning?”

I glanced at Monty. He was technically my boss, after all.

“About seven? If we meet at the café, Liz can make us all a coffee to take on the road.”

“Oh, can she now?” I said mildly.

“Yes, indeed, and being the kind, generous soul you are, you’d probably include a cheese and ham toastie. Or at least cake.”

I snorted and shoved him toward the car. “Let’s get going before you fall too far into that fantasy world of yours.”

He laughed. I nodded at Tala as she went back to her SUV, and then followed Monty. We were back on the road minutes later, with Mrs. Rankin an unhappy presence in the back seat. She didn’t say anything until we pulled into the parking area behind the café.

“I’m staying here?” Her voice was incredulous. “In a damn café?”

“There’s sleeping accommodation on the first floor,” I said as Monty stopped the truck, then jumped out and moved around to the rear. “This is the safest place for you to be if the dark spirit comes after you again. It’s absolutely smothered with magical protections.”

“Dark spirit?” she said. “I thought it was a witch?”

“It’s both.” I opened her door and helped her out of the truck. “Long story, but basically you’re toast if either of them get to you.”

Her face went pale again. “And is that likely? Will the protections here hold up?”

"Yes, they will. You can't leave the place, though, until we give you the all clear."

"That's going to be mighty inconvenient if I suddenly go into labor."

I blinked. "And is that likely to happen?"

"I'm due tomorrow."

Anger surged—not at her, but rather the situation she'd unwittingly found herself in—and I had to wriggle my fingers to release the sparks that burned at my fingertips. But I was having a hard time accepting that a damn dark spirit had more compassion and humanity than the witch who held her leash.

"Then let's hope your kid is in no hurry to greet the world," I said. "But just in case, I'll ask Tala to arrange for your doctor to be on standby."

"My sister is a certified midwife," she replied. "We'd planned for her to deliver the baby anyway, so it's probably best if she comes here, if that's at all possible. I would feel safer if she was with me."

So would I. I had absolutely no experience with babies, let alone the whole birthing thing. "As long as she doesn't mind a fold-down bed."

Mrs. Rankin smiled. "We've both slept in far worse in years past."

I unlocked the door, motioned them both inside, and then followed and turned on the lights so they didn't run into anything in the narrow hallway. "Ring her once we get upstairs, then, and we'll set things up."

"I will. Thank you."

Monty led the way, her suitcase in one hand as he climbed the stairs. Mrs. Rankin followed more slowly, gripping the handrail to both steady *and* haul herself up. That she struggled was no surprise, given she *was* due tomorrow.

I quickly dumped the backpack in the reading room and then followed, ready to give a gentle push if she faltered. She made it up the stairs a little out of breath but otherwise okay.

"Belle's room?" Monty asked, with a quick glance over his shoulder.

"Yep. The sheets have been changed, so it's all good."

Monty dropped the suitcase in Belle's bedroom, then stood aside as Mrs. Rankin waddled in. "Do you mind if I lie down for a while? It's a bit stressful."

"Sure," I said. "But ring your sister first, just in case."

She nodded and tugged her phone out of her pocket.

Monty glanced at me. "Will you be okay here alone?"

I half smiled. "Of course I will. Nothing is getting into this place unannounced. Not even a gnat."

"I know, it's just—" He hesitated. "I've got this feeling that now we've proven able to counter her creature—"

"Counter, not kill," I cut in. "Big difference."

"In the long run, I doubt it'll matter, especially when neither of them got the satisfaction of a kill this time."

"The hone-onna didn't *want* this kill."

He raised an eyebrow. "She's a dark spirit. They always want the kill."

"Not kids—not even unborn ones." I waved a hand. "Sorry, please do go on."

Amusement lurked in his silver eyes at the mock formality in my tone. "I think she'll intensify her efforts to kill everyone remaining on her list. Even if the hone-onna does continue to send us information, we can't protect or reach everyone."

"Perhaps, but the witch isn't going to be doing anything for the next twelve hours or so, at least." I might not know much about blood magic, but I had no doubt it, like most major spells, would take a serious toll on the practitioner's body. "It'll take time for her to recover from this casting."

"In normal circumstances yes. This witch isn't normal—I think that is becoming ever clearer."

He headed down the stairs. I followed him. "The thing is, there's nothing we can actually do about that until we find her altar."

"I know. I just wish there was some way we could alert possible victims."

"What, send out a reservation-wide warning?" I laughed at the thought. "Even if everyone did hear it, how many would actually admit to having an affair?"

"Well, none, but doing nothing is damnably frustrating."

"Then imagine how our head ranger is feeling."

He snorted. "Aiden is getting some much-needed thinking time. Let's hope he's using it wisely."

"He undoubtedly is, but there's absolutely no guarantee his decision will fall in my favor."

"He's a fucking fool if it doesn't."

I unlocked the back door and then gave him a quick, fierce hug. "Thank you. I appreciate the support."

And would no doubt need it, whether it be sooner or later.

"You're my favorite cousin," he said, voice a little gruff. "I don't want to see you hurt."

"Hurt is a fact of life, and in this particular situation, it's inescapable. And I knew that going in."

"Nothing is ever inescapable, Liz. He has the choice. It's just a matter of whether he has the balls."

I smiled. "He's an alpha wolf. He can't change that. Not for me, not for anyone."

He grunted—a clear sound of disagreement—then

kissed my cheek and left. I relocked the door, then headed back upstairs to make both Mrs. Rankin and myself a hot drink.

Her sister—Beverly—appeared two hours later. Once we'd all eaten—takeout, because I had no desire to cook this evening—I made up the fold-out sofa bed, then left them to it and headed downstairs. After making myself a big pot of tea, I reached out to the thread of wild magic that slowly circled the room. It responded instantly, pulsing with awareness and life as it wrapped gently around my wrist. It was from Katie's wellspring this time, not the larger one. I reached out, and she answered immediately.

Lizzie? Surprise echoed in her mental tone. *Is there a problem? Aside from the dark spirit that is currently on the rampage, that is.*

You could say so. Have you, through your threads, sighted any unusual activity in the Argyle or Rayburn Springs area?

Define unusual.

I couldn't help smiling. She very much sounded like Aiden at that moment, and pain stabbed through me. It wasn't until now that I realized he hadn't tried to contact me, not even to berate me for not letting him know how the bone reading went. Maybe he was still angry with me for dumping him at Ashworth's. And maybe, as Monty had said, he was using the time to contemplate what he wanted from our relationship.

If he wanted anything from it, that is.

We've a dark witch in the reservation—

Is she the reason the hone-onna is here?

Yes, I said, *and we believe she has a well-protected altar set up in a remote location near a mineral spring.*

I'll send out threads—

Only a couple, I cut in quickly. *We can't risk her realizing there's more to the wellsprings here than meets the eye.*

There is only one recognized wellspring.

Yes, but this witch has undoubtedly done her research, and she may well be aware of the main wellspring's resonance. She's clever enough to note the differences in the threads from your wellspring.

Katie was silent for a moment. *I can send a couple of threads from the main spring, but I do not have the control of them that I do with my own.*

Perhaps send one of yours accompanied by two of the others. That way, if she does spot them, she may just accept they're from the same wellspring.

After all, with all the protections around the main wellspring, she wouldn't have been able to examine it too closely —not without setting off alarms.

That might work. She paused for several seconds. *Gabe says that destroying an altar is no easy task and will require more force and knowledge than you can muster.*

I can muster a whole lot of force these days. There was no denying the lack of knowledge, however.

Yes, but you can't risk blowback staining the wild magic. Not given your growing connection with the main wellspring.

There, in one sentence, was confirmation of all my earlier fears. I drew in a deep breath that did little to actually calm the rise of tension. Though it wasn't like I could actually do anything to stop or even slow the ongoing merger. Not when I had no idea how it even really started, or why. It would perhaps have been understandable had the wellspring here been the one Mom had been sent to restrain and protect when she'd barely been pregnant with me, but it wasn't. But they *did* all have the same source—the deep earth—so maybe it was more the fact that this one had been similarly unrestrained when I'd first arrived on the reservation.

Monty will be able to destroy the altar—there is an entire unit dedicated to the subject at university, Katie continued, *but Gabe says it will take all his strength and that, by necessity, means you'll have to dismantle whatever protection rings she's running around the altar.*

I frowned. *As you've already noted, I don't have the knowledge. Not when it comes to a dark witch's magic.*

And while Monty undoubtedly knew the theory of dismantlement, he didn't have the experience. Ashworth and Eli undoubtedly *did*, but dare we risk pulling them off guard duty when the hone-onna still lurked out there?

Gabe says he'll guide you.

Via the partial merger again, I take it?

It was what we'd done to defeat Clayton. While Gabe's soul was irrevocably tied to the wellspring, he'd been able to partially merge with me—sharing my body space and senses to see the traps and spells that Clayton had set and guide me through them. It had drained us both, but it had been worth it.

And if it saved lives in this case, I was more than happy to give it another go.

Yes, Katie said. *It's the safest way.*

I nodded, though she was unlikely to see it given the thread was only being used as a communication method. *You'll send out the threads tonight?*

Within the hour. If anything is found, I'll contact you.

Thanks, Katie.

Welcome.

Her thoughts left mine. The thread unwound itself from my wrist and drifted away, though it didn't go all that far. Maybe Katie had told it to remain close in case she needed to contact me again.

I headed into the kitchen to check the stock levels and write up a list of what had to be ordered tomorrow, and then made a couple of different slices. Slices didn't keep forever, and there were five varieties in the cake fridge that would reach their use-by date over the next few days.

It was close to eleven by the time I took off my shoes and padded quietly up the stairs. The two women were asleep, and Mrs. Rankin was snoring quite loudly. Thankfully, my room was shielded against all manner of noise, be it physical *or* mental. It was one of the first things we'd done when we bought the place in order to give Belle refuge from the constant barrage of my thoughts.

After a quick hot shower, I tumbled into bed and was quickly asleep. For a change, my dreams were quiet. That in itself should have been warning enough.

Because at three in the morning, the wild magic woke me.

Katie had found the altar.

CHAPTER THIRTEEN

I sat bolt upright, my heart going a million miles an hour while my brain scrambled to catch up. *Katie? You've really found the altar?*

Yes. It's in the St. Leonard's forest area, just off one of the old walking tracks there.

I sent a quick message to Belle to get Monty out of bed and over here ASAP, and then hastily got dressed. *That doesn't sound like a very secure location. I thought it'd be more remote and deep in the forest.*

Or even in a damn mine. There were plenty of those about.

It doesn't need to be because few use the track, she replied. *That particular area was so heavily mined that even wolves need prior approval to go in there these days. Experienced guides do caving and mining tours over summer, but in winter the area is deserted.*

Which suggested the witch had done her research, and that the timing of her attacks were no mistake. I sat back down on the bed and tugged on my socks and boots. *So will we need a guide?*

No. I can guide you through the wild thread. You need to call it to you; this means of communication will drain us both too quickly otherwise.

I immediately did so. *I take it you're familiar with that area?*

No, but through my connection with the wild magic, I can devise a safe path.

If I fall down a mineshaft, I'm going to be pissed.

I won't let you fall down a shaft. She paused. *And if you do, I'll catch you.*

Hate to tell you this, but you're a soul locked to a wellspring. You can't catch anything.

She laughed. *I meant via the wild magic.*

That didn't fill me with a whole lot of confidence, given the ethereal nature of the wild magic. I swept up my phone and keys and headed out. There was a creak of springs, and then Beverly said softly, "Everything okay?"

"Yes. We finally have a lead on the witch who terrorized your sister. I've called in a friend and fellow witch—Belle—to keep an eye on things here, so if you hear a new voice, don't panic."

"I gather she doesn't need to be let in?"

"No. She's on her way over right now, so she'll be here before I leave."

"Okay. Thanks for letting me know."

I hadn't actually intended to, so it was just as well she'd woken up. I padded down to the reading room and filled the backpack with absolutely every magical charm and blessed item and every bottle of holy water we had. I had absolutely no idea what it took to destroy an altar, so overkill was a must.

Gabe said overkill probably won't be necessary if the

dismantlement and cleansing spells are done correctly, but it also won't hurt given what we're dealing with.

Always better safe than sorry has become my motto of late. I zipped up the now overstuffed pack. *The minute we start dismantlement, she's going to know.*

Yes, so speed is of the essence.

Speed often led to mistakes, in my limited experience. The growing closeness of Belle's thoughts told me she and Monty were only seconds away, so I slung the pack over my shoulder and headed toward the front door.

Contact me when you near Argyle, Katie said, then her awareness retreated.

I unlocked the front door but didn't move beyond the protections of the café's magic until Monty—once again in Aiden's truck—pulled up at the front. Belle jumped out, leaving the passenger door open as she strode across to me. "How's Mrs. Rankin?"

"Asleep and snoring."

"Just as well I'm not intending to sleep then." She gripped my arm. "I know I keep saying this, but be careful out there."

"Katie and Gabe will be with us. We'll be fine."

She groaned. "Will you stop tempting fate with proclamations like that?"

I grinned, squeezed her arm, and then ran over to the truck and climbed in.

"Where are we going?" Monty said as he pulled out into the empty street.

"Head for Argyle. Katie will give us more specific instructions once we get there. Gabe will help us disconnect whatever protection spells the witch might be running once we get close to the altar."

"Gabe? The dead husband?"

"Who's now a ghost and haunting the reservation. We did mention this, didn't we?" To be honest, I couldn't remember exactly what we'd told him. He knew about Katie, but not the second wellspring. Surely one of us must have mentioned Gabe in passing.

"Huh." He glanced at me briefly. "I've a feeling there's more to this story than what you're saying."

I shrugged. "There are many secrets in this reservation, and they're not all mine to tell."

He didn't say anything, but his aura suggested annoyance. I had a bad feeling I'd just set him on an information hunt, and Monty was the type not to let go until he'd uncovered every little secret.

We turned onto the highway and sped down to Argyle. It didn't take us as long as it would have during the day because the roads were all but empty, and Monty was once again making full use of lights and siren.

When we were a few minutes out, I reached out for Katie. *Just heading into Argyle now.*

At the roundabout, turn right, and follow that. When you reach St. Leonards—which is a blink-and-you'll-miss-it town —slow down and then turn right at Barkstead Road. Contact me again, and I'll guide you from there.

Her awareness departed again. Perhaps she was conserving both our strength. While I didn't yet have a headache, the promise of one was definitely lurking.

I repeated the instructions to Monty, and he nodded. We drove through Argyle's main retail sector at speed and followed the single lane road through the various twists, turns, and tiny towns. St. Leonards itself consisted of little more than six houses and a community hall. There wasn't a shop or even a post office. Monty glanced at the GPS and then slowed down and swung right into Barkstead Road. I immediately reached for Katie.

Okay, she said, *deepen the connection.*

I obeyed. It felt rather weird, because it wasn't just the telepathic link that strengthened but also a deepening of awareness and state. I was still me, but in many ways, I was also sharing all that I was with her—and vice versa. I also suspected it was *this* connection—one we'd done previously—that was responsible for the physical changes in me.

"Take the right fork up ahead," we said. "And kill the lights and sirens."

Monty did so, then shot me an alarmed look. "What's happening? You sound ... strange."

"Katie is with me, guiding me." This time, the reply was mine.

"How is that possible when you're not the one capable of spirit communing?"

"Long story, but it's happening through the wild magic." I paused, then we added, "The road gets rough and narrow up ahead. You need to slow."

He obeyed, then swore and wrenched the truck sideways to avoid a wombat that decided to stroll out in front of us. We skidded for several seconds before he brought it back under control.

The sheer thickness of the surrounding forest meant it was completely black out here; even if the moon had been out tonight, it was doubtful it would have helped all that much. The headlights, even on high beam, certainly weren't piercing the gloom too successfully. As for the road, well, rough and narrow was a definite understatement.

Katie retreated from our connection once again, briefly easing the physical toll on us both, but returned a few minutes later. We said, "Left-hand turn coming up. It's a tight fit."

Monty slowed and then, as the headlights picked out the turn, said, "That's not a fucking road–it's a walking track."

"The truck will fit."

He gave us a disbelieving look, slowed to a crawl, and carefully eased onto the smaller track. Branches scraped the side of the truck, and the trees were way too close for my liking, but we did fit.

We continued on at a snail's pace, Monty carefully guiding the truck down a path that was never designed for a vehicle this size.

After what seemed like forever but was probably only a couple of minutes, Katie's presence surged again, and we said, "Here. Stop here."

He did so, but didn't immediately turn off the truck, leaving the engine running and the headlights on while he studied the surrounding trees. "It's goddamn black out there. Even with flashlights, it'll be easy to get lost or fall down a mine."

"We won't let that happen."

He glanced at me, expression uncertain, then turned off the truck and climbed out. I did the same and swung the backpack over my shoulders and waited while he collected his pack from the back of the truck.

"Here," he said, offering me a flashlight.

"We don't need it. The wild magic guides us."

He dumped it on top of the hood instead of returning it to the rear of the truck. "Yeah, well, I'll still keep one. We may need it for the return journey."

"Oh, we definitely will," I said. "This merger is going to knock the hell out of both Katie and me, and I very much doubt either of us will be in any sort of position to guide us out."

Hell, I might not even be *conscious*.

"Then I'll pay close attention to where we're going."

Given he had very human eyes and senses, and the trees in place were a maze of similarly unremarkable trunks, we seriously doubted he'd succeed. But we held our tongue and, when he motioned us forward with a sweep of his hand, moved on.

Follow this path for five minutes, Katie said.

I glanced down and saw we were indeed on a track—one used by roos rather than humans, but a track nevertheless.

Her presence withdrew again, and I sucked in a deeper breath that did little to ease the slowly gathering ache in my head or the fear in my heart. But then, it was likely nothing would—not until we'd taken care of the witch who held the hone-onna's leash.

And maybe even the hone-onna herself.

Though it was inky-black amongst the trees, I had no trouble seeing. Katie's presence, however remote it currently was, had heightened my senses again. It was testament to just how far my sensory changes had to go before they truly reached that of a wolf.

When the five minutes were up, Katie came back online. *We're close to it now, but don't send out any sort of magical probe—she's laid intrusion spells.*

I stopped so fast, Monty had to do a quick side step to avoid me.

"The altar's just up ahead," I said. "But there's a network of warning spells between us and it."

He quickly scanned the area. "I'm not picking up anything just yet."

"Gabe says it's off to the left and its output is shielded," we said. "We can't risk a probe, and we won't see or hear it until we're almost on it."

If Gabe now haunted our connection, it would explain its sudden heaviness—and why my energy was fading at a faster rate.

I'm here if you need to syphon came Belle's comment.

Not unless it's absolutely necessary.

Or until you're almost dead, she grumbled, *because you're a pigheaded, stubborn woman.*

Takes one to know one, I replied, amused.

Concentrate came Katie's soft rebuke. Or Gabe's. It was hard to know which right now. *It gets dangerous from here.*

I sucked in another of those useless breaths and then slowly moved to the left, letting her senses guide me. After a few minutes, a very soft, somewhat irritating hum became evident.

"Hear that?" I said, glancing at Monty.

He nodded. "Its resonance suggests it's an alarm spell of some kind."

"Would she have used blood magic in its construction?"

"I'd have thought that overkill, but I'm also not a dark witch."

We'd only gone another couple of feet when the hum abruptly cut off. I didn't need Katie's sharp warning to stop. At first glance, there was no sign of a spell. It wasn't until I dropped my gaze and saw a slight shimmer that I realized the spells had been placed very low to the ground and were protected not only by scrub and rocks, but also by a covering spell. It had been so well constructed that the unwary—or those in a hurry—might not have even noticed it until they'd stumbled through it.

Monty squatted and studied the shimmer for several

very long seconds. "I can't see much thanks to that cover spell, but from the feel of it, it's going to take some strength to dismantle."

"You won't be dismantling it," we said. "You're the one with the knowledge and the means to cleanse and destroy the altar. We should handle this."

He shot me another of those incredulous glances. "I'm not sure—"

I reached out and grasped his arm. "Monty, you can't do everything, especially when you need to be fully powered to counter whatever protection measures our dark witch has around her altar."

He grimaced but didn't disagree. "So your plan is what, exactly? Because we both know that while you have the power, you don't have the knowledge to counter something like this."

"Gabe is going to partially merge with me. It'll allow him to see the spells clearly so he can guide me through dismantlement."

"Isn't merging with a spirit dangerous? What does it actually involve?"

"It's really not all that much different to me sharing sensory awareness with Belle. And she'll be in the background, keeping an eye on things. She'll split us if it becomes necessary."

He drew in a breath and released it slowly; it failed to budge the concern in his expression. "So, back to the current problem. I suspect there're multiple alarms woven into this bloody spell."

"Yes, but Gabe is confident we can get around them all."

"I hope that confidence isn't misplaced."

So did I. I hesitated, caught by a moment of uncertainty,

and then firmly reached out to Gabe. As Katie's presence faded into the background, his energy flooded the link and fused with mine. As before, it wasn't so deep that his spirit shared body space, but he could use his skill and direct my magic while seeing through my eyes.

And it still felt fucking weird. Felt like I was present in my body and yet standing apart.

You remain in control, Gabe said, *I'll only intervene as necessary*.

I knew that, but it didn't really help. Not before; not now.

I pushed the fear aside and concentrated on the spell that blocked our path. After a moment, we said, "Our best option isn't to dismantle the entire spell; it would take too much time and risk her becoming aware of our presence here. Instead, we'll just remove the cover spell and peel back the first five or six layers of the main spell. That should allow us to step over it without triggering it."

Monty nodded and motioned us to proceed. With Gabe's presence weighing on me heavily and guiding my actions, I carefully reached out and plucked the cover spell's initiating thread free. It felt foul—unclean—and my skin crawled. She might not have used blood magic in the construction of these layers, but it nevertheless stained her presence and her spells. And *that* suggested she'd been playing on the dark side for a very long time.

It took us five minutes to disconnect the cover spell, and its removal revealed the true complexity of the main one.

Monty sucked in a breath. "Fuck me."

"You're my cousin," I murmured absently. "It may be legal, but it would also be icky."

Monty snorted but otherwise didn't reply. Gabe studied the spell for several seconds and a wave of deep admiration washed through our thoughts. I could totally understand why—this spell was rich and deep, with a complex range of exclusions woven through it. Not only would no animal or bug trigger it, but it also treated regular humans different to witches and wolves. It would have taken her at least twenty-four hours to construct—if not longer—and meant Gabe had been right in wanting to avoid complete dismantlement. We simply didn't have the same luxury of time.

We reached out again, plucked the first thread free, and began to spell, the words falling silently from my lips, foreign and unknown. The initial layers were easy enough to detach and weave back through the threads lower down, but the deeper into the spell we got, the harder and more delicate the process became. Sweat trickled down the side of my face, but I didn't dare swipe at it. One wrong movement—hell, even breathing the wrong way right now—could prove disastrous.

Thankfully, the hum of the overall spell never altered, but by the time the initial trigger points had been dealt with, the little men with the hot pokers were back in business inside my head.

"Done," we said and pushed upright. "But let us go first, just in case."

I carefully stepped over the still-pulsing alarm spell, my breath catching deep in my throat and my heart galloping along so fast I swore it was about to tear out of my chest. Thankfully, the warning spell didn't so much as flicker. I glanced back at Monty. He followed me over the spell, echoing my movements precisely.

Again, no reaction.

Relief stirred, but it was Gabe's more than mine. Obviously, despite his outward confidence, he hadn't been one hundred percent sure the partial detachment would work.

And that relief might yet be misplaced. We were—magically *and* physically—a long way from being out of the woods just yet.

We continued on, our pace by necessity slow and careful. Only a few minutes further on, we came across a second alarm spell. I repeated the rerouting process, then swiped at the sweat stinging my eyes.

"I hope that's the last of them, because at this rate, I'm not going to have the strength to raise my own protection circle."

"You will," Monty said. "I have complete faith."

As have we, came Gabe's comment. *And you forget, I am with you, and I see what you cannot.*

Are we talking physical strength? Magic? Or something else entirely?

All. But now is not the time.

That was Katie, and, as before, she sounded altogether too much like her brother. Again the sadness stirred, but I ignored it and pushed on cautiously. There were no further alarm spells and nothing in the way of traps. Which didn't mean they wouldn't be here; we just hadn't sprung them yet.

The altar is fifty yards ahead, in a small clearing, Gabe said. *I suggest Monty create an outer protection circle while you do an inner one.*

Why not the other way around?

Because your circle will be the stronger of the two, thanks to the wild magic, Gabe said. *Let her waste time and energy dismantling Monty's circle before she gets to yours.*

But will the infusion of wild magic be enough to stop her?

That is an unknown, simply because up until now, no

witch has ever been able to use the wild magic in the way you can.

As far as we knew, anyway. It was possible, given the title of the book Eli was currently reading, that they had in the past. For reasons unknown, they'd not only stopped the practice but basically buried the knowledge.

I repeated Gabe's suggestion to Monty. He nodded and said, "Are there any more spells layered between us and the clearing?"

"There is one protecting the altar," we said. "But that's it."

"Then we'd better pick up the pace before she gets wise that something is happening."

"It'll take her time to get through this forest," I said.

"She's a dark witch. She can use a demonic form of transport. Or just send her creature."

Of the two, instinct suggested the second option was probably the safer. Instinct was obviously a little high on something.

The clearing was something of a mini amphitheater, with the steep but grassy sides running down to a flat, stony base. The altar had been placed in the middle of this and was very simply constructed—the two tall sturdy stones at either end supporting the black altar stone.

The stone isn't naturally black came Gabe's comment. *It's been stained that way over countless years by her sacrifices.*

Why on earth would she be dragging a heavy stone altar around with her? Why wouldn't she just create a new one at each location?

It may have some special significance to her. Perhaps after years of use, it has a resonance and power of its own, he replied. *Moving it would not be all that much of a problem to someone as powerful magically as she.*

I shivered and rubbed my arms, but it did little against the ice now gathering in my veins. The night was bitterly cold, but that ice was born from the fear that the three of us would not be enough to stop this witch.

Monty stopped beside me and swung off his backpack. Once he'd retrieved his spell stones, he said, "I'll run my circle around the edge of the clearing, as suggested. Do you want to start yours ten feet in and work in the opposite direction?"

I nodded, swung off my backpack, and tugged the small silk bag containing my spell stones free from the front pocket. These particular ones were rough-cut clear quartz; while Monty and most royal witches tended to use diamonds, quartz was cheaper and yet possessed very similar properties.

I tipped the stones into my palm and began the careful process of creating a protection circle. While Ashworth had taught me to make one without using these stones as an anchor, it wasn't one of my stronger spells and probably wouldn't last three seconds against this witch.

I placed each stone carefully, attached a multi-layered protection spell onto it, and then looped it back to the previous two stones—something I hadn't done before simply because I hadn't thought of it. I was only doing so now thanks to Eli saying during a conversation on protection circles that it helped strengthen the circle while stopping the possibility of breakage due to one stone being kicked out of line.

Once all the stones were lashed together, I added a glimmer spell to ensure I could find them all again, then stepped back and waited for Monty. He completed his circle a few seconds later and then activated it; the wave of his magic was so fierce and strong, it briefly burned my skin. He nodded in obvious satisfaction and moved down the hill toward me. Once he'd passed the line of my stones, I activated my circle but didn't entirely close it off, as Monty had his. I had a bad feeling I'd need to throw more strength into it before this nightmare was over.

Good circle came Gabe's comment. *It'll be interesting just how well the infusion of your personal wild magic copes against the power of a dark witch.*

If it doesn't cope, we're all going to be in deep shit.

Well, Monty and I were, at any rate. It wasn't like the witch could actually harm either of them.

I turned and followed Monty down the hill. The circle around the altar was visible and fairly simple looking, which had all sorts of alarms going off. After the complexity of the boundary alarms, why wouldn't she throw every spell in her armory at protecting the one item she could not afford to lose?

Monty obviously had come to the same conclusion, because he stopped a few meters short of the circle and crossed his arms.

"I'm not liking the look of that."

"No." I followed the line of threads around the island of stone. At the back of the altar—where she would have stood to bleed her sacrifice—there was a vague shimmer. It wasn't magic. It was something else.

An imp, Gabe commented.

Imps—or sprites, as they were commonly known—were lesser demons and were generally more mischievous than dangerous. They did have a tendency to throw things around, but there wasn't much in the way of debris around here for them to pick up and use.

Why would it be here? It's not like they're great guardians or anything.

Might be a messenger.

Of *course.* A witch strong enough to leash a hone-onna would easily be able to bend a sprite to her will.

I glanced over to Monty. "There's a sprite being held in the circle."

He wrinkled his nose. "No doubt primed to warn its master once we dismantle the circle."

And *our* protection circles had been designed to keep things out, not in.

"Can you stop it?"

"Either of us could, but the question is, should we bother?"

I frowned. "The longer she takes to realize we're here, the better it'll be for us."

"The minute I begin the cleansing ritual, she's going to know. Why waste energy when it'll only save us a few minutes?"

A few minutes could be the difference between life and death, but I didn't bother arguing the point. "I'll dismantle it then, while you get everything ready for the ritual."

He nodded and then squatted next to his pack, carefully unpacking his athame, holy water, salt, and various other bits and pieces.

I drew in a shaky breath that only invigorated the poker-bearing idiots in my head, and then began—with Gabe basically watching over my shoulder—to dismantle the final protection circle.

The minute the final thread fell, the imp screamed and shot away, heading for the tree line and darkness. Both circles shimmered as it went through but didn't otherwise react.

The countdown had begun.

Time was now of the essence.

Monty stepped forward and began the cleansing ritual. Just for an instant, I thought I heard a deep, horrified scream, and my gaze shot northward, searching the treetops and the sky beyond. Which was ridiculous, of course. Witches were capable of many things, but flying wasn't one of them. Not even via a broomstick.

Via demons, however? That was an entirely different prospect in this particular case.

Another scream, closer than before.

She was on her way.

And she was furious.

The ice in my veins grew stronger. I didn't want the confrontation that was coming, but I had no choice.

You're not alone, Gabe reminded me. *I'll be here.*

Another statement meant to comfort that really didn't. "You have five minutes, if that, before she hits us, Monty."

He didn't answer, but he did hear me, because he nodded as he slowly moved around the base of the altar, cleansing from the bottom up.

I watched him for several seconds, then swung around and marched up the hill. When I was ten feet away from my circle, I sat down and removed my shoes and socks. Neither Katie nor I could risk using the wild magic now, but there was one other way I could connect to the earth's magic without it being obvious. I'd done it a couple of times before —once to summon a wisp, and the other to track a missing wolf, though the latter had ripped the hell out of my strength.

I rose and dug my toes into the soft soil. There was a surge of power and heat, and suddenly I could feel the witch—feel her heavy steps on the ground. She was coming from Argyle's direction, running with unnatural speed, a dark and bloody storm that would break all over us in little more than a couple of minutes.

And she wasn't alone.

The hone-onna was with her. And while that wasn't unexpected, it did complicate things.

No, Gabe said. *It doesn't. It actually works to our advantage.*

And how did you come to that grand conclusion? I picked up my pack and began emptying its contents, placing the various charms, blessed items, and the bottles of holy water in separate clusters for easy, last-minute, last-stand grabbing.

Controlling her creature will take focus and energy. The minute she loses either, the hone-onna will attack.

I'm thinking this witch won't be that stupid.

That depends entirely on how much of a problem we are to her.

I guess it did. I pulled out both Belle's and my silver knives. They'd been blessed with holy water, so if I did have to use them to protect Monty or myself, they'd create a wound that would never heal. Of course, they'd also kill, but given my lack of experience when it came to using a knife defensively, I was more likely to stab myself in a battle than her.

I hadn't brought my athame—there was no way known I was about to foul her blade with the blood of a dark witch or even that of a dark spirit.

I braced my feet, toes burrowing into the ground again to ensure a constant flow of location data, and waited.

The dark wash of foul fury drew closer and closer, until her every step vibrated through me.

I flexed my fingers against the knife hilts, trying to ease some of the tension. It didn't help.

The dark witch burned through the first of her alarm spells. I tried to remain calm, but my heart raced so fast, it felt like one long scream.

I had no idea where the hone-onna was, because the dark witch's presence was all-consuming. But they'd obviously split up; no doubt they intended to hit our circles from two directions.

The witch burned through the second of her alarm spells. I shifted my feet, bracing as much as I could against what was to come.

Then she hit.

Hard.

Monty's circle bent around her body, shimmering fiercely before it rebounded and tossed her back. She screamed and began to spell, her hands moving so fast they were a blur. Or maybe *that* had nothing to do with the speed of her movements but rather the spell that was shielding her outline.

Another scream, this time from behind me. I didn't turn. I knew it was the hone-onna. Knew she was tearing at the spell, seeking to weaken it with both magic and a physical attack. Monty's circle pulsed brightly, each blow shimmering across the thread layers. They held.

For now.

We need to attack her, Gabe said. *We need to give Monty as much time as possible.*

I nodded, and his presence strengthened once again. The spell we created was a more complicated version of the repelling spell I often used. When it was done, we raised my hand and unleashed it. The witch saw it; she was always going to see it, because we made no attempt to hide it. But as she unleashed a foul-feeling counterspell, ours split, one portion smashing into her counter while the other went under and arrowed on, hitting her hard in the chest. It flung her off her feet and dragged her deep into the trees.

But not far enough. Nowhere near far enough.

We swung around, created another repelling spell, and cast it at the hone-onna. The dark spirit had more than enough time to see it, more than enough time to counter, but she did neither. She simply let the full force of our spell hit and cast her far away.

Because she didn't want me or Monty, and she certainly didn't want to stop the destruction of the altar.

She wanted the witch. *Badly*.

The leash, I said to Gabe. *We need to destroy the leash.*

If the leash is tied to the altar, we can't. Not until the altar is destroyed.

How would we know? I studied the altar through narrowed eyes. I couldn't see anything, but then, I wasn't really sure what I was actually looking for. *Gabe?*

It would resemble a twined rope of magic, possibly black or bloody red in color, he said.

I'm not seeing anything like that.

No.

The fall of fouled steps on earth vibrated up my legs. I spun, saw a blur of movement, then felt the burn of the spell that she'd flung at Monty's circle. I threw up a hand, instinctively protecting my eyes as the two collided. There was a pause as the two magics wrestled for supremacy, the hum of energy getting louder, stronger, until it was all I could feel and all I could hear. Then they exploded, lighting the sky with flashes of silver and purple. When the light faded, Monty's circle was gone. All that remained was the faintly glowing spots of his spell stones.

Which only left my circle between destruction and us.

The explosion did have one good side effect though—it had blasted away her covering spell. We could see the bitch now. Aside from the puckered and ugly scar down her cheek, she really could have been an older version of me. No wonder the hone-onna had attacked me.

She strode toward me, her fingers moving at speed as she wove another spell. I had no idea what it was, but it looked and felt damnably nasty.

My gaze dropped, and that was when I saw the thick leash of red and black spell threads attached to her wrist.

That, Gabe said heavily, *will take some undoing. I'm not sure we have the time.*

We have to try.

Yes. He paused. *We need dual attention. I can spell, but you'll have to keep an eye on what's happening.*

Before I could reply, she unleashed her spell. It hit my circle like a hammer, and it was obvious she intended to smash her way through my spell just as she had Monty's.

The intertwined threads of the circle gave ground to the blow and then rebuffed it. The force of both reverberated through my body and my brain, and for an instant, everything blurred.

I sucked in air and swiped at the moisture dribbling over my lashes. And yet despite the deep desire to avoid the brutal resonance of another blow, I didn't detach myself from the circle. The sheer strength of that first attack very much confirmed my earlier suspicion. I *would* have to push more energy into it before this fight was over.

Magic surged again, this time from behind. The hone-onna was back and joining in on the fun, even if unwillingly. Her blow sent another shudder through me, and I stumbled several steps before catching my balance again.

We had to break the goddamn leash.

The echoes of the spirit's attack had barely eased when the witch cast another. The bending in my circle was deeper this time, but it nevertheless repelled the would-be destroyer and remained intact.

But for how long?

Gabe?

Drop to the ground, he said. *Call on the earth to reinforce you if you need. I'll see what I can do about that leash.*

I dropped onto my knees, placed the knives on the ground in front of me, then quickly grabbed a bottle of holy water and poured it in a rough circle. If my circle fell, the holy water circle might be the only thing standing between destruction and me.

Gabe began to spell. Again, I had no idea what it was, but the threads of magic that formed in front of me were complex and multilayered. The witch screamed, but this time, it held a note of ... not fear, but certainly consternation. She knew what the spell was; knew what we were now attempting.

The force of the attacks heightened. My body shook and shuddered under every blow, but I kept my bloody gaze on the leash, watching, waiting, for something to happen as the strength of Gabe's spell increased.

The first thread in my circle gave way. The force of it rebounded through me, and I gasped, doubling over briefly.

I must see! Gabe shouted, the order echoing through every part of me.

My lungs were burning, my heart screaming, and my head felt ready to explode. I thrust my fingers deep into the soil, drawing on the strength of the earth—not to bolster the circle but rather me. If I didn't hang on, we wouldn't win. Monty was still spelling behind us, the ritual words filling the air with power. He hadn't even begun the spell that would permanently shatter the altar.

As the deep, wild warmth of the earth's magic flooded my system, my vision cleared, and I opened my eyes, staring resolutely at the witch. Just for an instant, her eyes widened, though I doubted it was fear. She was too far lost in darkness to ever fear someone like me.

Another thread in my circle snapped.

I didn't close my eyes. Didn't react. I just concentrated on the witch, on the bloody black threads that bound her to the creature who screamed and spelled behind us.

Gabe's magic climbed toward a peak. As another spell line collapsed on my circle, he unleashed it.

For an instant, nothing happened.

Then the witch screamed again, and the thread around her wrist began to burn. One thread disintegrated, then another, then another. Hope shot through me. It was working. It was goddamn working ...

The witch produced a knife, sliced into her opposite wrist, and began to spell.

Blood magic.

Another thread in the leash holding the hone-onna at bay disappeared, but it was happening far too slowly. If she finished that blood spell, we were done. I knew that. More importantly, Gabe knew that.

We had one choice. One hope.

We sucked in a breath and then scooped up my silver knife and cast one of the very first spells they'd taught us in school—a simple spell to transport an object.

We wrapped it around the knife, then, with a faint prayer to any god that might be listening, I punched a hole through my protection circle, and we cast the spell.

The knife tore from my grasp, sped through the hole,

and arrowed toward the witch. She was so wrapped up in her own spell that she didn't sense the knife's approach until the very last moment. She threw up her hand—the hand with the leash attached—as if to ward off the knife and protect her heart, but that had never been our target.

With one quick, brutal blow, the magic-enhanced silver knife sliced through flesh and muscle and bone even as it fused blood vessels.

She couldn't bleed out. Not if we wanted to get rid of the hone-onna.

The detached limb dropped inelegantly to the ground. For an instant, the witch didn't seem to notice, and her spelling didn't falter.

But with the leash no longer attached to a viable limb, the red and black threads withered and died. With them went any control the witch had over her creature.

The hone-onna screamed. This time, it wasn't anger; it was anticipation.

The sound must have cut through the witch's concentration, because her spell faltered. Her gaze snapped to the hand lying on the ground and then rose to mine. "Well played, little witch."

Her voice was calm. Accepting. Everything I hadn't been expecting.

She closed her eyes and waited. But not for long. The hone-onna hit her, tore into her, giving her no chance and no hope. She sucked the witch's life away even as she tore her apart. Then, as her soul rose from the bloody remnants of her flesh, the hone-onna consumed that as well.

A brutal end. A fitting end.

I closed the gap in my protective circle, then sat back on my heels and waited. For several minutes, the hone-onna didn't move.

Then she stirred—something I felt through my connection with the earth rather than saw.

"You help free." Her harsh voice rang with a mix of surprise and appreciation. "I hold deal. I leave this place, return to the city."

And with that, she was gone.

From this forest, from the area, from the reservation.

Behind me, Monty's magic peaked, and the altar crashed to the ground, shattering into a hundred different pieces, never to be reformed or reused.

Against all the odds, we'd not only survived but succeeded.

CHAPTER FOURTEEN

What happened after that was all a bit of a blur. I remember finding my spell stones and tucking them safely into the backpack. I remember the two of us stumbling back through the forest, my arm around Monty's waist and his around mine in an effort to keep us both upright.

I remember voices, and being picked up. Strong arms holding me close, the scent of musk and man filling my nostrils and warming my heart. Then nothing but the oblivion of sleep.

When I finally stirred, it was in a familiar bed—Aiden's rather than mine. No real surprise, given he was the one who'd carried me the last half-kilometer from the altar site. And yet there was a part of me that couldn't help but wish I'd woken in the hospital. The confrontation that had to happen would have been easier on neutral ground rather than in a place that held so many happy memories.

I pushed the thought away and stretched lightly. Various muscles twinged, but there'd been no major wounds or damage done this time. Even the armed idiots in my head had eased off, though they hadn't entirely gone.

The wind howled around the building, and rain pelted the wide expanse of glass to my left. The room was dark, but dawn wasn't all that far off—the song of the unseen moon was faint and distant, which meant it was riding low on the horizon.

The scent of coffee rode the air along with the faint wisps of wood smoke. The fire was ablaze—a good thing considering it was cold enough up here for my breath to condense.

I flung off the blankets, then rose and reached for the thick woolen sweater I used in place of a dressing gown. It was several sizes too big and hung on me like a sack, covering me from neck to knee. Sexy it wasn't. But sexy wasn't going to help right now.

I shoved my feet into my Uggs, then reached out for Belle.

How's Monty?

He slept almost as long as you did.

And how long was that?

Thirty-five hours. You did forty-eight.

Two days? I was out for two *days?*

Yes. I kept telling Aiden you were okay, but he wouldn't listen. That man really does care for you.

But is caring enough?

That, she said heavily, *is something only you can answer.*

In my heart, I already knew the answer. I briefly closed my eyes against the slivers of pain and hope that rose in equal measure, and then said, *How's Mrs. Rankin?*

She had a baby girl yesterday. She called her Elizabeth Fredericka Rankin, after the two people who saved her life.

A silly smile touched my lips. *Fredericka is a better option than Montague.*

Exactly what Monty said. She paused. *Ashworth finally tracked down a little information on the witch through the description I gave him. She was listed in the RWA's 'seize if sighted' list.*

Given she was using blood magic and a hone-onna to murder people, I'm surprised she wasn't on the High Council's most wanted list.

Apparently, no one knew she was capable of magic that powerful.

Then why was she on a seize list?

Because she escaped a psychiatric hospital some ten years ago.

And her murderous spree has been going on since then? That didn't seem possible.

Remember, we only became aware she was here after you almost got blown up in that caravan.

And once we *had* become aware, there was little point in the witch concealing the presence of her leashed dark spirit.

I headed out of the bedroom, but paused at the top of the stairs and flared my nostrils, drawing in all the warm scents rising from below. Aiden was sitting close to the fire. I slowly made my way down.

Good luck, Belle added softly and withdrew from my thoughts. *Oh, and in case you do decide to leave, we dropped the Suzi off there yesterday.*

Thanks. I stopped again at the base of the stairs. Aiden was sprawled on the sofa, lightly snoring. He was naked aside from a pair of boxer shorts, and the well-muscled planes of his lean body gleamed like gold in the flickering glow of the fire. My fingers itched with the desire to lightly explore the glorious length of him while I could, but I ignored it. I couldn't be distracted. Not again.

I popped four crumpets into the toaster, then made myself a cup of coffee. He stirred—something I felt more than saw—then sat upright abruptly. "You're awake."

"Observant of you," I replied, amused.

He laughed, pushed off the sofa, and strode toward me, sweeping me into his arms and a kiss that was as fierce as it was relieved.

"You had me worried for a while there," he said eventually.

"So Belle said." I placed a hand on his warm chest. Felt the beat of his heart under my fingertips, strong and steady. "But I'm okay, Aiden."

He dropped a kiss on the top of my head, then reached past me and plucked the crumpets from the toaster, placing them on the nearby breadboard. I grabbed the butter and cheese, while he retrieved the vegemite and turned on the benchtop toaster oven.

"Yes, but she wasn't seeing how gaunt you were." His gaze scanned me. "And still are."

"It's the cost of magic."

"So I was informed. Multiple times. Doesn't alter the fact it's worrying."

"I know."

I shrugged and silently buttered the crumpets. Once he'd smeared vegemite over them, we put on the cheese and then lightly toasted them. As breakfasts went, it was pretty close to perfect. Only a side of bacon would have made it better.

I picked up my cup and plate and followed him across to the sofa, but sat down facing him rather than beside him as I usually did. I took a sip of coffee, then put it on the nearby coffee table and said, "How did you find us up there?"

"Easy. All ranger vehicles have trackers in them, remember?"

I half smiled. "Just as well Monty decided to keep using your truck then."

"Yeah, and I'm not impressed with the scratches he's given her." His expression belied the annoyance in his voice. "When Ashworth and Eli felt the first surge of dark magic, it was a simple matter of contacting Belle to see what vehicle you were in."

"I take it the whole gang was with you?"

He shook his head. "Eli stayed behind to guard Mia, on the off chance it was a diversion."

Which gave me the perfect in on the conversation that had to be had. One we'd been avoiding for entirely too long now.

I munched on the crumpet for several seconds while I gathered my courage and then said softly, "So did you and Mia have time to sit down and talk?"

"Yes, and it didn't alter anything. I told you it wouldn't."

"I didn't actually expect it to."

He frowned. "Then why ask the question?"

"You know why, Aiden."

He sighed, the warmth in his expression losing ground to frustration. "Are we really going to do this now? When you're barely out of your sickbed?"

"We can't keep finding excuses, Aiden. We need to talk about us. About this relationship and what we want out of it."

"You know what I want out of it," he said in a gruff voice that held a distinct edge. "You. In my life, in my bed. For now, and for the foreseeable future."

"And the future we can't see?"

"Worry about that when the time comes."

I sighed. He still wasn't getting it.

"Aiden, I've spent the last few months of our relationship fearing Mia's return—fearing that she would be the one who would tear us apart—" I held up a hand to stop his comment. "But in truth, she was never the real threat. She was just a manifestation of the problem that lies between us."

"You being a witch rather than a werewolf," he said bluntly. "I don't care."

"But you *do*." I couldn't help the edge in my voice. "Otherwise, you'd be willing to take this relationship to its natural conclusion."

He didn't say anything. Maybe he simply wasn't willing to admit, even now, the truth we both knew.

"Damn it, Aiden," I growled, frustrated. "I love you. I think I fell in love with you that very first day, when you arrested my ass. I want nothing more than to build a life with you, but I can't do that. Not like this. Not when at any given moment you can decide that playtime with the witch is over and it's time to resume the mantle as alpha of your pack."

"I can't change what I am."

"No, but that was never the point. Katie fought the pack and your parents to marry the man she loved. Do you really think she would have done anything different had she not been dying?"

"Had she not been dying, the pack would not have approved."

"Do you think she would have cared? If you do, then you don't know your sister very well at all."

"Liz, listen—"

"No. I'm done listening. I'm done being patient. I'm done torturing myself with the possibility of loving a man who will never admit his feelings or truly commit to me. I want marriage, Aiden. I want kids. And if I can't have it with you, then this has to end. *Now*. I'm not going to spend the next one or two or however many damn years it is fearing that the next wolf who walks into the reservation might be the one you leave me for." Tears were tracking down my face now, but I didn't care. "I want more than that. I *deserve* more than that."

He didn't say anything for a very long time, then he slowly reached out and thumbed away a tear. "I don't want to lose you, Liz. I don't want to lose this."

"But what are you willing to do to keep it? Marry me? Commit to being a full-time life partner rather than just a bedmate? Because that's what it's going to take."

"Marriage is no guarantee of a happy ever after."

"No, but at least I'd know where I stand in your life. Right now, I'm in no-man's land. I'm a lover who shares your bed but not all of your life, and you certainly go to great pains to keep our relationship separate from your pack life."

"Because—"

"I'm not a wolf," I finished for him. "And for you, that will always be a major obstacle."

"It's not a new revelation, Liz," he growled, blue eyes glowing fiercely. "I've never said or acted in any way to make you believe otherwise."

"I know. It's my stupid fault for falling for a man whose heart was always beyond my grasp. But here we are."

He scrubbed a hand through his hair and looked away. "Damn it, Liz, please don't do this. Not now."

"Then when?" I asked fiercely. "Just when *is* the right time for you to break my heart?"

He cursed, thrust to his feet, and stalked across to the fire, holding out his hands to the flames, though we both knew they didn't need warming. Tension rode the muscles across his back, and his aura ran with a confusing mix of hurt, anger, and frustration.

"I don't want this," he growled.

"To be honest, Aiden, I don't think you really know what you want."

He didn't reply. He didn't look around.

I sighed, placed my unfinished crumpet back on the plate, then rose and padded over to him. His muscles tensed, but he otherwise didn't react.

"You know I'm right."

He didn't say anything.

"This is goodbye, Aiden."

"No." One word, gruffly said.

"Yes," I said firmly, though my heart and my soul were shattering.

He swore and swung around to face me. He didn't touch me. He didn't kiss me, though I could see the desire to do both burning in his eyes. "I need a run. I need to think."

"I won't be here when you get back, Aiden."

"Just wait for me. Please."

I didn't reply. He hesitated, then strode for the door, slamming it open and then slamming it closed with equal force.

I felt the shimmer of his change, the long lope of his steps as he chased the fast-disappearing night. Running away from the truth rather than searching for answers.

There were no answers. We both knew that. Not unless he was at least willing to meet me halfway.

I walked upstairs, got dressed, and then grabbed a bag and stuffed everything I could into it. The rest I could come back for either tomorrow or the next day. I hauled it downstairs, swept up my purse, and headed out into the wild night. After dumping the bag in the rear of the Suzi, I opened the driver door and climbed in.

What happened from this point on was up to him.

I reversed out of the parking area and slowly drove away.

And deep in the distance heard the anguished, broken howl of a wolf.

I knew exactly how he felt.

ALSO BY KERI ARTHUR

Relic Hunters Novels

Crown of Shadows (Feb 2022)

Sword of Darkness (Oct 2022)

Ring of Ruin (June 2023)

The Witch King's Crown

Blackbird Rising (Feb 2020)

Blackbird Broken (Oct 2020)

Blackbird Crowned (June 2021)

Lizzie Grace series

Blood Kissed (May 2017)

Hell's Bell (Feb 2018)

Hunter Hunted (Aug 2018)

Demon's Dance (Feb 2019)

Wicked Wings (Oct 2019)

Deadly Vows (Jun 2020)

Magic Misled (Feb 2021)

Broken Bonds (Oct 2021)

Sorrows Song (June 2022)

Killer's Kiss (Feb 2023)

Kingdoms of Earth & Air

Unlit (May 2018)

Cursed (Nov 2018)

Burn (June 2019)

The Outcast series

City of Light (Jan 2016)

Winter Halo (Nov 2016)

The Black Tide (Dec 2017)

Souls of Fire series

Fireborn (July 2014)

Wicked Embers (July 2015)

Flameout (July 2016)

Ashes Reborn (Sept 2017)

Dark Angels series

Darkness Unbound (Sept 27th 2011)

Darkness Rising (Oct 26th 2011)

Darkness Devours (July 5th 2012)

Darkness Hunts (Nov 6th 2012)

Darkness Unmasked (June 4 2013)

Darkness Splintered (Nov 2013)

Darkness Falls (Dec 2014)

Riley Jenson Guardian Series

Full Moon Rising (Dec 2006)

Kissing Sin (Jan 2007)

Tempting Evil (Feb 2007)

Dangerous Games (March 2007)

Embraced by Darkness (July 2007)

The Darkest Kiss (April 2008)

Deadly Desire (March 2009)

Bound to Shadows (Oct 2009)

Moon Sworn (May 2010)

Myth and Magic series

Destiny Kills (Oct 2008)

Mercy Burns (March 2011)

Nikki & Micheal series

Dancing with the Devil (March 2001 / Aug 2013)

Hearts in Darkness Dec (2001/ Sept 2013)

Chasing the Shadows Nov (2002/Oct 2013)

Kiss the Night Goodbye (March 2004/Nov 2013)

Damask Circle series

Circle of Fire (Aug 2010 / Feb 2014)

Circle of Death (July 2002/March 2014)

Circle of Desire (July 2003/April 2014)

Ripple Creek series

Beneath a Rising Moon (June 2003/July 2012)

Beneath a Darkening Moon (Dec 2004/Oct 2012)

Spook Squad series

Memory Zero (June 2004/26 Aug 2014)

Generation 18 (Sept 2004/30 Sept 2014)

Penumbra (Nov 2005/29 Oct 2014)

Stand Alone Novels

Who Needs Enemies (E-book only, Sept 1 2013)

Novella

Lifemate Connections (March 2007)

Anthology Short Stories

The Mammoth Book of Vampire Romance (2008)

Wolfbane and Mistletoe--2008

Hotter than Hell--2008